Rogue Faction Part 1

Xander Weaver

Rogue Faction Part 1

—For Mom and Dad—

You've given me a lifetime of support and encouragement.
Since saying *thank you* isn't enough, I give you this book.

Prologue

Onyx Gander, GmbH
19 years ago

The underground parking garage was virtually deserted at the late hour. What few cars remained were likely there for the night. The Cadillac CTS sedan was the object of the dark figure's attention as he watched from the shadows more than fifty feet away. He knew that car wasn't in for the night. In fact, its owner was due to depart at any moment.

Dressed in a long dark coat, the figure wore a matching fedora tipped low across his brow. He knew there were no security cameras in the immediate vicinity, but protecting his identity was paramount. He had too much riding on this operation, and it was critical that tonight's events never linked back to him.

He'd taken great care in examining the limited security of the underground parking structure and was certain he could exit without being discovered. Sadly, he felt less confident in the skills of the specialist contracted for the operation. While there was no question the man had a talent when it came to his craft, the dark figure had less trust in the small technician's ability to enter and exit the garage undetected. The dark figure had escorted him, as a result.

Watching the man work had turned out to be an illuminating experience. What the diminutive specialist lacked in social graces, he more than made up for in raw talent. He'd completed the complex job of wiring the target's car in record time, exactly matching the intricate specifications provided to him. But for all of his talent and quiet manner, the specialist had an unsettling way about him. As someone who worked with unsavory people as a matter of routine, the dark figure had found the tiny bomb technician unusually off-putting. It had been a relief to guide the man from the building after completing work on the car.

That left the dark figure alone to watch over the target's vehicle. The operation was only one component in the larger scheme of things, so for the rest to run like clockwork, it was critical that the charges in the car were triggered according to plan. The special charges that were wired around the interior of the vehicle's passenger compartment were designed with a purpose in mind—to send a message.

The wait was the difficult part. While the man had taken every possible precaution, the longer he waited, the chance someone would discover his presence increased dramatically. Remaining to witness the detonation was an unnecessary indulgence—at least, it would've been in any other case. This was a special situation in so many ways.

The man took a deep breath and watched the vapor cloud from his breath hang before his eyes. There was no circulation this deep in the parking structure, and the air tasted stale. Shivering, he turned up the collar of his coat against the cold. The frigid weather of Germany seemed to intensify this far underground. Stuffing his gloved hands into the hip pockets of his trench coat, his hand wrapped around the grip of a snub-nose .357 revolver. There was reassurance in knowing that the weapon was close, though for operations such as this, the suppressed .380 semi-automatic slung from a holster inside his coat was the better choice. Luckily, there wouldn't be cause to use either weapon tonight.

His left hand moved in his pocket and found the blunt shape of a steel sap. It was a small but powerful device, well suited for rendering someone unconscious or even shattering bone, depending on how it was swung. Again, it wouldn't be useful tonight, but it was comforting to have.

Flexing his knees and shifting his weight from foot to foot, the dark figure worked to stave off the cold as it attempted to stiffen his joints. He was fighting the urge to check his wristwatch when he heard the unmistakable sounds of footfalls on concrete. Straining to locate the source of the sound, a smile crossed his face. The footfalls were distinctive—delicate and female. The sound of sensible shoes—the type worn by a young mother with two infant daughters waiting at home. The footsteps moved steadily across the pavement, quickly drawing near.

The man stood motionless on the far side of a tall concrete support column. In his mind, he could envision the thin, long-haired woman moving steadily through the deserted garage on her way to the car. She would be bundled up against the cold, and eager to get behind the wheel and activate the heater.

When he heard the sound of a car door opening, the man dared to peer from the darkness. The blonde woman stood in the doorway of the Cadillac, placing a small bag behind the front seat.

Turning quickly, she slipped behind the steering column and swiftly pulled the door shut behind her.

Ducking back behind the pillar, the dark figure took in a deep breath. In his mind, he could see the young lady inserting her key in the car's ignition. A moment later he heard the car stereo blast to life. It was an ear splitting eruption that would send the poor woman's heart into her throat as she fought to find the power button and make sense of the disparity. She hadn't left the radio on when she'd parked the car earlier that morning.

The moment the stereo went silent, the dark figure cringed. Her action would trigger the first set of small dispersal charges. On cue, he heard four muffled 'pops' sound in rapid succession. The noise was followed instantly by an earsplitting shriek that seemed to go on without end. It tore at even the dark figure's heart. He counted the seconds in his head, knowing the woman inside the car would be experiencing pain that was unlike anything dreamt of by any sane mind. The figure placed his gloved fingers in his ears and pushed his back against the concrete pillar for support. But when his count reached seven and the second stage explosive hadn't triggered, he knew there was a problem. The primary explosive was supposed to trigger five seconds after the initial dispersal charges.

Though the dark figure had since ceased his internal count, the moment the ten-second mark was reached, a deafening explosion tore through the automobile. The car frame twisted with a white-hot burst of flames as every window was blown out at once. The man had just begun to ease his fingers from his ears and contemplate a contingency plan when the explosion caught him off guard. The air was knocked from his lungs, sending him to his knees while still trying to shove numbed fingers back into his ears.

The shell-shocked man pulled himself to his feet and peered around the support column. The car was a fiery ruin. Wreckage was scattered for fifty feet and flames were licking the low ceiling of the garage. The fire suppression sprinklers sat still and dry. Disabling them had been a simple matter.

Turning, the man walked quickly through the shadows at the back of the structure. He had the escape route down cold. Blinking against the acrid smoke that was already filling every cubic foot of the level, he was also fighting a dizzying ring in his ears.

Five seconds, he thought. The plan had been for the primary charge to detonate five seconds after the dispersal charge. The main detonation had been far too long in triggering. Had it been a mistake? No—a vision of the creepy little bomb technician crossed his mind and he knew the delay had been no accident. The savage little bastard had wanted the target to suffer far longer than had been necessary.

Distracted by his irritation, when the dark figure turned the corner he collided with a body rushing in the opposite direction. The woman bounced off him and crashed unceremoniously to her backside.

She looked up at him through wild eyes. "What happened! What was that sound? Is everyone alright?"

The woman was speaking German. It wasn't the dark figure's native tongue, but he spoke it fluently. Gnashing his teeth, he looked at the woman on the pavement before him. Reaching down, he took her hand and pulled her to her feet. "Fine, fine," he said in a calming voice as he looked into her eyes. "Everything is fine."

In a single blur of motion, the dark figure grabbed the woman's head. Placing one gloved hand under her jaw and the other on the back of her skull, he made a single violent twist. Her neck snapped as easily as if it was made of fragile balsa wood, and her body went limp between his hands. He laid her out on the concrete floor.

Pulling the sap from his coat pocket, the man leaned over the woman's collapsed form. He gave her a quick jolt across the crown of her skull with the blunt device, and eased her body into a position near the edge of the wall where they had collided. Placing the crown of her skull closest to the poured concrete wall, he made sure that the angle of impact looked appropriate before pocketing the sap once more.

Retrieving a shoe she'd lost in the tumble, he broke the two-inch heel from it before placing it beside her foot. None of this would hold up against an inspection from a talented investigator, but it would be enough to fool most authorities. As far as the dark figure's experience went, no one ever looked that closely. In any case, he wasn't worried. He'd left no evidence, and the assassination couldn't be traced back to him. The one person who could identify him now lay broken at his feet.

Without wasting another second, the figure stepped past the body and entered the stairwell. He walked calmly up three flights before exiting onto a nearly deserted city street. A dark, four-door BMW sat at the curb waiting for him. He slipped through the passenger side door and the driver pulled away without delay. Blending into the late night traffic, the car disappeared into the darkness.

Chapter 1

Kingston Waterfront
10:50 pm

The mosquitoes were eating Greg Boone alive as he lay concealed in his position at the tree line. While he'd experienced worse, the nasty little bloodsuckers only added to an already growing tension. Eyeing his wristwatch once more, he felt the muscles in his jaw tighten further. Sensing the stare of the man beside him, he resisted the urge to glare at the young field agent. "Having you eyeball me isn't helping matters," Boone chastised.

"Sorry, sir," the man whispered his reply in the darkness.

They'd been embedded in the same location concealed position for over three hours. Boone knew that the agent beside him was up to the challenges of the assignment, but they were behind schedule, and that knowledge was a dangerous test of his resolve.

It hadn't been long since the last COMM check, but Boone decided that even fruitless action was better than no action at all. So far, he and Agent Stubbs had been watching the parked Land Rover since its arrival more than thirty minutes earlier. The SUV was positioned in what might generously be called a parking turnout at the edge of a small sandbar that fronted the costal inlet. The edge of the parking area stopped just short of the crest in a small ridge. Beyond that ridge lay the waterline.

They could hear the sounds of heavy machinery in the distance. Light spilled through the tree line separating their scenic overlook from Kingston Wharf less than a mile up the road. The wharf was still fairly active, even at the late hour, as recently arrived freighters transferred cargo as part of the 24-hour operation.

"Overwatch, report?" Boone said quietly into his wireless bone conducting earbud.

The reply came quickly. "No new contact in the bay," Overwatch responded. "No unusual movement from the target."

By 'target', the voice was referring to the three figures in the Land Rover. At least one part of the operation was on track, Boone knew. When the four-wheel drive entered the lot, Boone had been able to identify one of the occupants using his night vision glasses. Kang Woo-jin was clearly visible in the backseat as the vehicle had passed Boone's position. Kang was at the waterfront to take delivery of a powerful new explosive that was in the process of being smuggled into the country. But while Boone's people knew that the explosive device was scheduled to arrive by ship, as well as the approximate time of delivery, they had no idea which ship carried the device. Since Kingston Wharf was a busy port, all Boone could do was wait for the package to change hands. Once it was in the open, his team would move to intercept.

Boone's stress was due to the fact that this operation was only the first stage in a larger and more complicated mission. He needed to acquire the explosive and deliver it to an undercover agent who had arranged to sell the device before the night was through. Unfortunate timing was causing increased concern because the delay in Kang's delivery was now behind schedule, and it meant that Boone's window of opportunity to meet his undercover man was rapidly drawing to a close.

"Polecat, do you copy?"

Boone rolled his eyes. His designation for this operation was yet another irritation. He sensed Cyrus's handiwork at play. The kid had been undercover and radio silent for six months, but somehow still managed to have Boone shackled with the most unfortunate of code names. "Polecat here, go ahead," he grumbled.

"I may have information regarding the delay, sir," the technician back at base reported. "We just monitored a radio transmission. It seems that one of the freighters was searched shortly after arriving in port tonight. According to the report, the search has only just now concluded."

"Sir," Stubbs said from beside Boone. "Do you think it's the freighter Kang is waiting on?"

Dumb question.

Boone offered a slight nod in the darkness. It would explain the delay, he reasoned. "Roger that, Control. I take it the search didn't turn up anything?"

"It seems that way, sir."

Adjusting the position of his night vision glasses, Boone studied the silhouettes inside Kang's SUV. Even from his remote position almost seventy-five yards off, Boone could see increased movement inside the truck.

"This is Overwatch, we have movement in the bay. I have two RIBs closing on your position."

A pair of Rigid-hulled inflatable boats…that stood to reason. With precious cargo, whoever was responsible for delivering the device would want a second boat for support, and the RIBs could launch fast and maneuver quickly in the bay. They were also a formidable weapons platform.

"Don't tell me," Boone whispered. "50's?"

"Affirmative, sir," Overwatch responded. "Each craft is equipped with a .50 caliber stationary gun on the bow. I count three tangos aboard each craft."

"Roger," Boone confirmed. "Teams one, two and three, prepare to take your assigned actions. We move when Overwatch gives the word."

Stoffer Airfield
10:56 pm

Standing in the middle of a spacious aircraft hangar, Cyrus Cooper watched a dozen mercenaries load cargo onto the hastily converted Airbus A319. A hundred of the commercial aircraft's 124 seats had been summarily torn out and thrown in a pile at the back of the hangar, allowing room for an improvised cargo hold. As soon as the plane was loaded, Cyrus knew that his time would be at an end.

"It seems that your friend is late," Aubin Sutter said, as he walked up behind Cyrus. "That doesn't bode well for you. It's a shame…I had such high hopes for your future."

Cyrus turned to look at Sutter. He was a solid looking man with short dark hair and several days' worth of stubble on his jaw.

Standing a couple inches over six feet, he likely weighed a little over two hundred. There was a grizzled brashness to him. He was a tough, dangerous man who knew how to handle himself. Cyrus had seen him fight more than once in the six months he'd been a part of Sutter's crew; there was a reason he was calling the shots.

Sutter's most distinguishing quality was the patch he wore over his right eye. There were plenty of rumors as to how the arms dealer had lost the eye, likely many of them started by Sutter himself. But out of Sutter's crew, only Cyrus knew the truth. Though he would never admit it, Sutter had lost it as a child while playing on his parent's vineyard in France.

Offering Sutter a disinterested grin, Cyrus slipped his hands into the pockets of his jeans, and shrugged. "I wouldn't call him my friend. He's really more of an acquaintance."

"I should think not," Sutter laughed. "He's going to get you killed, after all."

Refusing to cower before Sutter, Cyrus shrugged once again. "He'll be here. He still has a few minutes left. Don't worry." Though he never liked turning his back on Sutter, he knew it would make his point.

Cyrus turned slowly to take in the rest of the hangar. The massive front doors had been closed up tight, safe from prying eyes. The wide concrete floor was polished and coated with polyurethane. It gleamed white under the glare of the fluorescent lights high above. Most of the floor space was empty, except for the massive Airbus parked in the center. A steel wheeled staircase was pushed up against the forward cabin door, allowing Sutter's men to file in and out of the plane like hard-working ants from a dirt mound.

Making a slow circuit of the building's perimeter was a short bespectacled man. He walked at an awkward pace, his eyes moving across the outermost wall of the building. The bald top of the man's head shone with a glare that was almost as blinding as the polished floor. He was checking an array of explosive charges located at the periphery of the hangar.

Sutter followed Cyrus's gaze. "Does Eartzie's work on the perimeter concern you?" he asked.

"Everything that deviant troll does concerns me." Cyrus sent an accusatory glance back at Sutter. "You're out of your mind. Do you really think you can trust someone like that?"

The comment brought a laugh from Sutter. "This new thermobaric explosive is supposed to be something special. I need an expert on hand to authenticate the product your contact is delivering. Eartzie is the best. He's forgotten more about high energy explosives than you or I will ever know."

Slowly shaking his head, Cyrus kept his eyes locked on Sutter. "You're telling me you trust him? Have you been paying attention? He forgets to blink, for God's sake. The guy's got a head full of loose wiring—he doesn't give you the creeps?"

Cyrus saw the twitch under Sutter's good eye with that statement. Sutter looked back at Eartzie who was now on the far end of the hangar. The man was standing statue still, and staring at a blank spot on the wall. When Sutter's gaze returned to Cyrus, Cyrus saw a distinct lack of conviction for any argument he might make.

"Is there some reason you would rather I have someone else examine the device?" Sutter accused. "Is there something you're hiding?"

"No," Cyrus said flatly. "But we're talking about an extremely powerful explosive. One you intend to put in the hands of a nutcase who's likely to set it off just to *see* what the inside of his own face looks like. I think its poor judgment on your part."

The slight resulted in a deep guttural sound from Sutter; it was something akin to a growl. With a wave of his hand, he motioned to someone outside of Cyrus's field of vision. Cyrus knew he'd successfully distracted the man for a time, but it hadn't been long enough. The unmistakable feeling of two rifle muzzles being pressed into his back was enough to eliminate any doubt.

Sutter walked forward and pulled the pistol from the holster on Cyrus's hip. With a cold detachment echoing in his voice, he concluded, "Your friend isn't coming."

Chapter 2

Kingston Waterfront
10:58 pm

Lying prone at the edge of the warehouse roof, Wil Helinger was thirteen hundred yards away from the scene playing out on the distant stretch of sand. He had the wharf to his back—the distant sounds of heavy machinery were muted, but ever present. The powerful floodlights of the dock created a diffused glow to his rear, causing him to lie close to the roofline in order to avoid creating an unmistakable silhouette against the skyline.

Helinger's night vision glasses turned night into day, but without the green cast common to conventional night vision hardware. The goggles looked like a pair of sleek sunglasses crossed with a pair of low profile ski goggles. They slipped on over his ears like glasses, but wrapped tight to his face to keep the light from their heads-up display from spilling out into the night. They incorporated the latest in light enhancement technology and were slaved to the targeting system of the powerful .50 caliber long rifle mounted on a small articulated arm at his side.

Sliding his finger across the small touchpad that was built into the goggles and located over his right temple, Helinger's view of the distant area was magnified by a factor of 15. He watched as a pair of large, inflatable zodiacs materialized from the fog that had settled over the bay. No—not just any zodiacs. These were RIBs. There was a .50 caliber bolted to a stationary mount at the bow of each craft making them even more formidable.

Helinger reported the discovery. "This is Overwatch, we have movement in the bay. I've got two RIBs closing on your position."

He heard Boone grumble. "Don't tell me, 50's?"

"Affirmative, sir. Each craft is equipped with a stationary .50 caliber. I count three tangos aboard each boat."

"Roger that," Boone said. "Teams one, two and three, prepare to take your assigned actions. We move when Overwatch gives the word."

His finger sliding across the pad on the side of his goggles, Helinger increased his magnification further. Without taking his eyes off the targets below, he touched the small screen strapped to the back of his left wrist. A small red reticle appeared in the center of the heads-up display inside his glasses. When his eyes focused on the large gun mounted at the front of the first watercraft, the reticle slid across the display and centered in alignment with his focus. He tapped his wrist display and the reticle pulsed twice. When his eyes shifted to the position of the second heavy gun on the second boat, the reticle followed. He flagged the position of the second target with another tap of his finger. As each target was designated, a residual transparent marker remained over the target. Even as he turned his head, the markers moved along with the selected targets. It was as if the digital markers were pinned in cyberspace and only became visible as his gaze passed over the tagged physical locations. Helinger knew that the targeting system was able to maintain the lock on moving targets as well as stationary objects. So, if the crafts made a break for it, the targeting system would maintain a lock in spite of changes in angle, trajectory and distance.

Helinger went on to tag the twin engines of both inflatable boats, just as he had with their guns. The articulated .50 caliber long rifle beside him was slaved to his goggles and would fire on the designated targets the moment he triggered it. Unfortunately, the system was a prototype, and did have a limitation. He could flag only a maximum of five targets at one time. The two heavy guns onboard the boats were an obvious priority, but so were the twin outboard engines that powered each boat. If he put a round into each gun as well as each engine, he was still one shot short. He could only flag five of the six targets, which meant one of the engines would remain operational.

"Hold position," Helinger reported.

The boats were just making landfall. As they reached shore, a man leapt from each craft to drag it from the surf. When the second boat came to rest, Helinger found a solution to his problem. Re-designating the last target, he locked in the targeting scenario. The automated rifle fired depleted uranium rounds that were packed with 30% more powder than conventional ammunition. Since the targeting computer would compensate for wind shift, gravity, and even the friction of the round as it related to the weather conditions, recoil from the hot loads wasn't a concern. The final resting location of the second RIB had put both of its engines in line with each other. A single depleted uranium slug would tear through the pair of engines with ease.

Helinger watched as two new men from each craft leapt to the beach and joined the pair who had pulled the boats from the water. One man on each inflatable was left behind to wield the .50 caliber deck gun. Most importantly to Helinger, two of the men on the beach were struggling to carry between them what looked like a small thermal cooler. Helinger tapped another button on his wrist and the view from his goggles switched rapidly between thermal, electromagnetic and microwave displays of the men and the cooler.

"This is Overwatch," he said. "I have eyes on the prize. I'm ready when you are."

The four targets moved up the short stretch of sand. Two of them lugged the device while the other two flanked them, their rifles held at the ready. Three men were advancing across the beach from the opposite direction. They'd come from the parked SUV; one carried a small bag under his arm. He recognized that man as Kang.

The exchange was about to take place.

"This is Overwatch. Polecat, do you read me?"

The four seconds he waited for a reply felt like a lifetime, but Helinger already knew that something was wrong. "This is Overwatch. COMM check. Sound off."

No answer.

Shit.

Kang and his two men reached the four men from the boat. They were gathered in the middle of the small expanse of sand. Both boats sat at the waterline, a man standing at the ready behind each heavy gun.

Turning his attention to the parking area not fifty yards from the beach, Helinger saw the dark shapes of Boone and Stubbs as they cleared their brush-covered position and moved toward the crest in the small ridge separating them from the coast. Zooming the view of his glasses further, Helinger could see Boone's lips moving. He realized that Boone was trying to use the radio but wasn't getting through.

Watching carefully, Helinger saw Boone wave Stubbs off to the right as they made a slow advance on the ridgeline that blocked their view of the beach. When Boone turned to the south and looked directly at Helinger—a form impossible to make out in the darkness from that distance—Helinger knew it was time. Boone raised two fingers and pointed them at Helinger's assigned position. Helinger knew he'd just received the *Go* signal.

With a single tap on his wrist, the ceaseless clanking, banging and grinding of the late-night dock operations was shattered by five back-to-back thunderous explosions. From the corner of his eye, Helinger could see what looked like a single long flame leap from the muzzle of the .50 caliber rifle, as five rounds were unleashed faster than any human could aim and pull the trigger.

———————

Kingston Waterfront
11:01 pm

Boone took a quick look at his watch and felt his heart sink. They were officially behind schedule. He was supposed to have the package in-hand well before now. His meeting with Cyrus and Aubin Sutter was set for 11 pm. There was no question—Sutter was not a patient man. But if anyone knew how to stall, it would be Cyrus.

Boone took a deep breath and hoped the rest of the mission could be concluded without delay. "It's your call, Overwatch," he urged.

Boone watched as Kang and two of his men exited the Land Rover and headed over the ridge separating the parking area from the sandbar. The exchange was about to go down. Only Helinger had a clear view of all that was happening, although Team Two was ready to sweep in from the north and would have a partial view of the targets at the moment. Team Three would come in from the south, but they were literally buried in three inches of sand and couldn't move until it was time to spring the trap.

Boone noticed that Kang carried a large satchel. Whatever was inside was heavy, because the moment his boots hit sand, his stride became decidedly more labored. Giving Kang time to reach the men from the boats, Boone tried once more to raise the rest of the team on the radio. His first two attempts had gone unanswered, and he was growing more concerned with each passing second. A sick feeling roiled in the pit of his stomach as he counted the seconds that had passed since Kang and his men had disappeared over the ridge.

"COMM check," Boone growled. "Is *anybody* there?"

Stubbs met Boone's eye and shook his head. There wasn't even static—it was like the radio frequency had been smothered to the point of nonexistence. Pointing two fingers at Stubbs and making a motion to the right, Boone gave the signal to advance. There was no more time to waste.

Looking to the south, Boone eyed the dark roofline of the nearest warehouse on the wharf. Though he knew Helinger was there, he couldn't detect any trace of the man. Raising a hand, he pointed two fingers at Helinger's position.

A burst of light from the distant warehouse roofline was the first indication that Helinger had received the improvised command. A flame split the night a second and a half before the blast wave hit. Explosions sounded from over the ridge and down the beach. Boone and Stubbs were already charging for the vacant SUV and the beach beyond. Teams Two and Three would be closing from their respective positions of north and south.

Small explosions could be seen as Boone passed the Rover and crested the ridge with his rifle sweeping for targets. A massive explosion sounded before he could zero in on his first target. A ball of flame shot into the air producing a concussive wave that nearly knocked him off his feet. Though the burst of flame vanished almost as quickly as it had appeared, the denotation had raised the temperature of the air by a considerable margin.

Both boats were sinking to the waterline at their sterns, and still grounded at their bows. The intermittent explosions came from the ammo cans of .50 calibers cooking off in the small fires at the front of each boat. Understandably, each gunner left aboard was now little more than a pile of pink meat. Both men looked like jigsaw puzzles with half their pieces missing.

In the middle of the beach lay five additional bodies. Four were clearly fallen hostiles; it was obvious by their grubby clothes and discarded AKs. Two of the men were fragged, and in worse shape than the gunners left in the inflatable boats. Some kind of charge had detonated, catching the group of men at close range. Body parts were missing. The remaining pair of hostiles were in better condition—but only in the most relative terms. They, too, were clearly dead, though they would be heading to hell with all body parts still in place.

Taking in the scene, Boone was at a loss to find an explanation. Thirty feet away he saw the dark form of another body. He stowed the rifle on a sling over his back and pulled his sidearm. Rolling the body, he recognized the man was part of Team Three. He checked for a pulse, but found none. He wasn't surprised. There was blood—a lot of it.

Looking around quickly, Boone was shocked to find the body of Kang missing; not only that but the two Korean men with Kang were MIA, as well. The remaining two members of Team Three were also unaccounted for, and Team Two was nowhere to be seen.

His eyes probing the stretch of beach, Boone waved his hand at Stubbs. "Where in the hell did they go? Fleming is dead. Help me find Hobbs and Higgs!"

The dance of light and shadow cast from several small residual fires only served to confound the search. Everything around them seemed to be moving in the swaying shadows. A splash in the surf at the shoreline was subtle, but distinctive. Boone spun with his SIG raised and his finger already partially depressing the trigger. The contrast of his night vision glasses adjusted to see the form of a man lying in the slowly rolling waves.

"It's Hobbs!"

Boone pulled Hobbs from the surf, while Stubbs covered their position as best he could from the waterline. Boone tried his radio again, as he assessed the man's injuries. He still couldn't raise Team Two, Overwatch, *or* Command. Something was very wrong.

Examining Hobbs' limp form on the wet sand, Boone couldn't find any blood. Seeing the man's eyes suddenly flutter and then roll wildly in their sockets, Boone felt a flood of relief. He patted Hobbs on the side of the face and spoke sharply in hushed tones.

"Hey—Hobbs—are you with me?" He delivered another slap to the man's cheek.

Hobbs' eyes finally snapped open and looked at Boone— alarm clearly visible. Rolling onto his side, he vomited onto the sand. "Jesus, what happened?" Hobbs groaned.

"I was going to ask you that! What the *hell* happened? Where is everyone?"

Chapter 3

One of his men had just reported that the last of the cargo would be secured within the next five minutes. Sutter sent orders for the pilot and copilot to begin their preflight preparations. He wanted to depart the moment everything was in place. Glancing at the small balding man standing alone at the periphery of the loading zone, Sutter considered his options. He was reluctant to inform Eartzie—the addled bomb maker—that his latest toy, the experimental thermobaric explosive, wasn't going to arrive in time for departure.

Though he did his best to hide it, the bomb maker unnerved him. He was as small and unassuming of a person as Sutter had ever seen, but a few minutes in the man's presence was all it took to gather an overwhelming sense that he just wasn't *right*. He was quiet…too quiet. It was nearly impossible to engage him in conversation. Almost to the point where he made one wonder if he were mentally deficient, or otherwise absent. That sense was counterbalanced by the way the quiet man's eyes constantly moved to observe everything around him—even as his body remained unnaturally still. There was a disturbing intelligence behind those eyes when they fell on you, observant and predatory, completely at odds with the rest of his appearance.

Though he might seem quiet, Sutter knew that Eartzie was as dangerous a man as he'd ever dealt with. Possibly more so than most, since he was a bomb maker of unparalleled skill. And while Sutter was accustomed to dealing with deviant and dangerous men, the prospect of telling Eartzie that he would not have his prize left him more than a little apprehensive.

Frustrated and looking for an excuse to put off what he knew would be a very one-sided conversation, Sutter turned his attention to Cyrus. The young man was perhaps the greatest disappointment of all. Though he was always suspicious of new faces, Sutter had to admit that the kid had quickly found a place on his crew. He was young, capable, and smarter than his best four men put together. In so many ways he was the ideal new recruit, and Sutter had envisioned a bright future for him in his organization. Sadly, that wasn't to be. Arranging the sale of the thermobaric compound was Cyrus's big break, and it had fallen apart.

As much as he liked the kid, Sutter knew he couldn't let such a major slight stand. He would make an example of him. It was just good business… And if the gesture placated the mad bomber? Sutter figured he might sleep better at night, literally, not having to worry about a bomb having been hidden beneath his bunk for retribution.

Pulling the radio from his belt, Sutter took a deep breath and steeled himself. "Eartzie, can I have a word?"

Sutter watched the small bomb maker from across the hangar. Eartzie continued to stare at the wall without movement. As far as Sutter could tell, there was nothing there for him to see. "Eartzie, come in?"

There was still no response. No movement at all. It was chilling, and it made Sutter regret what he had to say even more. Still, there was no more time to waste. With a roll of his eye, Sutter brought his fingers to his lips and produced an ear piercing whistle that echoed through the open space. A half dozen of the men still working around the base of the aircraft staircase turned instantly. Sutter paid them no attention. After what seemed like several endless seconds, Eartzie pried his gaze from the wall and slowly turned in Sutter's direction. Gritting his teeth, Sutter waved him over.

The short balding man took his time, walking slowly across the center of the hangar. There was an odd manner to his gait, Sutter noticed. His legs moved with each step but his arms never swung to keep pace. Sutter swallowed hard and looked quickly back at Cyrus who simply shrugged as if to say, *I told you so.*

Sutter examined Eartzie's expression and found what he might call expectant eyes. It was hard to tell under the man's pale, bland veneer. "I'm afraid the deal has fallen through, my friend," Sutter said in a dry voice.

Eartzie stood silently, his gaze never leaving Sutter.

"I'm sorry for the loss of your prize," Sutter offered. "But you have my word, I will make it up to you. I'll find another source for the explosive." His focus settled on Cyrus. "And this one will pay for your disappointment," he promised.

After seeming to take a moment to consider the statement, Eartzie also moved his attention to Cyrus. Several silent seconds followed before he finally nodded in agreement. "Disappointment hardly seems a strong enough word. I had a new design in mind… Something truly exceptional."

The small man stopped, looking lost in thought for a moment before a crooked smile crossed his face. "Still," he continued, "it will be extraordinary. I think it can wait just a short time more."

The bomber seemed lost in his own mind again, perhaps enjoying some twisted amusement that only he could understand. Whatever mental imagery he'd conjured was clearly bringing far too much pleasure, and that brought a cold sense of dread to Sutter. The guy was a box of broken marbles. The idea of finding a bomb beneath his bunk suddenly seemed so much more plausible.

"Eartzie," Sutter said, with some trepidation. Eartzie was standing stock-still with a smile on his lips and a blank look in his eyes. Sutter felt the contents of his stomach churn as he realized that Eartzie was still enjoying whatever loony-tune amusement he'd conceived amidst their conversation.

"Eartzie!" Sutter repeated.

At this, Eartzie slipped from his delusion as smoothly as he'd transitioned into it. He looked at Sutter as if this sort of thing happened to everyone.

Sutter swallowed hard and tried not to show his growing discomfort. "Please arm the perimeter explosives," he managed. "It's time to leave."

This brought a slight nod from the small man.

Rolling back his left sleeve, Eartzie revealed a small touch-screen display. It was about three inches wide, two inches tall, and strapped to the inside of his wrist. He tapped a numeric code into the screen and the display changed to show a bank of tiny green dots.

Though Eartzie had never explained the device to him, Sutter was fairly certain he understood what he was seeing. The screen displayed approximately a dozen green markers. If his guess was right, each represented a separate explosive that was planted somewhere in the hangar.

He's been busy.

Dragging a finger across the screen, Eartzie moved a virtual slider from one position to the next. Sutter couldn't be sure what the control did, but it seemed fairly obvious when the green dots instantly turned red.

He'd armed the devices.

His eyebrows furrowing, Eartzie brought the wrist-mounted display closer to his face and squinted. The concern wasn't lost on Sutter. "What is it?" he asked. Moving closer to Eartzie, he tried to get a better look for himself.

After a few seconds spent staring at the display, Eartzie finally lowered his arm and directed his attention toward Sutter. "I'm not sure," he said. "One of my devices didn't arm properly." Without further explanation, the bomber turned on his heel and stalked off into the distance.

"He's not the cat with the sharpest claws," Cyrus chided.

This brought Sutter's attention back around on Cyrus. He looked at him for a long moment, and then glanced over his shoulder to confirm that Eartzie was still walking away. "He may be a little…eccentric…but he's the best in the business."

Though his words were confident, they lacked conviction. Even Sutter heard it this time.

"Are you kidding me? He plays with bombs *for fun*. Now he's even slipping at that. There's what, a dozen charges scattered around this place? And out of twelve, he messed up one? I don't know about you, but I don't like those odds. Are you sure you want this guy building you a bomb?"

Opening his mouth to speak, Sutter stopped short. He wasn't entirely sure what to say. After all, it was a fair point.

———

Kingston Waterfront
11:06 pm

"Polecat, this is Command. Do you read?"

Boone shot a look to Stubbs. He stood thirty feet away with his rifle at his shoulder, scanning the darkness for additional dangers. Stubbs shook his head, likely in irritation. His COMMs were finally back online, as well.

"What the hell is going on?" Boone growled into his microphone. "Where have you been?"

"Some kind of broad spectrum interference tanked our relay," the technician at Command explained. "Someone is using some kind of selective frequency jammer. I switched over to a modulating encryption over an out-of-band-carrier—"

"Cut to the chase. Are COMMs reliable, or not?"

"Affirmative."

Boone cursed under his breath. "Overwatch, come in?"

"I'm here, sir."

"The package is out of pocket. What can you tell me?" Boone's tone was calm and professional, but he was seething inside.

"Kang and two of his men moved south following the coast. Team Two was in pursuit. I lost sight of them once they reached the tree line. It's unclear from my vantage, but it looks like Team Three is out of commission."

Boone now had his hands full as the mission spun out of control. "Understood, Overwatch. Control, I need medics on site. I have one casualty, one missing, and one in need of immediate medical EVAC. Team Two, come in?"

Silence came from the communications channel.

"Team Two, does anyone read me?" Boone persisted.

The voice of the technician back at base filled the silent channel. "Wait one, Polecat. Let me open up the spectrum range a little wider. Team Two must have moved outside of the hundred-yard perimeter Overwatch is targeting with the uplink. I should be able to blanket your general vicinity now that I know what I'm dealing with."

"—anyone there?" another voice cut in a second later.

"This is Polecat, Team Two. COMMs have been restored. Give me a sit-rep."

"Target set off a charge on the beach and took out Team Three, as well as a bunch of his own men. He used the detonation as cover to escape south. We're tracking him now."

"Understood. Activate your locator. I'm on my way to you."

"Roger."

"Polecat, this is Command. Emergency medical is en route from fallback perimeter. ETA is three minutes."

"Understood," Boone confirmed.

Boone looked at Stubbs. "You're staying with Hobbs. Higgs is still missing. EVAC Hobbs and pull out once you've located Higgs. I'm with Team Two."

Stubbs responded over his shoulder without shifting his watchful eye from the darkness to their back. "Roger that."

Pulling a small display from his pocket, Boone saw a light indicating the position of Team Two several hundred yards to the south. Assessing the proper bearing, he took off in a sprint.

He radioed Team Two as he drew near. Sneaking up on armed soldiers was never a good idea, and Boone was moving too quickly to approach with a high level of stealth. As he closed in on Team Two, he picked up the distinctive mark of tire treads in his night vision glasses. The path snaked through the loose scattering of trees, but it was easy to follow in the shallow blanket of sand that clung to everything. Kang must've had several ATVs stashed at the tree line as part of some contingency plan. If that were the case, it meant that he had a full-fledged escape route set ahead of time.

Kang had a leg up on them.

Boone found Team Two gathered in a small clearing. One of the men was on his hands and knees working on something, while the remaining two had their backs to him and scanned the perimeter for ambush. Three large four-wheel-drive ATVs sat a dozen yards away, their mufflers ticking as they cooled in the night air. It confirmed Boone's suspicion regarding Kang's rapid escape.

"Report," Boone said as he joined the group. Even after running several hundred yards through the woods, he was barely breathing hard.

The man who was on his hands and knees was hovering at the edge of a large concrete ring set in the dirt at the center of the clearing. He looked up at Boone. "Kang and two of his men ducked in here," he said, pointing to the hatch in the center of the concrete ring. "We arrived just in time to see Kang drop through here, but the damn thing's rigged. I'm trying to figure it out now. I'll have it disabled in a minute, sir."

Boone considered all that had happened so far. Kang had been fully prepared for their ambush. Every second they lost was an opportunity for Kang to make good on his escape. The steel hatch lid wasn't locked. Agent Ryan had it pulled open about an inch and was working a pen light and a small mirror beneath it. They were wasting time examining the booby-trap.

Working while he talked, Boone pulled a small wad of C4 from the webbing of his combat harness and stuck a wireless detonator into the soft plastic explosive. He waved Ryan away and stuck the C4 into the gap Ryan had created. .

"Control," Boone said. "I need to know where this tunnel goes."

"Understood," Control responded. "The tunnel doesn't appear on any of the waterfront plans. We're trying to sort that out right now."

Boone gnashed his teeth. "Make it fast. Our target is making us look bad."

The three members of Team Two had joined Boone and moved away from the surface hatch. Without a word, Boone raised the handheld detonator and hit the trigger. When the C4 flared, it sent the steel hatch flying from its hinges and winging off into the night. The detonation fractured the wide concrete ring surrounding the portal and it started to crumble. A second later, a massive fireball leapt from the mouth of the tunnel, shooting like a geyser into the sky. Fist sized flaming splatters of gelatinous fluid rained down around Boone and his men.

"Holy shit," Jenson gasped. "That's napalm. Kang is one vindictive sonofabitch!"

It was some kind of napalm hybrid, Boone realized. It had been mixed with a thick viscous gel to increase its lethality. The bomb would've been enough to stop whoever tried to follow. But the napalm charge was designed to burn the human body with a fire that was damn near impossible to extinguish. If the bomb didn't kill them, even the slightest kiss from that napalm charge would put anyone down.

"God dammit, Control, I need to know where this tunnel leads!" Boone spat. He was standing at the edge of a gaping hole in the earth. Beneath his feet was a wide, concrete-lined tunnel that ran north and south. Not only was the hatch gone, but its surrounding ring had disintegrated in the pair of explosions as well. The hole he was looking into was at least eight feet in diameter.

Boone relayed the lay of the land back to Control. "This looks like a sewer system," he explained. It's a concrete-lined pipe about twelve feet wide running north and south along the coast. I need to know where it comes out."

"That's an affirmative," Control responded. "It's a storm water run-off system that was installed twelve years ago. Someone wiped the information from the digital records. It looks like your friend Kang is more resourceful than we gave him credit for. He must've deleted the digital files in preparation for this operation."

Grinding his teeth once more, Boone walked away from the gaping hole. "Stow the commentary, Control. I just need to know if he went north or south. I'm pretty sure he had a couple of ATV's down in the tunnel, and that means he's moving fast— whichever way he's going."

"This is Overwatch. How sure are you about those ATV's, Polecat?"

Boone looked down at the ATV he was currently sitting on. "Pretty damn, why?"

When Overwatch came back, Boone realized for the first time just how out of breath Helinger sounded. "Base transmitted me a schematic of the storm system you're accessing. I just popped a lid in the middle of the wharf and, other than standing in a foot of water, it's quiet over here. Either the target has come and gone, or—"

"Or he's gone north," Boone cut in. "Roger that, Overwatch. Scout the area. I'm sending Jenson your way, just to cover our bases. Command, I want teams moving on any location Kang could use to surface north of my position. Murphy and Stubbs are with me in pursuit. "

"Are you sure that's a good idea, Polecat?" Command responded. "If you're right and they have ATV's, you'll never catch them."

Looking to Jenson for the all clear, Boone triggered the electric start on the 750cc Honda 4x4 that Kang had used to travel from the ambush point to the tunnel entrance. Jenson had already removed the simple booby-trap charge on each of the three machines. He had also done a quick job on the electrical system to bypass the starter lock.

The idea of Command second-guessing him didn't sit well with Boone. He would have a talk with the mission controller once the operation was complete. "I've got that covered," he mumbled and feathered the throttle. Dropping the transmission in gear, his thumb goosed the throttle and the machine lurched forward. With a click of his left toe, he shifted into second and then third, accelerating as quickly as the machine could operate. The engine roared as he opened the throttle fully just before reaching the lip of the hole in the center of the clearing. The front end of the heavy machine lifted by only a small degree before the ATV plummeted into the darkness below.

Chapter 4

Kyle Murphy was Team Two's demolitions expert, and even he'd been impressed by Greg Boone's efficiency in disabling the booby-trap at the mouth of the underground tunnel. The use of the explosive charge had not only disabled the trap left by Kang, but it had cleared the way for their team to enter on the discarded ATVs. There was a potential added bonus—if Kang heard the explosion, he would expect his trap to have claimed the lives of at least some of his pursuers.

The three ATVs rocketed through the wide underground tunnel in single file. Boone led the charge with Murphy in the second position, and Robert Ryan bringing up the rear. They were making good time. Boone set an aggressive pace, his 4x4 driving hard against the nearly two-foot deep stagnant water that blanketed the bottom of the tunnel. They were driving with their headlights extinguished being that their night vision glasses afforded a superior view. The heavy all-terrain vehicles were powered by beefy four-stroke motors that were quiet under normal circumstances, but given the cramped acoustic confines of the underground environment, the engines sounded like stock car engines.

There was an inherent danger to this plan, Murphy knew. They were sacrificing stealth for speed, plus the tunnel constituted one massive choke point. Odds were good that they wouldn't catch Kang by surprise. Murphy knew that he, Boone, and Ryan would be sitting ducks if they couldn't subdue Kang and his two men with utmost efficiency. His ATV jolted as it crushed some unseen debris beneath the water. He felt the rifle strapped to his back shift, as he leaned to the left and corrected the slight skid of the machine. At least he had the rifle and the SIG strapped to his hip. Murphy only wished there was something they could do about the noise they were making.

Boone's left hand rose into the air and closed into a fist. Murphy noticed instantly as the speed of Boone's ATV began to slow. Following suit, he eased off his own throttle. Relaying the signal to Ryan on the machine behind him, Murphy avoided touching the brake and let the swamp water surrounding the wheels bleed off his machine's speed.

Sliding from the left side of his ATV, Boone pulled the rifle from his back and took a knee in the water. The muzzle of his M4 covered the distant darkness to their twelve o'clock. Murphy took his cue and slipped into position on the right side of Boone's quad. His knee sunk into the stagnant swamp water with barely a thought, as he pointed his own rifle down the tunnel.

"What did I miss?" Murphy asked. "I must've lost my earbud when I dropped into the tunnel."

Boone's answer came as a whisper. He never removed his gaze from the distant darkness. "Control says there's a fork up ahead. You can bet Kang knows we're onto him. We sound like we're riding jet skis up this goddamn pipe."

"You're thinking ambush?"

That brought a grim nod from Boone. "It's what I would do. Plus, Control says it's another mile before this system reaches a gap large enough for a man to crawl out of. We have a team there now and Kang hasn't shown."

Murphy understood. Kang would likely make his stand. "He's got to know that we'll have people waiting for him when he surfaces. There's no getting away now. Why would he—"

Boone held up a hand to silence Murphy's whisper. He was receiving another transmission through his earbud. When Boone's eyes widened and turned to the tunnel roof directly over their heads, Murphy knew they were in trouble.

Boone spoke through clenched teeth, this time in less of a whisper. "Apparently, we're now right underneath one of the smaller costal inlets."

His eyes following Boone's gaze to the ceiling, Murphy's hand instinctively sought the fanny pack strapped to his waist. He was the team's demolitions expert, and he had a sinking feeling that he knew what was coming next. "Kang doesn't plan on taking this tunnel to the end of the line, does he?" he grumbled.

"Would you?" Boone quipped.

Murphy sensed Ryan silently behind him. His M4 was leveled across the fender of the ATV, and he'd been staring into the darkness throughout the entire conversation. From the look in his eyes, he hadn't heard what was said.

Murphy read the question in Ryan's eyes, and responded. "He said Kang's going to flood the tunnel and drown us like rats."

His eyes narrowed at the thought, but Ryan said nothing. He looked back over his shoulder for a long second and then back to Murphy. Ryan spat the wad of chew from his mouth. "I never liked water park rides. What's the plan?"

With a grin, Murphy turned back to Boone. He could see the wheels working behind the boss's eyes and hoped he had a trick up his sleeve.

Kingston Waterfront
11:17 pm

Standing on the rear cargo rack of his Honda ATV, Kang Woo-jin secured the last strip of narrow det cord and completed the irregularly shaped circle on the ceiling of the tunnel. The loop was about an inch wide and six feet in diameter. The detonator snapped into place straddling the cordlike material. He knew he was being pursued, but once the charge was triggered, millions of gallons of seawater would flood the tunnel and bring an end to those giving chase.

Jumping from the ATV and landing with a splash in the knee-deep water, Kang adjusted his night vision headset to check on the progress of his men. His equipment was the more conventional, bulky design with a two-inch lens protruding from the front of goggles. Everything he saw was cast in shapely contrasted shades of iridescent green. One of his men had taken shrapnel when Kang set off the satchel charge on the beach. The fool knew the plan; he just hadn't been fast enough on his feet. Now he was losing blood at an alarming rate and was guaranteed not to survive the next stage.

When Kang left his SUV to meet the delivery team on the beach, he didn't know about the sting operation, but he'd been prepared for an ambush just the same. The satchel he carried with him to the water's edge had contained the agreed upon two million dollars in bearer bonds, as well as his contingency plan—a kilogram brick of Semtex.

The trap was sprung the moment Kang and his two men stepped within twenty feet of the team that had arrived on the zodiacs. Kang wasted no time. He threw the satchel to the member of the delivery crew who stood furthest from him, and snatched the cooler sized box from the hands of the couriers. He'd then flung himself to the ground and triggered the charge inside the satchel. SWAT team members had already been sweeping across the beach from the south. When the charge detonated, it nearly vaporized the man who was holding it, but it was the payload of ball bearings that killed the remainder of the landing party. At least one of the SWAT members had been killed in the blast, and Kang had seen two more SWAT members knocked out into the surf before he'd managed to find his feet and make for the tree line.

Stashing the three all-terrain vehicles in the brush had been a gamble that had paid dividends. There'd been a chance of some backwoods hillbilly finding the machines prior to the exchange, but the simple camouflage nets had proven effective.

After setting off the charge, Kang and his two men had made for the tree line and retrieved the four-wheelers. From there, it had been only a short ride to the hatch where they gained access to the underground tunnel. Three more ATVs were waiting for them inside the passage. After that, they'd made good time. The most dangerous portion of the backup plan was only moments away, but Kang felt confident that his adversaries wouldn't see his dodge coming. They would expect him to exit the tunnels at the first junction either north or south of where he'd entered the system.

"Are the restraints secure?" Kang asked his man in their Korean tongue.

"I am fastening the cargo netting now," the man replied over his shoulder as he worked. He was linking a thick mesh of nylon webbing to steel eyelets that were anchored deep into the concrete wall.

Kang's view shifted to his wounded man. The short Korean was young, in his mid-twenties at most. Though his night vision didn't afford a view that included color, Kang could see the young man's lower chest and abdomen were wet with a fluid much darker than the water that had splashed over every inch of him. He was bleeding out. In fact, Kang wasn't sure how the boy had remained upright this long.

"You should have been faster on your feet, my friend," Kang said. "Let me help you into your harness. We will get you out of here and then find you some help."

Kang led the young man to the tunnel wall where a five-point harness had been bolted to the concrete just like the cargo netting. A buzzing could be heard in the distance, and Kang looked to the south in search of the source of the noise. He saw the uncertain look on the face of his healthy subordinate.

"Don't worry," Kang said. "Their pursuit was a foregone conclusion. Just secure the box and strap yourself into your harness. I can't get the device out of here without you."

The man nodded and went to work as instructed. Kang turned back to the wounded boy who was trying to pull the first of the restraining straps into the buckle. "Allow me," Kang said. His hands moved quickly, buckling three fasteners to hold the man in place.

As soon as the last buckle latched, Kang saw the boy's weight sag against the harness. His eyes were rolling listlessly, teetering on the edge of consciousness. Kang pulled the Velcro flap back on the small pouch that was sewn into the harness, and freed a long tube with a breathing regulator on the end. He slipped the device into the injured man's mouth and pressed the button on the side of it. The hiss of flowing oxygen was unmistakable. Shooting a glance over his shoulder, Kang ensured that the healthy man was still busy with the task at hand before deftly releasing the carabineer on three of the four lag bolts securing the harness of the injured man to the wall. His death would be more merciful this way.

The distant buzzing sound was growing more distinct. Kang could make it out clearly now—the sound of approaching ATVs. *His ATVs.* How they'd gotten them into the tunnel was anyone's guess, but he was impressed. After hearing the detonation of the charge he'd left behind on the tunnel entrance, he'd dared to hope that the pursuing force had been completely eliminated. The explosion had been larger than expected after all, giving him added hope the napalm gel had done a number on the pursuing force. He flipped the power switch on the detonator in his hand, and smiled. It wouldn't matter in the end. If the bomb hadn't gotten them, the water would.

Seeing that his prize was secure in the cargo netting bolted to the wall at his side, it took Kang only seconds to strap himself into his harness. His subordinate was already secure. It would take only a second to trigger the det cord on the tunnel ceiling, and it wouldn't take much longer to flood the tunnel for a mile in each direction.

Kang was just slipping the regulator into his mouth when he realized that the buzz of approaching ATVs had ceased. His eyes narrowed through the goggles as he leaned around the cargo net. Peering into the darkness, he searched for his enemy.

Chapter 5

Stoffer Airfield
11:09 pm

Having been relieved of his gun was the least of Cyrus's problems. From the looks of things, the plane would be ready for takeoff at any moment. The copilot had completed his external examination of the aircraft only a moment ago, cursory as it was. Eartzie was the key. Cyrus needed to keep Sutter's attention on the bomb maker. It was his motivation for relentlessly needling Sutter regarding his decision to team up with the madman.

"I'm not kidding," Cyrus continued. "You haven't noticed the little guy's facial tick? He's getting worse. Now his bomb doesn't even arm properly? What more proof do you need?"

As Sutter fixed him with a penetrating stare, Cyrus knew he was never going to turn one psycho against the other. That was fine. Glancing back at Eartzie, he was fairly certain he only needed another few seconds.

Sutter's gaze followed that of Cyrus and fell back on Eartzie who was squatting down along the wall a hundred yards away on the far end of the hangar. There was a sudden violent flash of light, and Eartzie simply ceased to exist. Even before the deafening sound of the explosion reached Cyrus's ears, the man had disintegrated into a cloud of red mist.

The explosion caught everyone off guard—everyone except Cyrus. He'd worked hard devising a way to outsmart the mad bomber at his own game. So when the detonation took place, he was already in motion.

Putting all of his energy into a violent spin to his right, Cyrus felt the rifle muzzle slip away from the left side of his back. He shoved out with his right hand and knocked aside the remaining gun. At the same time, he swept wide with his right leg, knocking the feet from beneath one of the two guards. As the man went down, Cyrus effortlessly snatched the M4 carbine from his failing grip and fired point blank into the torso of the last guard standing.

Jumping back and swinging the butt of the rifle, Cyrus heard the unmistakable sound of crushing cartilage as the stock connected with the nose of Aubin Sutter. Sutter had his Colt 1911 halfway from the holster when he took the blow to the face. The impact sent the Colt skittering across concrete, as Sutter's legs folded and he dropped to his backside—his eyes glassy and stunned.

One immediate threat remained; the guard Cyrus had knocked to the floor.

Showing amazing dexterity and economy of motion, Cyrus took a wide swinging step to his left and brought the rifle to bear. Two shots rang out through the hangar as both bullets found their mark in the guard's heart. The guard had his handgun free from his holster, but had only just begun to raise it in Cyrus's general direction when death came for him.

Shouts erupted from the fuselage of the Airbus A319. Sutter still had a dozen men, each well trained and even more well-armed. Cyrus didn't like those odds, so when the first soldier arrived in the doorway of the aircraft, he didn't waste time with a warning shot—he hit the man with a double tap to the chest. As the dead body tumbled to the base of the mobile staircase, Cyrus could see the churning mass of additional soldiers struggling to move away from the aircraft door, already seeking cover further inside the plane.

The soldiers were held back for the moment, but it wouldn't last. They would realize they could fire on him from inside the aircraft soon enough. He didn't have much time.

"You sonofabitch!" Sutter snarled from his position on the floor. Blood was pouring from his nose and had already covered the lower portion of his face, drenching him to his collar. "I'll kill you for—"

Taking the weight of the rifle in his left hand, Cyrus lashed out with his right fist to deliver a devastating blow to the center of Sutter's face. There was a loud snap; blood splattered in all directions. This was followed by a hollow 'thump' when Sutter's head bounced off the concrete a half second after he collapsed onto his back. His eyes rolled slowly around while he struggled to hold onto consciousness.

With a sharp shake of his wrist, Cyrus flung what he could of Sutter's excess blood from his hand and onto the floor. What remained, he quickly wiped on the leg of his jeans. Hearing more noise from inside the aircraft, he quickly pulled the rifle to his shoulder and peppered the empty doorway with a series of rounds.

That should keep them pinned down for another minute.

Unfortunately, he needed a more long-term solution.

He found the answer to his problem when he glanced at Sutter sprawled out a few feet away. It took another second to find a way to reduce some of the variables. When he was done, he had the makings of a solid, if somewhat messy, plan.

Cyrus retrieved Sutter's discarded Colt 1911 from the floor a few feet away. It was lying amidst about a dozen loose ball bearings that had managed to roll from the far end of the hangar. They were still coated in a fine layer of *Eartzie*. Cyrus cringed, then pulled the M4 rifle strap over his shoulder and secured it behind his back. Racking the slide of the 1911, the round that had been in the chamber ejected and leapt into the air. He caught the unfired round in what looked like a well-practiced maneuver. He wasn't the least bit surprised to find there had already been a round in the chamber.

Standing over Sutter's semiconscious form, Cyrus considered the bullet in his hand. It had a wide copper casing and was capped with a full metal jacket, Teflon tipped solid point slug. He finally tossed the .45 caliber round down where the heavy live round impacted audibly with Sutter's chest. "I've got to say," Cyrus said with amusement. "You're going to wish you'd gone with something smaller, like a 9mm."

With that, he fired a shot into the meaty portion of Sutter's right thigh. This brought the man instantly back to consciousness. His eyes flared wide as he gasped in shock and struggled to pull himself into a sitting position.

Sutter choked in anguish, and he looked livid. But when Cyrus glanced in Sutter's eyes, he didn't see an opponent who was out of the fight. The goal here was to reduce the number of threats, not escalate things. He needed to take him down another notch.

Directing his attention back to the plane, Cyrus saw a face and a gun barrel appear in the corner of the aircraft doorway. Cyrus responded by raising the 1911 and firing off three quick shots. He paused before following with two more rounds. All five slugs had made solid impacts within the entrance of the aircraft. He hadn't been trying to hit anyone this time, but needed to keep everyone pinned down so he could get moving.

Looking back at Sutter, Cyrus fired one more round, this time into the man's left foot.

With Sutter now screaming like a wounded animal, Cyrus finally saw what he needed in Sutter's face. Tears streamed down his cheeks as he fought the pain. Blood flowed freely from his leg and foot, but since Cyrus had been careful to avoid his femoral artery, Sutter wouldn't immediately bleed out.

Pulling the belt from around his waist, Cyrus tossed it to the injured man. "If you want to live, you'd better tie off both legs," he warned.

Sutter set about using the belt as a tourniquet for his leg wound. When he was done with that, Cyrus knew he would need to use his own belt on the other leg to stem the flow of blood from the foot on the opposite side. For the remainder of the operation, Sutter would be too busy maintaining the tourniquets to cause any additional grief.

That left the dozen soldiers on the Airbus.

The 1911 was empty, its slide locked open following the last shot. Cyrus flipped the release and let the chamber slam shut before holstering it in the back of his jeans. He pulled the M4's strap free from his shoulder and once again peppered the doorway of the aircraft with rounds, targeting a wider area for good measure this time. The thin skin of the fuselage surrounding the door would do nothing to stop the rounds, and it would force the gutsier members of Sutter's crew to reevaluate the foolish plans they were no doubt in the process of making.

Snatching Sutter's discarded handheld radio from the ground where it had fallen, Cyrus tapped the transmit button. "Thompson, this is Cyrus. Do you read?"

The passing seconds seemed like an eternity. Then, Cyrus noticed movement through the cockpit window.

"This is Thompson." His voice was shaky, and Cyrus couldn't blame him. "What the hell's going on out there Cyrus? Did you just shoot the boss?"

"Sure did," Cyrus said. He couldn't suppress his smile. "Tell me you haven't had the urge to shoot the arrogant bastard a time or two?"

This brought another awkward silence.

"Maybe once or twice," Thompson finally admitted. "But civilized people don't do stuff like that, Cyrus. Are you feeling alright, man?"

The circumstances nearly made Cyrus laugh. He knew Thompson to be a pretty decent guy. He figured that Cyrus had lost his mind and just started shooting. His concern would've been touching had he not been working for one of the world's most notorious arms dealers.

Cyrus settled for shaking his head. Someone like Thompson should be running a Walmart, not flying aircraft for a gunrunner. What sort of twisted wrong turns in life had brought someone like him to this strange crossroads?

"Do me a favor, Thompson?" Cyrus asked. "Could you put me on the aircraft wide intercom? Your boys are in a lot of trouble right now. I think it's only fair to explain the situation before they do something they'll regret."

This resulted in another pregnant pause, one that made Cyrus wonder if Thompson was still there. That was, until he heard the distinctive sound of an uncomfortable man taking a very deep breath and swallowing down a dry throat.

Thompson just needed a minute to process all that was happening around him.

While he waited, Cyrus hunkered down behind Sutter's big black Escalade for cover. No one had opened fire from inside the aircraft yet, but it was only a matter of time. Hell only knew what sort of party favors were stocked away in the expanded cargo hold. Once Sutter's soldiers realized how well armed they were, things would get messy very quickly. Cyrus hoped to preempt that situation with his radio call to the pilot.

"Go ahead, Cyrus." Thompson returned. "You're on the ship wide COMM."

That meant it was Cyrus's turn to take a steadying breath before keying the transmit button.

"How're we doing in there, guys?" he addressed the soldiers en masse. "If you would please direct your attention to the starboard windows, you will notice that the boss man is down for the count. He has been relieved of his command—"

While Cyrus was talking, one of the more creative members of Sutter's team took it upon himself to slip into the shadowed corner of the open fuselage door with a sniper rifle. It was a clever move, but the conditions weren't dark enough to provide him proper cover. Plus, Cyrus had anticipated such a maneuver was coming.

Even as he was continuing his address of the crew, Cyrus pulled his head back behind the Escalade and readied the M4. The sniper had a scope that gave him an advantage over the M4's iron sights, but the scope had a distinct disadvantage as well in that it limited the shooter's field of view. It was something Cyrus could use to his advantage.

While the sniper lay prone in the shadows of the aircraft doorway, Cyrus slipped around to the rear of the SUV and readied his rifle with his free hand. At the last moment, he abruptly ceased his address of the crew, pulled the M4 tight to his shoulder, and peered around the quarter panel of the Escalade.

Cyrus rested his shoulder against the SUV to steady the shot, and quickly brought his target into view though the peep sight. He heard a cry from inside the cabin of the aircraft. Spotters watching from windows had seen him and were trying to warn the sniper.

They were too late. Cyrus squeezed the trigger. His rifle barked and the target slumped, even as the report echoed through the confines of the hangar bay.

"As I was saying," Cyrus continued as if nothing had happened. "You folks are under arrest. You have the right to remain silent. Should you refuse this right, you're welcome to go up in a fiery blaze of senseless glory. The choice is yours. But, just so you can make a fully informed decision, I think it's only fair to disclose the C4 charges currently distributed along the underside of your aircraft."

Cyrus went momentarily silent, giving everyone a chance to let the revelation sink in. "While you're pondering that, I'd like to remind you fellas that you're sitting on two tons of armaments at the moment. So, while fighting your way out might hold a certain appeal, please keep in mind that every bit of that shit is also incendiary. And since I know a few of you gentlemen are a little slow on the uptake, let me put that another way: You're sitting on enough explosives that, should you piss me off, even DNA won't be useful in identifying your remains."

Cyrus watched the doorway of the plane, but there was no further movement. He caught activity in the occasional passenger window, but that was to be expected. He'd given them a lot to think about and discuss.

A rather cruel idea crossed his mind, and Cyrus couldn't help himself. He tapped the transmit button once more. "You folks don't have to give me a formal answer," he prodded. "I'll assume you're willing to sit tight for the moment unless you show me otherwise. But if I see a single face appear in that doorway, smiling or otherwise, I'll take that as your collective decision and send you all straight to Hell. Please don't test me." He was grinning—he just couldn't help it.

Setting the radio aside, Cyrus ejected the magazine from his rifle. There were two rounds left, plus one in the chamber. If they called his bluff, he would have to hold off what was left of a dozen heavily armed men with three shots and an empty 1911. He knew it was a hell of a gamble, and he had never considered himself a betting man.

The radio chirped with static. "Okay," Thompson said, from the other end of the radio. "I think you made your point when you blew up the little bald guy. We're not moving. Just don't blow us up too, *okay?*"

Exhaling a breath he didn't know he'd been holding, Cyrus chuckled. "That sounds fair to me," he agreed.

Kingston Waterfront
11:20 pm

The roar of the approaching ATV was unmistakable. The engine noise filled the confines of the tunnel; although he couldn't yet see them, Kang knew that his pursuers were fast approaching. He smiled and flipped away the safety catch on the remote detonator. They wouldn't arrive in time. The onslaught of water would kill them as surely as any bullet.

Taking a deep breath through his regulator, Kang tapped the trigger button on the small remote and braced himself for the violent rush of water.

But no explosion came, and no water resulted.

Kang's focus shot to the small remote in his hand. The small LED light was clearly visible in the green cast of his night vision headset. Likewise, he could see the light on the tiny receiver detonator attached to the roof of the tunnel only a few yards away. He tapped the trigger several times, rapidly as his pulse began to race. The light on the remote flashed with each tap, but there was no flicker from the light on the receiver.

No!

Kang didn't know how or why the charge wasn't working, but his well laid escape plan hinged on the rapid flooding of the tunnel. His pursuers were drawing nearer—judging by the sound, the ATVs were uncomfortably close. Movement was visible at the south end of the tunnel.

Throwing the useless trigger away, Kang snatched the Glock from his waistband and chambered a round. The cargo netting containing his prize was secured to his left, providing him some cover against what was to come, but at what cost? The thermobaric compound had been secured for travel inside a steel case that was coated in a thick, buoyant, plastic polymer material that would keep it afloat. But would the material stop bullets? While a few well-placed rounds wouldn't trigger the explosive, they could allow the liquid portion of the compound to leak out and become useless.

Pressing his heels against the wall behind him, Kang arched his back for a better view around the box and its netting. The harness was tight, but it gave him just enough movement to swing his gun past the obstacle. He opened fire immediately.

The moment Kang opened fire, so did his associate. The man was confined to a harness on the opposite side of the cargo net, so he suffered no obstructed view. He also had no cover. He would quickly fall to enemy fire if they couldn't take down their pursuers with the utmost efficiency. Kang knew that no support would come from the man to his right. He'd already lost consciousness, if he wasn't already dead.

From the darkness came the source of the vicious growl: a lone ATV charging at them down the center of the tunnel. The machine had its headlight off—a necessity, Kang realized. Since both sides of this battle relied on night vision optics, neither could afford to be blinded by the limited usefulness of a single headlight. The machine kicked up a sizable wall of water as it bucked the two foot deep flooding and advanced in four-wheel-drive.

Kang fired off an entire magazine in the time it took the machine to draw near. Ejecting the spent mag and slapping a fresh load home with practiced ease, he fired again while two thoughts crossed his mind for the first time. Why had no one returned fire? And why was there only one ATV attacking?

The large Honda 4x4 swerved back and forth in the tunnel as it kicked up a wall of water with its wide front end. But even as it zigged and zagged, it did so only with the slightest of adjustments. It was less like the rider was trying to avoid the gunfire, and more like he was fighting for control of the machine.

The ATV continued its attack at a ceaseless pace until it smashed into the back of the ATV Kang had left parked beneath his ring of det cord. At the moment of impact, when the forward motion ceased and the wall of water abated, Kang saw there was no one on the driver's seat. The engine roared unchecked as the 4x4 continued to buck and push against the parked machine as if it had a mission of its own.

Kang's brow furrowed as his eyes searched the tunnel to the south. Still, he saw nothing. A loud *pop* returned his attention to the Honda. The machine's seat went spinning up into the air, apparently of its own accord. When the unmistakable form of what could only be a pair of grenades rolled from under where the seat had been, a curse caught in the Korean's throat.

Shouting as he fought with the restraints confining him to the harness, Kang's words were lost to the sound of the ATV's over revved engine and the crunching of plastic and metal as it fought for a way over or through the obstruction.

Only one of the restraining buckles remained when the flash bang grenades detonated simultaneously. The phosphorescent blast of light and bone rattling explosion relegated to the tight confines of the tunnel were overpowering. The combination hit the Korean like a metaphoric freight train and sent him tumbling into unconsciousness.

Chapter 6

The rustic countryside passed below, unseen by Greg Boone, as the Bell 412 helicopter charged through the night sky. He fought the urge to check his watch once more, knowing that it would do him no good. Nearly an hour overdue for his meeting with Cyrus and Aubin Sutter, his failure had put Cyrus in an unwinnable situation. Everything they knew about Sutter said that he wouldn't suffer the delay with any degree of understanding. Though Boone now had Kang in custody and had control of the thermobaric compound, sadly, his last task of the night would be to retrieve Cyrus's body from the meeting location.

Boone's side of the operation had suffered casualties, but they were losses he would deal with in time. Members of his field teams knew the risks and accepted them each time they went on assignment. Cyrus had known the risks as well as anyone, but somehow Boone knew he would suffer the death of the young agent more acutely than others he'd lost in the past. He'd recruited Cyrus and been responsible for every stage of his training. And though the kid had an innate talent for the work, Boone realized that it had been his failure that put Cyrus in a corner from which there was no escape.

A voice in Boone's headset jarred him from his self-recrimination. "Two minutes to the LZ, sir," said the copilot.

With a dry swallow, Boone looked to the three men who accompanied him. Team Three was entirely out of commission. One man was dead and two were severely wounded. The support team had moved in on the beach after he and Team Two left in pursuit of Kang. The unconscious body of Billy Higgs had been found adrift in the surf. Both Higgs and Hobbs had survived, but from what Boone had been told, both would be a long time in recovery.

Kang's tunnel escape had been stopped short by a thin margin. When the support team was clearing the beach, they'd discovered a selective frequency jammer hidden in Kang's SUV. Rather than deactivate the unit, Boone had the device recalibrated to block all but Coalition frequencies. At the time, he'd hoped to prevent Kang from contacting whomever he might rendezvous with to make good his escape. The decision turned out to have lifesaving consequences when the jammer prevented Kang from triggering the charge he planned on using to flood the underground tunnel.

Realizing that he and his men were about to become easy targets as they approached Kang's position without defensive cover, Boone's team rigged up one of their ATV's as a Trojan horse. They used a pair of rifle straps to tie the handle bar grips to the rear cargo rack. That, and the fact that the machine was essentially running headlong down a wide pipe, made it easy to keep the unmanned machine on course. Binding the ATV thumb-throttle into a wide-open position had taken only a single zip-tie. Boone had only ridden the machine about forty feet—long enough to get the 4x4 into third gear and make sure its course would hold true. Then he bailed, watching the machine until it disappeared beyond the range of his night vision glasses.

Murphy had rigged a small charge to the latch mechanism under the four-wheeler's seat. They'd pulled the pin on flash bang grenades before wedging them under the seat. Once the machine reached its target, Murphy triggered the small charge and sent the seat flying. The flash bangs had detonated seconds later. The effect of the detonation in the confined space, and in such close proximity to Kang and his men, had been devastating. Kang and one of his men were rendered unconscious by the percussive blast. The remaining member of Kang's team was pronounced dead at the scene, likely having succumbed shortly before Boone's attack on Kang's position.

In the end, Boone had taken Kang without having to fire a shot. Sadly, it wouldn't be enough to save Cyrus Cooper. Boone gnashed his teeth once more at the thought of his error, as the chopper set down on an open stretch of grass at the east end of Stoffer Airfield. Boone and his team piled out of the aircraft. He watched as the chopper lifted off seconds later and disappeared into the night. It wouldn't return until he radioed the 'all clear'.

A black Chevy Suburban was waiting nearby. The team silently took up positions and the SUV pulled away without any of the four men uttering a word. A somber mood was shared by all. Everyone understood what they were here to do, and for as much as each man wanted to see this operation come to an end, Boone knew that none of them was in a hurry to address this last task.

Stoffer Airfield
11:56 pm

The black Suburban pulled up to the ten-foot chain link fence that circled the aircraft hangar. The hangar was a massive arched structure—utilitarian, but modern and recently constructed. Boone slid from the back seat of the four-door vehicle and took a look at the building. They were still about fifty yards out. The gate had been left wide open and there were no guards in sight.

These were not good signs.

Stubbs slipped from the back seat, pulling his M4 and a compact MP5 along with him. The Chevy's internal dome lights had been disabled prior to their arrival.

Looking over his shoulder, Boone's eyes met those of Stubbs. The man looked skeptical. He didn't like the look of things either. Boone gave him a nod and Stubbs ducked inside the fence, sweeping right before disappearing into the darkness. Murphy and Jenson went through the gate, taking the left flank and vanishing just as quickly.

Sitting in the passenger seat of the Chevy, Boone accepted the FLIR imaging unit Ryan passed him from the driver's seat. The device would pick up heat sources inside the building and should make it easy to identify potential threats and targets.

"Three, in position," Stubbs reported over the COMM from somewhere in the darkness.

"Four is good to go," Murphy also responded.

"Two is set," Jenson radioed.

With some trepidation, Boone activated the FLIR imager. He aimed the tiny lens through the windshield and panned it over the face of the aircraft hangar. Only two heat sources stood out. One was clearly a water heater; the other was the distinctive form of a man. At this, Boone's heart sank. He knew his worst fears were becoming manifest. He'd hoped for multiple heat signatures. It would've indicated that Sutter and his men were still on site. If only one warm body was present, it was surely a dire sign. Sutter was long gone.

What if this signature is Cyrus?

It was as illogical as it was unlikely. Sutter wouldn't leave Cyrus behind unless the kid was dead.

But then who would the last heat signature be? Airport security? Why would Sutter leave anyone behind?

Boone wasn't leaving until he knew for sure.

Just before he pulled the imaging lens down from the dashboard, he realized there was another unusual reading. The device showed human body heat temperatures in a distinctive red color. Cold zones were displayed in shades of gray. Anything between black and white was some sort of ambient thermal rating. Temperatures of 60°F or above would take on a subtle yellow color and grow redder from there. So, the orange amorphous blob registering on the north wall was a mystery. It was a shade of orange that was fluctuating constantly. Boone couldn't tell what he was seeing. It was large, oddly shaped, and indistinct.

And the fluctuation?

Then it clicked…

Fire—or fire damage!

Tapping his earpiece, Boone reported the unusual discovery. "I register one warm body. We can't be sure if it's a tango or a friendly, so let's use caution in there, boys."

Ryan closed the case on the FLIR device, and tossed it over his shoulder into the back seat. Facing forward, he dropped the gear select into 'drive' and slowly advanced through the perimeter gate.

As they approached the front of the hangar, Boone knew that Jenson, Murphy, and Stubbs would be doing the same on foot, moving in from the flanks. The fact that no one had greeted them confirmed what he already knew. They were alone here. Alone, except for the one mystery body inside the hangar.

Stopping the SUV twenty yards shy of a service entrance set beside the massive overhead hangar door, Boone was surprised to find the smaller door standing wide open. Why not, he supposed. The gate had been open as well.

Chapter 7

Boone had his gun drawn, as he slipped through the door and into the hangar. The lighting was poor, but not so bad that he needed his night vision gear. Somewhere in the distance music played, but he couldn't make out the tune. Only a few of the overhead lights were in use. They were at the far end of the hanger, shining brightly upon the glaring white body of an Airbus A319.

Boone moved in on the aircraft, advancing down the center of the structure. At the same time, he sensed Ryan somewhere to his right, moving in lockstep with him. As the Airbus came fully into view for the first time, Boone was puzzled by what he saw. A mobile staircase was positioned against the main fuselage door just behind the cockpit, and the doorway appeared to be peppered with bullet holes. All of the passenger window shades were open, and the front windows were empty. The back two thirds of the windows appeared to be blocked with cargo.

Parked near the base of the staircase was a black Cadillac Escalade. Its four windows were down and the rear hatch was open. The music Boone heard was coming from the Escalade's sound system; now that he was close, he could hear it clearly. It wasn't loud, but it was easy to make out from within fifty or so feet of the vehicle. He couldn't recall the album, but it was one of *Social Distortion's* newer albums. Boone was well acquainted with the band because Cyrus had played their albums to death during sparring sessions.

However, none of this was the strangest of what there was to see. Spread out across the floor in front of the Escalade were at least a dozen automatic rifles and nearly two dozen handguns of varying makes and calibers. They were neatly arranged on the ground, as if someone was taking inventory of some eclectic collection. Scattered among the mix of armaments was an assortment of hunting and combat knives, a few tactical vests, and even a half dozen smoke and fragmentation grenades.

What the hell is going on?

Cyrus's most recent report had explained that Sutter had acquired an Airbus and that he would be using it to leave the country with his latest shipment of hardware. But if the jet was still on the ground, where in the hell was Sutter?

Boone observed the strange circumstances as all of these questions filtered through his mind. He caught sight of Ryan surreptitiously moving toward him from his right. And based on the look crossing his face, he was asking himself the same questions.

Stoffer Airfield
12:06 am

A wide smile crossed Cyrus's face as he stepped from the doorway of the Airbus A319. He stood at the top of the staircase and looked down at his friend and mentor as the man examined the strange display spread across the hangar floor. After disarming the mercenary clan, Cyrus was at a loss to amuse himself, so he'd set about taking inventory of the confiscated weapons. He didn't say a word as he watched Boone examine the scene; nor did he react when he saw Ryan moving in from the periphery. Both men seemed equally confused by what they were seeing.

A moment later, when Boone's attention shifted, his eyes caught sight of Cyrus at the top of the staircase. Boone's gun instantly rose and acquired him as a target. Cyrus slowly raised his hands in a defensive gesture; a mischievous grin already slapped on his face. "It would be a shame to shoot me now," Cyrus admonished. "I've worked hard to stay alive this long."

Boone's mouth fell open. He started to speak, only to stop himself before finding the words. Almost an afterthought, he seemed to realize that he was still pointing his weapon. Lowering it, Boone offered a shocked, if reluctant, grin.

"How're you doing, kid?" Boone finally managed to ask.

The question brought a laugh from Cyrus. "All good here, boss! Oh, we're clear, by the way. You can call the rest of the team in, if you like."

Shaking his head, Boone tapped his earpiece. "I've got eyes on Cyrus. The sonofabitch is alive and well. Establish a perimeter. I don't want anyone sneaking up on us."

With a nod, Ryan took his cue. He headed back toward the entrance to join the rest of the team and set up a perimeter.

Cyrus watched Ryan leave and considered Boone's orders. "Are you expecting trouble?"

Exhaling a long breath, Boone made eye contact. "It's been a really long day. We're weak on the perimeter. I lost half my team in Kingston. I don't want to be caught with my pants down if Sutter shows up."

Cyrus quickly descended the staircase and approached Boone. "I was afraid things went south when you didn't show on time. That's not like you. How bad was it?"

"Fleming didn't make it."

Cyrus could see the pain in his friend's eyes. He hadn't been in the game all that long, comparatively speaking, but he'd been on operations that lost people. It wasn't easy. Doubly so for the man in charge.

"Two more are badly injured and on their way back to the States right now," Boone concluded.

"I'm sorry to hear that," Cyrus said quietly. He knew Boone took these things to heart. It was part of what made him a good man and a great commanding officer.

"But you don't have to worry about Sutter," Cyrus continued. "I've got him. He's not going anywhere."

The remark caused Boone's brow to furrow.

"It's true," Cyrus confirmed. Boone's visible skepticism made him want to laugh, but it wasn't the time. "When you were running late I had to improvise. I took Sutter prisoner, then leveraged him against the rest of his men."

Boone didn't look convinced.

Shaking his head, Cyrus couldn't understand the man's doubt. "See for yourself," he urged. "I put everyone on ice!"

Cyrus was already leading Boone across the hangar to the wide stainless steel door on the long, box-like structure running along the back wall. On the way, they passed the still smoldering remains of one of the exterior service doors. There was a wide breach in the wall through which the night sky was plainly visible.

Boone stopped short, looking at a charred white shoe off to the side.

"Oh," Cyrus said with a somewhat sheepish grin. "I forgot to mention that. Eartzie didn't make it."

Without elaboration, Cyrus kept walking.

When they reached the heavily insulated freezer door, both men stopped. "Ten men, plus four dead, and Aubin Sutter. Sutter didn't go quietly so he's going to need medical attention," Cyrus reported in a tone that was all business.

Thinking about that for a moment, Cyrus decided to revise his statement. "Scratch that. Better have a medic standing by. Sutter went down hard. You should have someone here when you pull him out of the freezer if you want to keep him viable."

Boone just stared at him as if he were speaking another language. Cyrus banged his fist on the freezer door. "How're we doing in there?" He yelled.

This brought a rousing chorus of profanity from inside the freezer. It was accompanied with the clamor of fists and feet smashing against both the door and the sides of the thick freezer walls.

It made Cyrus laugh. He couldn't understand the kicking and pounding. It was incredibly unlikely that the door would give under the weak onslaught. Sutter's crew wasn't the sharpest bunch, and Cyrus found them amusing. What possible good could all of the fuss do?

He supposed that the career path "mercenary" didn't require a very high score on a high school aptitude test. Then again, he'd spent six months undercover with most of those clowns. It was actually a wonder that some of them knew which end of a gun to stand behind when pulling the trigger.

When Cyrus pulled back from his personal revelry, he realized Boone was staring at him.

"What the hell?" Cyrus finally demanded. "Just say what's on your mind so we can get the hell out of here. What did I do wrong?"

Boone burst out laughing. "Wrong? From where I'm standing you didn't do a damn thing wrong!"

Boone turned and walked away, shaking his head and mumbling to himself. He left Cyrus there wondering what the laughter was all about.

Cyrus jogged to catch up.

"I gotta be honest, kid," Boone explained. "My mission was a goddamn disaster. I had three men down. Then we got here an hour behind schedule, I was sure I was coming to collect your corpse!"

Cyrus walked beside him. He still didn't see what Boone was so worked up over.

"You're going to make me spell it out?" Boone demanded. "You're a dick, you know that?" He was grinning.

"Fine!" Boone continued. "I send you undercover with a world class arms dealer. The guy is a Grade-A asshole. Every agency knows it. I figured there was no way you'd get inside his group in the first place. But you had to prove me wrong. Not only did you get inside, but you brokered one hell of a deal! You got Sutter to pull you in on the biggest operation he's touched in five years. He called you in on an op he was working with Eartzie, of all people! That SOB's on the wanted list of every agency on the planet—and you talked your way onto *that* crew?

"All fine and good. But you did it by telling Sutter that you could deliver a new prototype explosive? I knew we were asking for trouble when Monica insisted on a pair of back-to-back ops, but you said you were game. The entire point was to use the meeting to get a tactical team within reach of Sutter. But when I drop the ball and miss the meet, you just scoop them all up *on your own?*"

Boone stopped walking and put his hand on Cyrus's chest, stopping him as well. "Cut the bullshit kid—how'd you do it? How'd you roll up Sutter, Eartzie, and all the king's men by yourself?"

Cyrus shrugged. "I rigged one of Eartzie's perimeter bombs. When he tried to activate the perimeter, one of them failed to arm. That kind of thing looks really bad for a pro like Eartzie. He might be crazy, but he's still a professional. He still takes—err, took, pride in his work. So when he went to check on the device, he found a simple oversight and fixed it quickly. He didn't look close enough to see that I'd spliced the wires and added a 9-volt battery to one of the leads. As soon as he plunged the detonator pin into the plastique, the thing vaporized him. I just played on his professionalism and vanity."

"What about Sutter's men? There must've been a dozen or more."

Cyrus smiled. "That was easier. I shot Sutter in the leg and foot, then trapped his men on the plane."

Cyrus liked to keep things simple. Boone didn't go for it.

"Quit screwing around. How'd you trap them on the plane?"

"Fine," Cyrus sighed. "Sutter was going to kill me when you didn't show. I think he waited until everyone was on board so he wouldn't draw attention to the way he'd been stood up. I killed the two men guarding me, then put two rounds in Sutter. I told the guys on board the plane that I had it rigged. If they didn't surrender, no one would be able to ID their bodies. I gave them some time to think about it."

"How'd you manage to rig the plane ahead of time?"

The question brought a sheepish grin from Cyrus. "I didn't do anything to the plane—they just didn't know that. While I was letting them think it over, I moved the staircase away from the plane and pulled the explosives from a few of the places where Eartzie rigged the hangar. By the time the guys onboard made up their mind, I had the fuselage rigged for real—just in case they called my bluff.

"The next thing you know, I had everyone disarmed, in the freezer, and locked up nice and tight."

"And you put them in the freezer because…"

Cyrus took a deep breath. He was hoping to avoid saying the words. "I thought I might have to go looking for you. You're never late. Something had obviously gone wrong."

Boone took a long look at Cyrus. Then he looked back at the massive white aircraft. He seemed to be taking his time and contemplating the extent of Cyrus's extended plan.

"All that on a bluff? And all of it improvised when I didn't show up on time?"

"It wasn't all a bluff," Cyrus offered. "I eventually made good on my promise about having the plane rigged to blow."

Boone laughed.

After a few moments of silence, Boone finally tapped his earpiece. "Murphy, I need you inside to arrange transport for a dozen prisoners, plus medevac and security for a high value detainee."

He looked back at Cyrus, offering a pale grin. "You're something else, kid!"

Chapter 8

Somewhere over the Atlantic
5:20 am

Cyrus had watched Boone for the better part of an hour. Only minutes after the Coalition's Gulfstream G650 lifted off for home, Boone placed a call using a handset that was hardwired into the onboard communication system. Whatever was being discussed, Boone was doing a lot of the talking. And while the plush accommodations of the Gulfstream did a remarkable job of reducing engine noise, the constant muted rumble of the jet turbines and whistle of the air across the fuselage were just enough to keep Boone's words from Cyrus's ears. Whatever was being said, Boone looked as tired as Cyrus had ever seen him. The call only seemed to be wearing him down further.

Looking to the rear of the cabin, Cyrus examined the scene for perhaps the fifth time. He still found the view every bit as satisfying. The lavish leather seats at the rear of the Gulfstream had been removed, allowing for prisoner transport accommodations. In this case, it was a pair of unpleasant looking steel framed chairs that were bolted to both the deck plating and the rear bulkhead of the cabin. The seats were reclined at approximately a thirty-degree angle and offered no padding whatsoever.

A prisoner was secured to each of the primitive looking chairs; both men shackled hand and foot and bound to the arms and legs of the seat with heavy leather straps. A hood had been pulled over the head of each man, but telling them apart was a simple matter. Sutter, on the right, had at least fifty pounds on Kang and was nearly a foot taller. Sutter also had broad shoulders and thick arms. Seeing Kang beside him—especially with both of their faces obscured—made Kang look like a child sitting beside a grown man.

Cyrus found the comparison amusing and wondered if it had anything to do with the frustration Boone had over capturing Kang. All he knew for sure was that Boone's operation hadn't gone according to plan, and that his commanding officer was chafing over whatever had happened. They had ex-filtrated so quickly that Cyrus hadn't heard the details of Boone's operation. He now felt anxious for his friend to get off the phone so he could bring him up to speed. It wasn't like Boone to let an op go sideways on him.

Still examining Sutter and Kang at the far end of the cabin, Cyrus's eyes were drawn to the thick bandages around Sutter's leg and foot. Though he'd inflicted the wounds as a means to an end, he now had to admit—at least to himself—that they'd also served a secondary purpose. Even at the time he'd considered the idea to have long term tactical value—though he wasn't sure those higher up the food chain would ever agree.

The gunshot to the leg and foot had put Sutter out of the game and placed Cyrus in control of the aircraft hangar. The pair of injuries left Sutter too busy maintaining his tourniquets to be much of a problem. But since day one of the six-month undercover operation with Sutter's band of merry men, something had bothered Cyrus. His mission was to infiltrate the operation and gain Sutter's trust. The Coalition wanted to learn everything they could about his business and his clients. The more information Cyrus could gather, the more leverage they would have once Sutter was in custody. The goal, he'd been told, was to roll up Sutter and his crew, eliminating the entire operation in a clean sweep. They would take down Sutter's entire client list in the process. Unfortunately, it was that final objective that had always bothered Cyrus.

Taking down Sutter was easy enough. With Cyrus on the inside, the Coalition could grab him at any time. But if the Coalition was after Sutter's clients, it meant they were after terrorist organizations and warlords—Sutter even supplied arms to small nations. There were small time thugs on the client list, but most of the groups Sutter brokered for were heavy hitting outfits. Moves against the organizations on Sutter's ledger would constitute a massive undertaking. The way Cyrus saw it, there was only one way they could bag any of Sutter's clients, let alone do any real damage to the bulk of his client list. Sooner or later, the Coalition brass would consider Sutter for catch and release. They were looking to turn him—to use him as a double agent.

After six months undercover with Sutter, Cyrus knew better. If the Coalition offered Sutter a deal, he would take it and find a way to leverage the situation to his own advantage. Cyrus knew he would never talk the Red Queen out of making such a deal; she'd lied to him about his mission objective, likely because she foresaw his objections. The gunshot wound to Sutter's leg, and more specifically his foot, had been Cyrus's attempt to work around the problems associated with any kind of catch and release arrangement.

Sutter had always prided himself on the .45 caliber Colt 1911 he carried. Much like the story of how Sutter had lost his eye, the provenance of the weapon changed depending on who he was trying to impress at any given moment. Nonetheless, it was the caliber of the sidearm that had come back to haunt him, and not the story of its acquisition. The large caliber round had done a fair amount of tissue damage to his thigh—the wound had bled heavily and required considerable attention. But it was the shot to the foot that had ensured Sutter would never again walk without a limp. The heavy round had shattered several of the delicate bones in his foot. If he was turned and released back into the world as a double agent for the Coalition, Sutter would have a constant reminder of his situation and another war wound to explain to his clientele.

Cyrus knew it wasn't a brilliant plan, but he knew Sutter. The arms dealer wore his eye patch like a badge of honor, proudly telling fabricated stories of his loss to anyone who would listen. Cyrus had come to recognize each variation of the story for what it was—a tale of how Sutter wished he'd suffered the disfiguring injury. It meant he was always at odds with not only the disfigurement, but also how he'd received it. Cyrus had simply given the man something more to think about. It wasn't just a new lie to tell, it was an ever present reminder of his place on the food chain.

If he was honest with himself, Cyrus knew he was more concerned with the way the Red Queen manipulated his involvement in the operation. She didn't need to lie in order to get him to do his job. In fact, the better question was, why did she feel the need to lie at all? And if she was lying about this operation, what other hidden ways might she be manipulating him?

———————

Boone hung up the phone with a loud click and a deep sigh. He sagged against his seat and rubbed his eyes. After taking a long look at the pair of prisoners at the rear of the cabin, he turned his attention to the duo guarding them. A soldier clad in black tactical gear sat in a fold-down jump seat to the side of each hooded detainee. Both guards were sharp and alert, their full focus centered on the motionless forms of their charges. It was a dull, thankless job, Boone knew. He was glad he didn't have to spend the long hours staring at a pair of unconscious prisoners.

Moving from his seat by the phone, Boone walked to the front of the cabin and dropped into the wide, swiveling leather recliner beside Cyrus. He strapped his safety belt and rubbed his tired eyes once more.

"You're popular," Cyrus said, tipping his head in the direction of the phone a few seats away.

Boone rolled his eyes. "The Red Queen. She wanted to debrief while we were en route."

Cyrus grinned at Boone's use of Monica Fichtner's nickname, and Boone realized he'd used it without thought. Shaking his head in tired frustration, Boone couldn't hide his smirk. The nickname had spread quickly through the ranks of the Coalition, though no one dared use it Monica Fichtner's presence. Boone had no doubt that Cyrus was responsible for the moniker. It wasn't until the name really took hold that he felt compelled to ask about its significance. Until that point, he'd never heard of the evil artificial intelligence from the 'Resident Evil' movie series. He had to admit that the ruthless, robotic quality of an A.I. was a pretty accurate depiction of their leader. It was no wonder the name had stuck and spread so quickly.

Now even *he* was using it, Boone realized.

"What did I do to warrant these first class accommodations?" Cyrus asked. There was an uneasy look in his eye. Boone read it as suspicion. "I always ride the freight transport back with the rest of the team. Something's up. What's going on?"

Boone eased his seat back. "Monica's got a Brainstorm Session scheduled for first thing in the morning. Apparently the meeting is a priority; even your debriefing is being postponed."

Cyrus seemed to consider that for a moment. Boone saw his eyes narrow.

"What does that have to do with me?" Cyrus offered a suspicious glare.

Boone grinned. "Seems you're sitting in on the meeting with me."

"The hell I am!" Cyrus grumbled. "Six months! Six months under. I'm going home. I've got a long-standing date with *my shower* and *my pillow*. If Monica thinks I'm going into the office when I get off this plane, she's got another thing coming."

"Come on. Think of it as a promotion."

"Is that what this is? Why? What did you do?"

Boone shrugged. "You've offered some great insight in the past. I just made sure Monica and Clayton knew where the ideas were coming from. You've got yourself to thank for this unwanted invitation."

Closing his eyes and slouching in his chair, Cyrus still didn't seem at ease. "Why doesn't this feel like an invitation?"

Boone couldn't suppress his smile. It was a fair observation. His attendance wasn't actually optional. "Think of it as a trial run. If you really don't want this, all you have to do is fail to be your normal, resourceful self."

Cyrus fell silent for nearly thirty seconds; long enough for Boone to start feeling nervous. He didn't want to force the issue. Thankfully, when a mischievous smile spread across Cyrus's face, Boone knew something had turned things in his favor.

"Reid's going to have a fit over this, isn't he?" Cyrus asked. There was a glint of amusement in his eyes.

Boone laughed. "What's his problem with you, anyway?"

"I wish I knew. It's like he looks for opportunities to give me shit. I have no idea what's behind it."

"Let me worry about Reid," Boone said. "Are you in?"

Cyrus offered a shrug and only a slight nod of his head—one that lacked any enthusiasm. "Why not? I get to see the Red Queen in action. It might be worth the loss of a little more sleep."

There was something about the look in Cyrus's eyes when he spoke—it gave Boone pause. It was no secret Cyrus wasn't a big fan of Monica Fichtner, but the two rarely interacted directly. Though Cyrus never said as much, Boone couldn't help but wonder if putting them in the same room might be a mistake.

"Is this another one of the Red Queen's tests?"

Boone shrugged. He honestly didn't know the answer.

Chapter 9

The Gulfstream touched down at the Coalition's private airstrip to find a multi-car prison escort waiting to take Sutter into custody. Less than five minutes after the jet had rolled to a stop, Sutter had been awakened and led from the aircraft. A medical technician examined him before he was shackled in additional restraints and loaded into the back of an armored prison transport.

A few minutes later, the same process was repeated with Kang. The transport this time was handled by people from the CIA. Cyrus recognized several of the black suited men taking possession of him. Once Kang's hood came off, Cyrus saw the thick spool of gauze that was wound around his head to cover insulation that had been inserted in his ears. When Boone had explained that they'd blown out both of Kang's eardrums, Cyrus thought he was exaggerating. Apparently, that wasn't the case.

A dark SUV was also standing by for Cyrus and Boone. It took them directly to Coalition Command at Memorial Tower.

Cyrus considered the unfairness of it all as he stood in the small kitchen nook and poured himself a large cup of thick, dark coffee. Not only had he been denied the comfort of his own bed, but rumor had it that the Red Queen was already looking to task his team with a new assignment.

Taking his coffee and heading down the hall, Cyrus reached his office door and swiped his keycard across the striker plate. At the sound of the mechanical latch, he entered.

Everything was just how he'd left it half a year earlier. The office was so small that there was barely enough room for both him and the desk. One small file cabinet was wedged in the corner. No photos or documents adorned the plain, utilitarian off-white paint on the walls. There were no bookshelves or decorations of any kind. None of those things mattered to Cyrus; he never spent time in the office anyway.

One thing had changed, he realized. A short stack of files sat in the middle of his desk. The only new addition to the office was the thin layer of dust that coated all surfaces. Months of neglect would do that, he decided.

The files were the reason that he and Boone had been contacted before returning from their last operation. Whatever information was contained within the three file folders, it was the reason for the urgent Brainstorm Session.

What could be so important?

Dropping into the chair behind the desk, Cyrus flipped open the top folder. It was an information dump pertaining to a potential operation. It was like many similar cases he analyzed between field assignments. Before an operation went live, the facts of different cases were put before a team of senior agents and analysts for review. The idea was to gather insight based on disparate portions of data that had been assembled. Then, based on a review of the case, the Coalition would either take on the operation, or farm it out to the intelligence or law enforcement agency best suited for the situation.

During his earliest days with the field team, Boone had put a lot of info dumps—or gists, as they were sometimes called—in front of Cyrus and asked him for evaluations. At the time, Cyrus didn't realize that the cases Boone put before him were for past operations. They were scenarios that had already played out, or led to events that had already taken place; some with varying degrees of success.

To Boone's surprise, Cyrus's analyses of the closed cases included insights that were not among those gleaned by the operatives who originally preflighted them. Boone quickly discovered that Cyrus had a knack for finding anomalies in the data and offering information that had been missed by agents before him.

This led to Cyrus's rapid promotion and involvement in the vetting of live cases. At first, Boone couldn't get his immediate boss, Thomas Clayton, or Clayton's boss, the Red Queen, to allow Cyrus access to the necessary raw intelligence. Still, Boone knew that the process would benefit from Cyrus's observant eye. To that end, he started taking files to Cyrus after hours. After turning up a few high value insights, Boone finally leveled with Clayton and the Red Queen. Cyrus was given access to case files on a regular basis. Until now, he had never been a direct part of their so called Brainstorm Sessions.

Cyrus still wasn't sure his newfound involvement was a positive career move. His current circumstances were a prime example. He wanted nothing more than to get home to bed and enjoy some much overdue rest and relaxation. Still, even as he flipped through the first file, he couldn't deny that what he saw intrigued him. Every case was like a puzzle. Every story was unique. No matter what was in the file, there was always more going on than immediately met the eye.

That was his secret for finding the details hidden in the data dumps. It was human nature to get stuck on the most likely story presented by the evidence. But in so many cases, the data didn't tell the whole story, or at least not right away. It was easy for an investigator to be led down the wrong path. For Cyrus, the trick was to look at the data and find the story buried within—the less obvious tale that didn't immediately spring to mind when looking at the clinical facts. Looking at the data from alternative perspectives was the key to asking the right questions, and those questions were crucial to any investigation.

All of this led to the three data dumps spread out before Cyrus. Though he'd contributed to the Brainstorm Sessions many times in the past, he had always done so from behind the scenes, using Boone as a conduit to convey his insights. He was about to walk into his first actual meeting—and there was a catch. The Red Queen wanted both him and Boone to take a look at the data and then discuss their thoughts at the 8:30 am meeting. That didn't leave him much time. It didn't even leave him enough time to fully digest *one* of the cases, let alone all three.

The Red Queen wasn't one for realistic expectations, but even by her standards this was unusual. Furthermore, had she chosen, these files could've been transmitted to them aboard the Gulfstream. While it was obvious that there was something more going on, Cyrus couldn't yet tell what it was.

Still, the deadline was quickly approaching. Whether he had completed review of the files or not, the meeting would start in less than fifteen minutes. He decided to hit the first case hard and soak it in. Hopefully, while everyone was discussing that case, he would find the time to review the remaining pair.

Cyrus knew Boone had the same files on his desk at this very moment, and was pretty sure Boone would be taking the same approach.

What was the real point of the meeting? It had to be some kind of test.

It was as if the Red Queen was trying to intentionally catch him unprepared.

Chapter 10

Walking into the conference room, Boone was disappointed to find everyone but Cyrus already on hand. The Red—*shit!*—Monica Fichtner, that habit was going to bite him in the ass one day, was already in place at the head of the table. To her right was Thomas Clayton, her second in command. Across the table from him was a newcomer, Charlie Greene. She was a bright eyed, dark haired young woman who had very recently been put in charge of Logistics. Boone had met her only once—briefly, just prior to her promotion. This was her first time attending a Brainstorm Session.

Boone hoped that today's session would prove to be one of the group's better days. Sometimes the meetings grew heated. When tensions escalated, things grew increasingly unproductive. Since Charlie was attending for the first time, and since he and Cyrus were functioning on little sleep, Boone had hopes of getting out the door in short order.

Beside Charlie sat Luke Reid, head of Tactical Operations. While Boone headed Field Operations, Reid was responsible for tactical support for Boone's men. That basically meant that while Boone ran things offsite, Reid was responsible for quarterbacking the live operation from headquarters over the communications relay. Reid was a good man, but Boone sometimes found himself butting heads with him over the most pointless of issues. He wasn't very flexible, and field operations were all about being able to adapt to situations in a quick, fluid manner.

Placing the short stack of folders on the table, Boone slid into a chair at the foot of the table, opposite Monica. As he sat, her eyes rose to meet his. "Good morning," she said. "Pleasant flight?" There was a small smile on her lips. It was a mirth that didn't touch her eyes.

All the warmth and compassion of a tarantula.

"Fast and smooth," Boone offered. "Sutter didn't have any complaints."

It was an attempt at a joke. Sutter had been bound and sedated for the entire trip. She knew as much. They all did. The unfortunate fact was that, if Monica had any sense of humor at all, no one at the office had ever witnessed it.

However, Boone's crack at the arms dealer's expense did raise a chuckle from both Reid and Clayton.

"It's good to finally have the sonofabitch behind bars," Clayton responded. He was visibly gnashing his teeth at the thought. It was understandable; Clayton had a deep-seated hatred for Sutter. Though Boone didn't know the details, he understood that Sutter had somehow wronged Clayton early in his career.

"Truth be told, I wouldn't have shed a tear if the bastard didn't make it through the operation," Reid offered. "Maybe you should've had a talk with the kid before you sent him under with that gang."

Boone wanted to let the comment pass. He knew Reid was just making a joke, but he also knew he was half serious. "That's the thing about Cyrus," Boone said. "When I give him an order, he'll do his damnedest to follow it, despite what he thinks of the people he's working with—or for."

Reid nodded with understanding, then his eyes darted to meet those of Boone, as he realized the veiled slight.

Yup, still too slow on the up-take.

"Where is the kid, anyway," Reid demanded. An edge had entered his voice, and Boone realized he'd just done Cyrus a disservice by raising the man's ire before the start of the meeting.

Charlie shift uncomfortably in her seat at the corner of the table. Reid's tension wasn't lost on her.

"He'll be along in a minute," Boone said simply. "He just had the raw data for three cases dumped in his lap. He makes a point of reviewing the files before he offers an opinion. We should all be as vigilant."

Whoops.

Boone was on a roll. He saw Reid's lips draw tight at the reference to the last Brainstorm Session. In that meeting, Reid had made a swift and decisive judgment regarding a potential operation. At first, his decision had seemed sound. That was, until Boone pulled out the report Cyrus had written based on his examination of the same data Reid had referenced. In the end, the group had sided with Cyrus's analysis—a recommendation that was in polar opposition to that of Reid's. And while Boone knew that Reid had secretly hoped for the resulting mission to collapse in failure, it was actually completed by the Coalition's most novice field team, and to great success. The operation had unfolded exactly as Cyrus had predicted based on the information he'd been presented.

While Reid knew he had to maintain a working relationship with Boone, Boone knew that Reid had no such problems starting trouble with Cyrus.

"Tell me again why Cyrus is even involved?" Reid asked of Monica.

Oh, don't ask that!

Monica Fichtner glared over the edge of her glasses. She seemed to realize that the look had not proven a sufficient enough answer, and elaborated. "I think Cyrus's most recent analysis was proof that we could benefit from his insight, don't you?"

Boone tried to hide his smirk.

Ouch! Ask a stupid question…

Boone could see from the look on Reid's face that he was about to boil over. Pressure was building; it was only a matter of time before he blew. Glancing at his watch, Boone wondered if he could get Reid's hissy-fit out of the way before Cyrus arrived.

"Miss Greene?" Boone asked. "Would you do me a personal favor?"

Charlie Greene was looking increasingly uncomfortable with each passing moment. Boone wanted to do something about that and deal with Reid at the same time.

Charlie met Boone's eyes, likely unsure what to say in such a charged situation.

"Cyrus Cooper should be here any moment," Boone explained. "Unless I miss my guess, he'll be in the hallway not far away at this moment. Would you be so kind as to intercept him and delay him for about five minutes?"

Charlie looked confused by the request. She clearly didn't know how to respond.

Boone glanced at Clayton. He was watching events unfold with what could only be described as a morbid curiosity. Monica, for her part, was so absorbed in the paperwork on the table in front of her that she didn't even notice what was going on. No, Boone looked closer. That wasn't the case. She wasn't all that engrossed in the paperwork. She, too, seemed to be waiting to see how things played out. She just didn't want to participate in what was happening.

Bureaucrats.

"I was just thinking that, if you stepped outside for a moment and delayed Cyrus in the process, we might be able to settle something in here and make for a more comfortable and pleasant working environment in the process," Boone explained to her.

She seemed to realize he was giving her a chance to leave the room before he dealt with Reid and his issues. Nodding, she immediately rose from her chair. It was an opportunity she would readily accept.

Even as the door closed behind her, Boone had his attention focused on Luke Reid. "*What in the hell is your problem?*" he demanded.

"Problem? I don't have a problem!" He was instantly defensive. That was good. Defensive people made mistakes.

Clayton looked on, an aura of fascination spanned his entire face. Monica continued to work through her files. There was no way she was oblivious to the conversation at this point.

Fair enough. Game on!

"You've been all over Cyrus's case ever since he joined the team. Now that he's part of this group, you're acting like he's invaded your sandbox and kicked over your sandcastle." Boone was growling at the man. He refused to raise his voice, but his ire was up all the same.

"I know you've taking a shine to the kid, but he's not qualified to contribute in this capacity. It's that simple!"

Boone took a deep breath. It was bullshit, but Reid was responding in a more cogent and rational manner than he'd anticipated.

Reid's case was less reckless than Boone had expected. Still, Reid represented a persistent roadblock. He would continue to butt heads with Cyrus at every turn unless the equation was altered in some way. The only thing Boone knew for sure was that Cyrus had the same innate talent for data analysis as he did for fieldwork. He wouldn't allow such a valuable asset to go underutilized.

"You're just frosted that *the kid*, as you call him, made you look bad at the last meeting," Boone needled.

This brought a pulsing vein to the surface of Reid's forehead. He looked ready to bear his teeth and snarl.

"One lucky instance—and I stand by *my* analysis! My profile would've been equally effective. But you keep talking up your pet monkey like you'll win a set of steak knives if he gets promoted! He doesn't have the experience, and he doesn't have the skills needed for this job!"

Boone took a slow, deep breath, and watched Reid for a moment. Reid appeared to fervently believe he was making valid points. It was almost like he wasn't privy to the same mission reports Boone had read, let alone the reports Boone had personally filed. The success of Cyrus's last half-dozen undercover assignments very clearly spoke for themselves. No one survived in the field by being lucky. Boone was sure that Reid had some other axe to grind; he just had no idea what it might be in regards to.

Maybe it was something he should speak with Cyrus about directly. He must have some idea why Reid had it out for him. Still, Boone knew he needed to deal with this situation here and now.

"You think Cyrus isn't up to the job?" Boone asked finally. "I say put your money where your mouth is."

Though Reid looked unsure as to what that meant, there was a light in his eyes. He liked the idea of having done with all of this. "What do you have in mind?"

"This meeting constitutes his test. Cyrus has three gists, and he's had less than thirty minutes to evaluate the lot. I haven't had time to read *any* of the damn files, for that matter. You, on the other hand, know everything about the cases we're about to discuss. At the close of this meeting, we put it to a vote. If those on hand don't believe Cyrus has made a valuable contribution to the session, then he's out. He'll have no input on future sessions and won't consult on mission plans."

Reid was already nodding his head.

"Not so fast," Boone warned. "If, at the end of the meeting, it's decided Cyrus *is* a valuable member of this group, you *never* voice a negative or disparaging comment regarding him again, whether in his presence or not."

At that, Reid's head stopped bobbing. The terms were no longer quite so agreeable. None of them were life or death, but he was at least fully considering the ramifications of a loss.

"One other stipulation," Boone clarified. "Both you and I are prohibited from voting as to Cyrus's value to this group."

Nodding one more time, Reid made his decision. "Agreed!"

Boone sat back in his chair, idly rolling his Zippo lighter in his hand. While he had no doubt Cyrus would prove his worth, that wasn't enough. He needed a way to stick it to Reid and really drive his point home.

Considering this, a mischievous smile spread across his face. It was the perfect idea. He literally held the solution in the palm of his hand.

Laying the lighter down, he pushed it across the table toward Reid. "Why don't we make it a little more interesting?" he offered.

Eyeing the lighter as if it might bite him, nonetheless, Reid seemed intrigued.

"Pick any pocket on your vest," Boone clarified, his glance shifting to the tactical vest Reid wore. It was riddled with over a dozen pockets, compartments and mysterious stashes, where the man could secure assorted field gear. "By the end of the meeting, Cyrus will tell you which pocket contains the lighter."

Reid was weary, but interested. "And if I win?"

"You keep the lighter."

The man's eyebrows arched at the implication. Reid was aware of the lighter's provenance. It had been a gift to Boone from his wife on their wedding day nearly twenty years earlier. And though she had succumbed to cancer only a few years later, that lighter was Boone's treasured, ever-present reminder of everything they had once shared. He had carried it with him every day since they'd been wed. And while Boone was not prone to sentimentality, or displays of emotion, those who knew him were well aware of the lighter's significance.

The apprehension in his face was palpable. Reid swallowed hard, his eyes focused on the lighter the entire time. Boone knew his case had been made and that, with this wager, Reid now knew the full extent of both his confidence and conviction.

"If you win?" Reid asked, almost fearfully.

Boone answered without pause. "You give me your A.T.F. badge."

Like the lighter, to most it seemed like a trinket. But Boone knew that Reid prided himself on the work he'd done with the Bureau for Alcohol Tobacco and Firearms, prior to joining the Coalition. He'd risen through their ranks faster than any field team commander in the institution's history. He'd outlasted many of his commanding officers, and his name was still regarded with reverence within the Bureau. That badge was more than identification to Reid, it was a trophy representing years of dedication and hard work.

He quickly looked at Boone, before letting his uncertain gaze fall back on the worn and faded chrome finish of the old Zippo lighter.

"Or you can back out now, no harm done," Boone persisted. He wanted the man to step up. He needed to drive his point home once and for all. "But, either way, you're backing the hell off the kid."

"Fine," Reid agreed. There was a halfhearted, uncharacteristic cracking in his voice. He reached out and accepted the lighter.

"But I don't want you seeing where I stash it. I don't need you signaling him in some way," Reid clarified.

Monica Fichtner cleared her throat and drew the attention of everyone at the table. "This is an interesting wager, gentlemen. But as head of this organization, I'd like to think I have some say in this matter. Am I wrong?"

Reid looked instantly chagrined. The rebuke was tame by Monica's standards, so Boone already knew how she would rule on the matter. But a nearly inaudible stammer from Reid, combined with his reluctance to meet the Red Queen's eye, told Boone that his associate had yet to gain a measure of the woman in charge. Boone, for his part, looked to her with patient eyes and remained silent.

"Very well," Monica said finally, after a moment's deliberation. "Play your game. I'm rather interested in the outcome, myself."

The decision brought a wide smile to Boone's face. Troublingly, Reid seemed suddenly infused with a burst of confidence. It was as if he held some secret that he planned to use against Cyrus.

This is going to be interesting.

Boone rose from his chair. "Guess I'll go find Cyrus. I sent a pretty young thing out there to delay him. Knowing that kid, we might not see him for hours."

Boone was chuckling to himself and shaking his head, as he headed for the door. But silently, he harbored concern for whatever was bringing Reid increased confidence.

Chapter 11

Memorial Tower
8:33 am

Rushing down the corridor with a sheath of file folders tucked under his arm, Cyrus was painfully aware of the time. He was already late for the meeting. And, while part of him wanted to tell those waiting that they could all just kiss his ass—he was fresh off a jet, returning from a six-month long operation—another part of him was still driven. He wanted to get in there and hit the ground running.

As he rounded a corner, Cyrus literally collided with a short brunette woman wearing a dark suit and high heels.

"Excuse me!" Cyrus said, dropping the folders and catching her by the elbow before she fell to the floor. She'd stumbled on her heels while reeling from the sudden collision.

The woman collected herself. She seemed 'off' somehow, maybe confused. As she pulled her disheveled hair back from her face for the first time, Cyrus saw that her cheeks were pink. She looked flustered. More so than should've resulted from the impact.

"Are you alright?" he asked, with some caution. "Do you need to sit down?"

She looked around. First at the files scattered on the floor, then at her shaking hands. Finally, her eyes met his. They struck him as being the most unique shade of green he'd ever seen.

When their eyes met, there was a flash of recognition, as if whatever had distracted her had finally evaporated, making way for clear thought. "I'm sorry," she said quietly. "I wasn't watching where I was going."

He gave her another moment. He could see there was more on her mind.

"You're Cyrus Cooper, right?" she asked.

"My reputation for klutziness precedes me," he said with a warm smile, offering his hand.

She laughed, and they shook. "Charlene Greene—my friends call me Charlie."

Cyrus knelt and started collecting his files. "It's nice to meet you, Charlene," he said, while he did it. "I'm sorry to knock you down and then run away, but I'm actually late for a meeting."

"Oh, no. Call me Charlie," she said. "And that's the funny part. I was on my way to find you. Greg Boone asked me to delay you for a few minutes while he dealt with an issue in the conference room. You're not late at all!"

Cyrus stopped what he was doing and looked up at the young woman. And she *was* young. Not all that much older than he was. He guessed her age at mid- to late-twenties. That was interesting. People gave him a hard time for being the youngest guy in Field Operations. But it seemed younger faces were popping up all over the Coalition.

"*Dealt with an issue?*" Cyrus asked.

Charlie's face blanched. "Uh…I probably wasn't supposed to mention that part—now that I think about it."

She suddenly looked very uncomfortable.

"I guess I wasn't supposed to tell you 'that part' either," she admitted.

Her demure attitude brought a sincere grin from Cyrus. "You're not a very good liar, Charlie. That's not an ideal quality in a spy. Are you sure you've taken a job with the right agency?"

Her eyes bulged at his insinuation, before squinting as if considering his words. When the sparkle touched her eyes and the smile crossed her lips, Cyrus knew she realized he was just giving her a hard time.

"That's sort of a relief then, since I'm not a spy," she explained. "I took over as head of Logistics while you were out on your last operation."

The realization brought some satisfaction to Cyrus. This meant they would be working together in the future. It wasn't an unpleasant thought. And based on what she'd just said, it sounded like they would be attending the Brainstorm Session together as well.

Grabbing the last of his folders, Cyrus cocked his head in the direction of the conference room. "I think you're going my way?" he asked.

"Ah…" she stammered. "Boone wanted me to have you wait a few minutes. How do we know if it's been long enough?"

"If I know Boone, it's been long enough."

As if on cue, Cyrus looked up to see Boone step from the doorway at the end of the hall. Boone met his glance, then looked at Charlie standing beside him. He rolled his eyes dramatically and motioned for them to get moving, before ducking back inside.

Chapter 12

After watching Charlie slip into her chair at the opposite corner of the table, Cyrus took his spot between Thomas Clayton and Greg Boone. Clayton and Monica Fichtner were the two unknowns in this equation, as far as Cyrus was concerned. Boone had recruited him into the Coalition, and after that he'd been his training officer. Most recently, Boone had led half of the missions Cyrus worked after graduating from probationary status. Luke Reid was potentially trouble. Cyrus knew the man didn't care for him, but he'd never figured out why. Reid seemed to have a chip on his shoulder.

That left Clayton and the Red Queen as the wildcards. He didn't know what to expect from them. The Red Queen ultimately ran the Coalition. She was the shot caller and the public face of the small, elite agency. She was the one to deal with any political fallout created by Coalition operations. She was also, more often, the one to reap the political rewards gained from their hard work. In Cyrus's short time with the agency, he'd come to realize she was almost as skilled at ducking the fallout as she was at leveraging success to gain favor with the powers that be. She was a ladder climber, and she saw her lofty position as head of the Coalition as another sizable stepping stone in a path to even greater personal wealth and glory.

Thomas Clayton's goals seemed to be largely in line with those of the Red Queen. The man was an experienced bureaucrat in his own right, though Cyrus had him pegged as more of an opportunistic brownnoser who'd gained his position as second-in-command more through fortunate timing and efficient ass kissing, than actual intelligence.

Charlie Greene was an unknown factor at the moment. Her promotion to Head of Logistics had been a complete surprise; the result of some sort of dust-up over the course of Cyrus's six months in the field. She was young, attractive, and had struck him as very sincere. He couldn't help hoping that the job didn't drive that last quality from her. Most of those who made up the Coalition, field agents and headquarters staff, had a tendency to be rather hardcore. The place seemed to attract individuals either genetically predisposed toward having no sense of humor, or Type-A personalities complete with broomsticks surgically implanted deep within their colons.

Still, there might be hope for Charlie. Only time would tell.

"Why don't we start the meeting by reviewing our most recent field operation," the Red Queen began. She'd finally set aside the stack of papers that had occupied her attention, and Cyrus watched the woman's eyes pass slowly around the table as if appraising everyone present.

Her gaze finally settled squarely on him.

Figures.

"Your report made for an interesting review," she said, with a trace of humor. "I understand that the operation *did not* go according to plan?"

Meeting her eyes, Cyrus knew better than to demur. He called her the Red Queen for a reason. It was a name she'd earned thanks to her clinical, often cold, interpretation of raw data. It had nothing to do with her hair color, though that was an amusing coincidence.

"I wouldn't say that," Cyrus countered. "The mission objectives were achieved with a minimal loss of life."

The Red Queen's lips tightened into a humorless smile. Her glance moved briefly to Boone before once again settling on Cyrus. Leaning forward, she rested her elbows on the table before speaking in a humorless, robotic fashion. "I don't recall the mission objectives including the detonation of one of the suspects—or any parameter that required my undercover agent to bring the remainder of the arms smuggling outfit in single handedly."

"But, you see, that was the very first thing I learned about field work," Cyrus explained without giving an inch. "As they say, no plan ever survives contact with the enemy. In order to be successful, it's necessary to adapt. I simply adjusted the plan and adapted to the fluctuating mission parameters."

She rolled her eyes. "You're going to tell me that blowing up the bomber…what was his name? Yurgie?"

"Eartzie," Boone clarified. It was his first contribution to the discussion.

"Eartzie," the Red Queen growled. "Whatever! You're telling me that your *fluctuating mission parameters* prompted the immolation of a *human being*?"

"It's completely detailed in my report, ma'am," Cyrus responded calmly. He refused to be drawn into an argument with the boss, but he stood by his actions.

She sat back in her chair. He could feel her glare; she studied him as if searching for something specific. What that might be, he had no idea.

Finally the Red Queen nodded. It was as if she'd come to some sort of personal decision. "The man, this Eartzie, was a deviant. He cost countless lives and left untold more in ruin. In truth, you very likely saved the taxpayers a great deal of money by eliminating the need for a trial. There would've been countless extradition issues, as well. I am relieved that you killed him for the right reasons. According to your report, it was actually quite creative, using the man's own bomb against him."

Cyrus wanted to explain that, more to the point, he'd used the man's pride against him. It had been the bomb that killed him, but it was Eartzie's utter confidence in his own work and unwillingness to double check that work, that actually cost him his life. Had the man taken even a few seconds for a closer look at the wiring of the explosive charge, he would've realized that it had been tampered with.

Six of one, half–a-dozen of the other.

The Red Queen was happy, so Cyrus let it go.

"I'm really more concerned about the failure of the first part of the mission," she said, as her glare fell upon Boone.

Cyrus could tell by the complete lack of reaction from Boone that he'd considered her focus to be only a matter of time.

It was clear that the Red Queen expected Boone to explain himself. But since she hadn't actually asked a question, Cyrus knew Boone wouldn't play her game.

"Fine, let us try it this way," she muttered, also realizing Boone wouldn't respond to anything less than a direct question. "What the hell happened out there? Why was your part of the operation so far behind schedule?"

Boone shrugged. The full report had been submitted, even before their flight back from the EU had touched down in the States. Everyone at the table was already well versed on everything that had happened, Cyrus knew. The fact that she was rubbing their noses in these details was only a matter of posturing.

"As Cyrus explained," Boone said, "situations in the field are fluid. This one was simply more fluid than most."

When Boone left it at that, Cyrus found himself suppressing a grin. Boone could have pointed out that his team had successfully captured Kang Woo-jin, as well as recovered the thermobaric device, but he didn't bother. For his part, Cyrus knew that the loss of Pete Jenson and the injuries sustained by Team Two were a sensitive subject for Boone. He just hoped that the Red Queen was wise enough not to press those particular buttons.

Luke Reid cleared his throat and placed his hand atop the short stack of papers on the table before him. "There's no such thing as a routine field operation," he said, with a tone of finality. "We can plan all we want, but there will always be at least some degree of chance involved. That's why we need our best men out there."

Reid was clearly doing his best to shift the discussion to a more productive track. "Since we already have three new cases to deal with, why don't we have at 'em?" he urged.

The man's attempt to move things along earned him a disapproving look from the Red Queen—the gesture wasn't lost on Cyrus. The truth was, it was more than he expected from Reid. The attempt to waylay the boss's diatribe was impressive.

Maybe he did it out of respect for Boone? He was smart enough to know it would be good to have Boone owe him one.

"Fine," the Red Queen acquiesced. "What's our first case?"

Flipping open the first of the folders before him, Thomas Clayton joined the conversation for the first time. He'd kept his figurative 'head down' through the entire prior ordeal.

"We have an ecological group sabotaging industrial machinery down in Florida," Clayton explained.

This brought a derisive snort from Reid. "Since when does something like that land on our desks?"

The rest of the group began examining copies of the file in question, as Clayton explained the situation.

"The FBI has uncovered multiple links tying the group's funding to bank accounts ultimately belonging to China and North Korea," he began.

"North Korea again?" This surprised even Boone. "What would they want with a group of tree-huggers?"

Clayton nodded. "The money trail would've been impossible to track given conventional technologies, but our friends over at The Well have been using their new toy. Apparently, they were running some new tests and turned up this little nugget of information."

"Excuse me?" Charlie Greene chimed in. "What part of Florida does the ecological group currently operate?"

It was an odd opening question, but Cyrus thought he knew why their logistics specialist had focused on that fact.

Luke Reid, on the other hand, wasn't seeing what Cyrus and Charlie were. Turning in his chair, he looked at Charlie as if she'd just appeared out of thin air. "What in the hell does that have to do with anything?"

Raising a hand to mask the smirk that had instantly spread across his face, Cyrus waited for Charlie to respond. But when her complexion paled at Reid's cold statement and unkind words, Cyrus realized that she wasn't yet accustomed to the man's caustic ways.

Charlie swallowed hard. She looked like a deer caught in the headlights of an oncoming car, clearly unsure how to react given the circumstances.

"I ran into Charlie in the hall on the way here," Cyrus interjected. "We discussed this case briefly. She explained that, given the influx of money from communist states and the group's geographic location, we should look closer. There are likely links to smuggling from Cuba, since it's also geographically convenient and there are similar ideologies involved."

While all eyes were on Cyrus, he saw Charlie take a slow, deep breath, and then another. She was finding her center. He just needed to buy her a few more moments.

"And with Florida already overrun with drug smugglers," Charlie said, as she jumped back into the conversation quicker than Cyrus expected. "Authorities are hardly going to look too closely at the local tree-huggers, as you call them, when they have *real criminals* to worry about. It sort of makes a local ecological group the ideal front for smugglers moving shipments into the United States."

Monica flipped through a folder that presumably contained additional case information. "She's right," she concluded. "The group's activity has been confined to the southern portion of the state. There could very well be a link to Cuba. It's worth looking into."

Everyone at the table considered the unorthodox theory. Even Reid, sitting beside Charlie, seemed to be reconsidering the idea with renewed interest. "That's actually not a bad plan," he admitted. "But what would three communist countries be working to smuggle into the U.S.?"

"Unknown," Clayton replied. "But that's the case before us. We need to decide what to do with it. Do we take it on ourselves and open an investigation, or is this something better left to another agency? Maybe the D.E.A., since they already have a strong presence in that area and a great degree of latitude with which to operate? Or perhaps the A.T.F.? There's a good chance the Reds are smuggling some kind of weapons. Maybe even supplying them to some sort of anti-government groups already on U.S. soil. If that's the case, the A.T.F. will know the players. Hell, we could even throw this one over to the CIA and let them begin the investigation with the financial transactions being made outside the country."

As the conversation shifted into the plusses and minuses of keeping the investigation in-house versus sending it off to another agency, Cyrus's attention returned to the stack of files on the table before him. This operation would be a quagmire of political red tape. He would stay as far away from it as he could. Maybe one of the other cases would be more to his liking.

Chapter 13

Memorial Tower
8:50 am

The debate continued. It wasn't unusual for these meetings to run for hours, but Boone hoped this wouldn't be one such event. He was jet lagged and already feeling the physical aches and pains that followed every mission that involved combat. Plus, his patience was starting to fray. To start the morning with Monica second-guessing his mission when he was literally just off the return flight, had nearly been too much. And when she'd started the meeting by crawling up Cyrus's ass? Boone had stifled the urge to throttle the woman right then.

Still, Cyrus had handled Monica with more professionalism than Boone thought anyone could muster given the circumstances. In fact, the more he considered it, Boone realized that the young agent had played her like a finely tuned instrument. First of all, Cyrus hadn't cowed to her condescending tone. Doing so would've laid the groundwork for the future of their professional relationship. Nor had he shown her too much patience. That would've been a nearly equal mistake. Instead,

Cyrus had briefly explained the facts as they'd appeared in his written report, and then stood by them. Best of all, when she pressed him as to why things had not gone to plan, Cyrus had rather eloquently explained to her that, in the field, *shit happens!*

That confrontation alone had brought Boone's morning out of the gutter. He'd been relying on a massive infusion of caffeine to sustain him, but that little display had done far more to brighten his dark mood.

Even the operational questions Monica leveled at him were a minimal irritation by that point. Monica had started the meeting confrontationally. She was a live grenade just looking to go off in their faces. Yet, right out of the gate Cyrus managed to place the pin back in that figurative grenade, effectively pacifying her for the remainder of the meeting.

As Boone sat there content in his amusement—the discussion surrounding the Florida based ecological group being nothing more than white noise in his ears—his eyes fell on the group's newest member. He hadn't even known that Joe Lieberman was being replaced. He had no idea when Charlie Greene had taken over the position. It was a rare situation when a field operative needed to speak with the head of Logistics. The Logistics Department contained several dozen agents. Even Boone didn't know exactly how many people were on staff, but an entire floor of the building was dedicated to them. All he knew was that they were available 24/7, and the field operations guys had immediate access to them from anywhere in the world. These were the people who could arrange transportation, accommodations, safe houses, munitions—just about anything a field agent needed. In many ways, they were an operative's lifeline. They made sure the grunts had the tools they needed on the job.

That Cyrus seemed to have hit it off with the young woman wasn't at all surprising. The kid had a way with people. At least, when he wanted to. Boone had seen him go from a stone cold killer to someone who could sell an air-conditioner to an Eskimo in the blink of an eye. It was one of the reasons he was so efficient undercover. He could be anyone he needed to be.

It also wasn't lost on Boone how the kid had pulled Charlie's butt out of the proverbial fire, either. She'd frozen when Reid got in her face. And while Boone was fairly sure that the conversation Cyrus claimed to have had with Charlie had never taken place; nonetheless, the kid had been on the same wavelength as the young woman and covered for her brilliantly.

Now she had settled in and seemed exceptionally comfortable with the conversation regarding the potential placement of agents in southern Florida.

Boone suddenly realized that he no longer had any idea what was being said. He had fully tuned out the group.

Caffeine. I need more caffeine, if I'm going to make it through this damn meeting...

Chapter 14

The group was still discussing different methods for dealing with the ecological group, but Cyrus had tuned out that conversation. He was most often tasked with the cases that no one knew how to handle. There was no shortage of options when it came to the issue in Florida, so he moved on to the remaining cases. Due to the time crunch, he'd never had a chance to review the associated files.

The second report did little to pique his interest. It looked like an open and shut case of industrial espionage. There were high value properties involved, but none of them fell under the Coalition's purview. The case centered on plans for a revolutionary new mining device—essentially intellectual property. It was a deep core drilling and mining technology that would allow for the extraction of rare earth elements from the depths of the earth that were never before reachable. It was an interesting case, but it was largely a legal issue in the end. Not the sort of case that necessitated Coalition involvement.

The Coalition's mandate was varied and wide ranging, but many of the cases Cyrus had been tasked with involved cutting edge science or technology; the sort of new breakthroughs that had world-changing ramifications. Case in point, the mission he had just returned from: Kang Woo-jin, a North Korean brokering a deal that included a revolutionary new thermobaric explosive. It was a fuel-air bomb that was an order of magnitude more devastating than any explosive its size, and it was undetectable using any current tests.

And while the operation had spiraled into something larger than he or Boone had originally intended, the opportunity to capture Aubin Sutter, Kang Woo-jin, and Eartzie the bomber, was simply too appealing to pass up. Curiously, the Red Queen quickly adjusted the mission parameters and made Eartzie the primary target of Cyrus's undercover operation. Certainly things had gone a little off the rails before the end of the mission, but in the end they had brought two of the three men back alive, closed down Sutter's operation, and captured two tons of illegal armaments. The fact that a deranged bomb maker didn't make it through the operation could hardly be considered a strike against the mission's success. They would chalk it up as another win and move on.

Cyrus would've preferred one good night's sleep in his own bed before being assigned to the next case, but that didn't seem like it was meant to be.

Reading through the rest of the file detailing the industrial espionage investigation, Cyrus made a note in the corner of the manila folder. He then moved on to the last of the three case files.

Debate over the Florida operation continued without him.

The third case caught his attention from page one. His blood flowed faster as he read further. It was exactly the sort of case that fell within the Coalition's purview, and just the type of strange situation that he found interesting on a personal level.

According to the information provided, a Russian scientist had been experimenting with different ways to augment human memory. And though the file didn't detail as much specifically, based on the invasive details in the report, Cyrus guessed that the Coalition had been keeping an eye on the scientist for some time.

The name of the scientist in question: Rutger Voss. Born and raised in Russia, the man had studied a wide range of specialties at universities all over the world. He even did post-doctorate work at Cal-Tech, in the United States. Following the death of his wife approximately twenty years prior, Voss had taken his family and left where he was working in Germany, moving to the Isle of Kapros. He'd resided there ever since.

Looking further, Cyrus was both surprised and impressed to find Voss's name listed on over two-dozen pharmaceutical patents for drugs used in the treatment of Alzheimer's disease, as well as a number of other neurological disorders. According to the cross-referenced information on Voss, he was apparently one of the world's foremost experts in cognitive research.

The more Cyrus read, the more fascinated he became. Though he had yet to find what landed Doctor Voss on the Coalition's radar, he was enamored with the work the man was doing. Cyrus suddenly deeply regretted leaving his laptop back in his office. He couldn't wait to get out of the meeting so he could start doing more extensive research on the man.

Turning the page, the Coalition's interest became manifest. Voss was working on a device designed to capture memories directly from the human brain. It seemed Voss believed that such technology would lead to breakthroughs in numerous memory and mental health related areas. For the first time, therapists would have the ability to literally put themselves in their patient's minds, seeing and experiencing the actual events that had scarred them. Not surprisingly, such a technology would have applications in the area of law enforcement. No longer would there be any question of a person's guilt or innocence. Not if technology existed to review a suspect's memory as easily as the files on a computer hard drive.

Voss's latest project was ambitious. And if successful, it wasn't a stretch to see how it would prove useful in espionage. The ability to directly access the memories of another person was, in many ways, the ultimate weapon. It would allow access to an enemy's greatest secrets. And despite all of its potential benefits to mankind, Cyrus knew the technology would be seen—first and foremost—as a weapon. Offensive or defensive, it would become a weapon no matter what.

But none of these benefits touched the primary intent and Voss's ultimate goal, if his stated objectives were to be believed. He wanted to use the technology to gain practical clinical insights. He was building a tool he could use to examine the nature of memory loss in Alzheimer's patients. And, if memories could be captured and reviewed, perhaps they could be saved, even archived, giving patients stricken with the disease a chance to regain what they had lost.

As strange as it sounded, according to the notes Cyrus was reading, all of the research Voss was doing was conducted with Alzheimer's research in mind. He'd been working for decades on memory-related studies. But as Cyrus flipped further through the file, he still couldn't find the one piece of information he believed to be missing. There was no mention of a relative or friend linked to Voss—someone directly affected by the disease that had brought about his passion for the endeavor.

As detailed as the file appeared to be, Cyrus knew that it didn't hold the entire story. Something had spurred Voss's crusade, and Cyrus felt oddly compelled to discover what drove the man.

Reaching the last section of the report, Cyrus scanned the details. He could hear the debate over the Florida operation winding down. It would take only a few more moments to complete his review of the file.

But when his eyes fell on the last pages, Cyrus felt his stomach drop and the room begin to spin. Looking more closely, he hoped there was some kind of mistake. In spite of himself, he knew that wasn't the case. He found himself suddenly unable to move further down the page. His eyes blurred as his mind drifted, confronted with circumstances that he never could've foreseen.

This changed everything.

It didn't matter what the Red Queen had to say, Cyrus knew he would be taking this assignment for himself. He would settle for nothing less.

Chapter 15

It was a relief that the discussion was over. As far as Boone was concerned, he didn't care who dealt with the tree-hugging little communists down in Florida. And for the life of him, he couldn't figure out how they'd managed to debate the issue for so long. Worst of all, they were only one third of the way through their agenda.

Not for the first time this morning, Boone considered himself lucky to work in the field. Even these short interludes, being stuck at the office, were enough to drive him insane. He just wanted to get out of the building before he snapped and shot someone.

"Alright," Clayton said, with some satisfaction. "That brings us to the second case. It looks like we're dealing with industrial espionage on a massive scale. If we take a look at the preliminary evidence—"

Boone began rubbing his temples. There would be no stopping the headache that was taking root.

Just kill me now…

"Ah, actually," Cyrus interrupted. "It just looks like industrial espionage. Keystone Global went to a lot of trouble to make it look like someone took their intellectual property for a ride, but it's just a smokescreen."

The room dropped into silence for the first time since everyone had taken their seats. All eyes were on Cyrus. The kid was receiving a blank stare from Clayton, a look of complete confusion from Monica, and Luke Reid seemed as if he'd sniffed something foul. To her credit, Charlie Greene remained genuinely interested.

No one knew what Cyrus was talking about.

"Do you care to clarify?" the Red Queen asked, finally breaking the silence.

Boone could see that there was something on Cyrus's mind. But knowing the kid as he did, it didn't seem to be the case on the table. He seemed to be in a renewed hurry to get out of there—a sentiment which Boone could wholeheartedly sympathize and agree with.

Looking at Cyrus more closely, Boone began to reassess that evaluation. The kid had something on his mind. Maybe he wasn't worried about getting out the door after all.

What are you up to?

"Yeah, sorry," Cyrus said, moving on to explain.

He stood up and advanced slowly around the room as he spoke. It looked like he was working off some kind of anxious energy. Though he spoke clearly and decisively, Boone could tell that Cyrus's mind was focused on another matter.

"While you were going over the last case," he said to the room as a whole, "I had a chance to read up on this one. We didn't have access to these files on the flight in, so this was my first opportunity to read the last case cover-to-cover. If you take—"

"Wait!" Reid interrupted. "Go back a second. Did you just say you read this case, *cover to cover?*"

Cyrus nodded.

"Just now?"

He nodded again.

Reid opened his copy of the report and fanned through at least fifty pages of densely typed information. "You couldn't possibly have read all of this just now."

Boone rolled his eyes. He was about to lose it. "Are you kidding me? Are you trying to derail the conversation? At this rate we'll be here until lunch! What the hell difference does it make if he read it all just now?"

Slamming the folder shut, Reid glared at Boone. "When I hear bullshit, I call bullshit! That's the point. There's no way he read the entire gist while we were sitting here."

Boone rubbed his temples again. Reid wasn't going to let this go. Of course Cyrus had read the file. Boone had watched him read the goddamn file. In fact, he'd watched him read the last two remaining files. But no good would come from bringing that up now.

"Oh, for the love of God," Boone finally conceded. He glanced at Cyrus. "What's the second full sentence on the third page of the report?"

All eyes turned to Cyrus who just stood at the edge of the table looking uncomfortable. "Are you kidding?" he asked.

Boone shook his head and said nothing.

When Cyrus didn't immediately answer, a wide grin spread across Reid's face. "See! He can't answer the question."

Clayton chuckled. "You expect him to recall the exact contents of the file from memory? Come on."

Cyrus was still standing, having stopped his random pacing of the room. He turned and walked to the bright floor-to-ceiling windows that overlooked an expansive duck pond twelve stories below.

"Of course he can't answer that question," Charlie grinned.

When all eyes turned to her, she made a point of flipping to the third page of the report before holding it up for the rest of them to see. It was a technical drawing, a blueprint of Keystone Global's data server vault.

"There *is* no second sentence on page three," she clarified.

Boone made no effort to hide the smile as it spread across his face. He did, however, contain the chortling laugh he felt welling up from within.

Looking to Cyrus who still had his back to the group as he stared out the window, Boone decided to let the spectacle play out. "Cyrus, if you please?" he urged.

He heard Cyrus exhale with some resignation. "If we apply the same criteria to page four of the report, it reads: 'Keystone Global employs multi-factor authentication in the form of biometric locks as well as ten digit personal identification codes'."

Boone watched with amusement as Reid rifled through his folder in search of page four. He nearly burst out laughing, watching Reid's lips move as he read silently through the page. For their part, the Red Queen and Clayton were also reviewing page four, although they managed to do it without moving their lips.

Reid looked pissed. He fanned through the stack of paper and selected a page at random. "Who is Keystone's head of security?" he challenged.

"Renfield Cabott," Cyrus answered without missing a beat, his back still to the group.

Boone burst out laughing. Charlie Greene joined in, though she looked chagrined at having let the boisterous response unexpectedly slip free.

After an awkward silence, the Red Queen finally cleared her throat. "Fine. Now, if we can dispense with the parlor tricks, perhaps Mister Cooper can finally enlighten us with his analysis of the case?"

Cyrus spun on a heel and continued his slow circuit of the room. "As I was saying," he glared at Reid.

Oh, that won't earn him any points.

"There's a lot of evidence pointing directly at Keystone's chief competitor, McMullin Shift LLC, as having raided the Keystone server farm and stolen proprietary secrets. When that data was compromised, Keystone lost a major related contract with an undisclosed client. If you look at the value of that contract and consider the technology that Keystone was developing, as well as who their only high value client has been within the last half decade, it becomes clear that the client in question was the Pentagon. In any case, the entire theft was a sham. I'm willing to bet that McMullin Shift never had any interest in Keystone's intellectual property, let alone made any effort to breach their security."

"That's bullshit guesswork," Reid mumbled. "You can't possibly know that based on the report."

"It's all there," Cyrus promised.

Clayton looked dubious. "Do you care to explain?"

Cyrus did. "Among other things, McMullin Shift LLC, specializes in next generation security systems. First of all, they have no product that directly competes with the intellectual property that Keystone is accusing them of stealing. But even more telling is the clumsiness of the intrusion. McMullin literally employs the most brilliant security researchers that money can buy. Yet, according to the report, the exploits used to gain access to the Keystone's server farm were unsophisticated and guaranteed to leave a trail."

All eyes were on Cyrus, but no one seemed to be following his logic.

"McMullin has the best and the brightest; yet, they used a clumsy and amateurish attack on their competitor that was guaranteed to lead directly back to their doorstep? That's absurd. When someone looks close enough, I think they'll find that Keystone orchestrated the security breach themselves. If we take a closer look at the contract they had with the D.O.D., there will be some kind of stipulation that lets Keystone off the hook if they fall victim to industrial espionage. There will be an emergency provision that guarantees Keystone some kind of payout as a contingency.

"Keystone suffers a breach, then points the finger at McMullin, and the entire project ends up scrapped."

Boone watched as the Red Queen's eyes narrowed. She was seeing the ultimate destination of Cyrus's logic. "Why would Keystone subvert their own contract with the government? Certainly any such emergency provision would net them less than the delivery of the final product."

Cyrus nodded at her. He stopped his slow circuit of the room and dropped a hand firmly on Luke Reid's shoulder. "Care to field that one, Luke?" he asked.

Reid sat stock still, clearly uncomfortable at being called out. The kid had guts, putting Reid on the spot after what he'd just done to him. It was fitting, but it was ballsy.

"I'm betting," Cyrus concluded, "that if we look close enough, we'll find that Keystone couldn't make good on the contract. They couldn't make their product work. So they set up this little scam to defraud the government—cheat the D.O.D. out of a sizable chunk of change, figuring they could still capitalize on their failure if they played their cards right."

After a few moments of silence, Boone saw the Red Queen smile. She was concurring with Cyrus's assessment. Devious and clever, the chances were very good that Keystone had orchestrated the entire affair.

"Let's put Antzak and his team on it," the Red Queen said to Clayton. "There's no sense in putting a field team in place for this. Mister Cooper is very likely correct. We can let the lawyers sort out this mess. We have far bigger fish to fry."

Chapter 16

Memorial Tower
10:12 am

Cyrus's plan to push through the 'Keystone Caper' had been bogged down in the group's slow moving back–and–forth. He knew that if Reid had just kept his mouth shut and not tried to embarrass him, things would've progressed more efficiently. And while Cyrus didn't like others to know about his eidetic memory, at least in this case, it had helped put Reid in his place.

Still, for the life of him Cyrus couldn't figure out what he could've done to antagonize the man and provoke such persistent aggression. Reid seemed fixated on undermining, or at least embarrassing him at every turn.

All of this was the least of Cyrus's concerns when the group finally moved on to the third and final case. It was the case he'd been pushing the group toward with all available energy since the moment he finished reading the file. Despite his best efforts, it had proven a slow and painful process.

And then, when they finally reached the case, the group opened up into a great discussion. Cyrus was infuriated. They were simply rehashing the information that was contained within the report. Nothing they discussed led to anything new or brought any additional insight.

While the research Voss was conducting was commendable, the Red Queen believed it was incumbent upon the Coalition to monitor his work and track his progress. Should his technology come to fruition, it would be a substantial benefit to medical science, but it also represented a far-reaching threat to national security. As such, she dictated that his work fell under Coalition purview.

First and foremost, they needed to understand the current status of Voss's work.

And now, after all of the talk and debate, Boone's solution was to bug Voss's home and office. Unfortunately, the building where Voss both lived and worked was a literal compound, completely segregated from outside contact. The building sat on its own power grid, and had onsite capabilities to produce its own electricity and fresh water in case of emergency. In addition to this, Voss employed a private security force that patrolled and defended the facility.

All of which seemed like paranoid overkill, until the history of the Voss family was taken into account. Rutger Voss's wife, Eleanor, had been killed in a car bombing nearly twenty years prior. At the time of the bombing, Rutger and Eleanor were both employed by Onyx Gander, GmbH—a German-based research and development group with offices all over Europe.

According to the information provided, authorities had never concluded whether Eleanor or her husband had been the target of the bomb. Since they were both employed by the same firm at the time, and both were high ranking senior staff members, both had access to sensitive and proprietary company information.

Cyrus was familiar with Onyx Gander. The company didn't make headlines, but it was well known within intelligence circles. The company dealt with all forms of cutting edge research. They were involved in everything from next generation military systems to the latest in experimental medical research. Given the sort of research Voss was now conducting, it wasn't any surprise that he'd worked for Onyx Gander earlier in his career.

After the death of Eleanor, according to the files, Voss had spiraled briefly into a fit of depression. He left his position at Onyx Gander, and little was known of the man for nearly a year until he resurfaced on the Isle of Kapros, off the west coast of Norway.

From what Cyrus could infer from the data, Voss must've made some sort of impression on the small nation's imperialistic leader, King August Casper Borden, II, because Voss was allowed access to a squat industrial tower located in the heart of the capital city. The short concrete and glass complex had once been home to the French embassy in Kapros, until an unfortunate falling out led to the King expelling the French from the island nation more than a decade earlier.

Following the death of his wife, Voss left Germany and made the island his permanent residence. He moved his family into the defunct French embassy and quickly remodeled the facility to meet his needs. The building became both his home, and a state-of-the-art research facility. His work at Onyx Gander had made him wealthy and, over time, he parlayed that wealth into an even greater fortune. His work created technology that generated revenue in the form of patents that continued to bolster the balance of his investment portfolio.

But for all of Voss's successes, the loss of his wife seemed to have made an indelible impression on the remainder of his life. According to reports, in the last twenty years he rarely left the compound, and he absolutely never left the island. The compound was staffed twenty-four hours a day by a team of highly trained bodyguards, and the number of visitors admitted to the facility was few and far between.

While the reports stated that it was never clear if Eleanor Voss was the intended target of the bomb that killed her, Rutger Voss seemingly feared for his safety and that of his two daughters, Natasha and Anna. But what the reports didn't specify one way or the other was if there had ever been any additional threats to the family. It was unclear whether the pervasive level of security surrounding Voss and his family was justified, or simply the work of an overprotective—perhaps, paranoid father.

Voss's security-conscious nature seemed contradicted by the fact that one of his daughters was a professional tennis player who competed in tournaments around the world. She was always escorted by a contingent of security personnel, but it seemed odd that Voss would allow her to travel and participate in public tournaments if there was, in fact, a threat to her safety.

It was a paradox Cyrus would decipher once he gained access to Voss's compound. Was the man a cautious and protective father, or an irrational and unpredictable man? While Cyrus had personal reasons for suspecting the former, he wouldn't bet the operation on a hunch. Only time would answer the majority of his questions.

All of Voss's security presented a great deal of trouble when it came to keeping close tabs on his progress. Current intelligence indicated that Voss's early experiments with memory recording had proven promising. Taking the technology to the next stage would involve prolonged neural captures, and a more advanced method for displaying the captured experiences. So far, all of the information they had was sketchy and vague, but it was enough to convince the Red Queen that the project was worthy of Coalition attention. The group needed to get up-to-date information—ideally, real-time updates—if they were going to keep proper tabs on Voss's work. The technology he was developing was both groundbreaking and powerful. But until it was complete, it was useless. The Coalition needed to know when the technology was perfected so it could be the first to acquire it.

But for everything that Cyrus read, there was nothing to indicate Voss had any intentions for his work beyond the obvious medical applications. This was a first in Cyrus's experience. Every case he'd worked since joining the Coalition had involved some sort of cutting edge technology or weapon that needed to be kept out of the so-called 'wrong hands'. Voss was the first target of an investigation that appeared to be working toward a legitimate, altruistic goal. As a result, the sort of surveillance and oversight that was being suggested seemed more like an invasion of privacy than anything else.

"Our biggest problem," Reid explained, "is that the facility is completely autonomous. It has no hardwired connection to the outside. No phone, no internet—hell, not even power or plumbing! The building was designed to be entirely self-sufficient."

"That's not our biggest problem," Boone countered. Where Reid's voice was raised and animated, Boone remained calm and collected.

"Our biggest problem is this man," Boone continued. He slid an 8x10 color photo to the center of the wide boardroom table.

"His name is Ian Dargoslav. He's retired Spetsnaz: Russian Special Forces. He served with distinction in the military and, upon discharge, started doing freelance security work."

Boone paused for effect, or maybe to consider his next words. As he did, he scanned the faces of the room. "This guy's smart, he's well trained, and since he's spending Voss's money, we know he's well-funded. We can expect the security inside this building to be top notch. You won't get anything less from Dargo."

The Red Queen perked at the statement. "Dargo?"

With a grin, Boone nodded. "Dargoslav? Ian Dargoslav is more commonly known simply as, Dargo.

"Before he signed on to work for Voss, he made a name for himself in freelance—built quite a reputation, actually. Prior to being hired away by Voss, Dargo actually worked *with* Voss and his wife at Onyx Gander, in their security division. Anyway, since we know he's responsible for Voss's security, even planting bugs in that lab isn't going to fly."

"You really think Dargo could find them?" Clayton asked. He sounded skeptical, but it didn't sound like he was going to push the point.

"I guarantee it," Boone confirmed. "And that wouldn't be the worst of it. Say we're able to gain access and plant bugs. When Dargo finds them, he'll know something's up. He'll circle the wagons and increase his defenses. After that, any shot we have at even getting close to Voss's work goes right out the window."

Boone's statement brought an unconventional idea to Cyrus's mind. He kicked it around for a few moments, weighing the merits of voicing it—in front of this group in particular.

Why not?

"Would that be the worst thing?" Cyrus asked, making eye contact with Boone.

Boone met his gaze, but it was obvious he didn't grasp the idea. When Cyrus scanned the rest of the faces in the room, he realized that no one understood his thinking.

"What if we get Dargo's hackles raised? Get him to circle the wagons, or raise his shields—call it whatever you want. But if you think that getting Dargo to go on high alert is enough to keep us out, then maybe that's the simplest solution to the problem. If he's good enough to keep us out, then he's good enough to keep everyone out. Problem solved."

The silence in the room was consuming. At first Cyrus thought everyone was considering his idea. From the look on Charlie's face, she seemed to appreciate the simple efficiency of the plan. But when he moved on to see what Reid's response might be, he found the man staring blankly at the surface of the table.

That was odd.

Boone, for his part, appeared strangely uncomfortable with the suggestion. Still, Cyrus couldn't read anything specific from his physical response. Clayton, not surprisingly, simply looked to the Red Queen in deference.

The Red Queen closed her eyes and exhaled. She shook her head slowly. "Securing the technology isn't the primary goal. Our objective is acquisition of that technology."

Leaning back in his seat, Cyrus considered her words. He took a few long seconds to let the implications of the statement sink in fully. Like his most recent job involving the sale of the new thermobaric technology, if it had made it onto the open market, the technology could have been utilized by anyone, anywhere, provided they were willing to pay the right price. The objective had been obvious and straightforward. Acquire the technology before it hits the market, thereby keeping it out of "the wrong hands."

That had been how the mission was explained to him upfront. Hell…that was how every mission was explained to him. But factoring in what the Red Queen was admitting now, he realized he'd been fed a line each time he was sent undercover. The last time around, the primary objective hadn't been to keep the explosive formula off the market; it was to acquire it for the United States—or maybe just the Coalition.

Not only did the idea rankle him, it forced him to re-evaluate everything he'd done since joining the agency. No wonder the Red Queen had been upset that he'd killed Eartzie. It was likely that she wanted to acquire him, as well—use him as an asset for his expertise.

The idea struck him as demented.

Cyrus took a deep breath and tried to temper the irritation at being manipulated by considering a positive counter argument. Maybe those things didn't matter because all of the positive mission objectives, as he knew them, had still taken place. He'd still taken dangerous people out of play. He'd still kept powerful and deadly weapons out of the wrong hands.

But it made him reconsider what actually constituted who those 'wrong hands' were.

Plus, being exploited in such a way was patently wrong. He wasn't a drone. He was owed the truth.

Containing his reaction, Cyrus looked to Boone. He found verification of his suspicions in his friend's eyes. Boone looked uncomfortable and guilty. As if he knew all of the things Cyrus now realized and felt ill-at-ease for his part in misleading him.

As much as the indignation threatened to tear him apart from the inside, Cyrus kept it bottled up. He set the frustration aside and compartmentalized it. Looking at the open file folder before him, several dozen sheets of paper were splayed across the narrow section of table for easy access. This was what mattered right now. He needed to keep his eye on the prize—to focus on this specific mission. It was critical that he make this operation his own. He needed to find a way inside Voss's high security compound, and he needed the Coalition to want him to be the one inside.

"Acquisition is the primary objective," Cyrus repeated. He let the rest of it go. It was an issue he would deal with at another time.

"And bugging the compound is out," he continued. "If Dargo is as good as we think, he's going to be sweeping for bugs on a regular basis." He looked to Boone. "And we can't piggyback surveillance on existing hardwired connections because that's all filtered or free standing?"

"Exactly," Boone confirmed. "You can bet he'll be scanning for any outgoing transmissions, as well."

"Then we need someone on the inside," Cyrus said matter-of-factly.

Reid burst out laughing. "Just like that?" he virtually giggled. "If it were that easy, do you really think we would all be sitting here right now?"

Cyrus saw Boone make eye contact with him and then smile. The man leaned forward in his chair and rested an elbow on the table.

"Try to contain yourself, Reid," Boone said, as though he were talking to a small child. "I think what Cyrus is trying to say is that he has something in mind."

Not wasting a moment, Cyrus leafed through the stack of paper, pulling a single document free and sliding it beside the color 8x10 of Dargo from earlier.

"This is my ticket in the door," he said, with some satisfaction.

"*Your* ticket?" the Red Queen snapped, a degree of venom touching her voice. "May I remind you that I am solely responsible for making mission assignments? I assess the objectives, examine the resource expenditures, and decide who is allocated to each operation!"

Oh? Perfect.

In light of what Cyrus had just learned about the way he'd been manipulated on his past missions, he had real concerns. Foremost was Boone. The man had been his recruiter, then his training officer, and then his mentor—ultimately teaching him everything he knew about tradecraft. After putting such unflinching faith in the man, Cyrus needed to know if it had been Boone's choice to mislead him at such a pervasive level.

Now it was clear who to hold accountable. It seemed the Red Queen deserved the moniker more fully than Cyrus had ever realized.

"The hard part will be finding someone qualified on such short notice," Cyrus said. Though a proud smile threatened to cross his face, he held it back. He had her right where he wanted her—this mission had to be her idea. He didn't trust anyone else with the operation, so he had to turn the tables and manipulate her, with the most delicate precision possible.

Chapter 17

For the love of all that was holy, Boone was glad the meeting was finally over. The Red Queen had disappeared from the room with an efficiency that was impressive, even for her. Even her sycophant lapdog, Clayton, had been hard pressed to ride her wake as she passed through the door.

With some degree of pride, Boone enjoyed the way Cyrus had left the woman with no choice but to put him in charge of the infiltration of Voss's compound. Still, he couldn't understand why the kid was so anxious to get back out in the field. Undercover operations were hard work, mentally and physically draining. He'd literally just returned home from a long job, and he was vying for another operation already?

Something's up.

Charlie Greene gave Cyrus a pert smile, as she stepped past him on her way out of the conference room. "I'm sure I'll be talking with you," she said in an amused voice as she went.

Cyrus grinned. "Count on it," he said to her back as she left.

Incredible. The kid was already making time with the cute new head of Logistics? *Oh, to be young again.*

That left only Boone, Cyrus and Reid, still seated at the table. All three men sat looking at each other as if they had unfinished business to discuss.

Cyrus was the first to break the silence. He sat back in his chair and dropped his hands in his lap. Looking across the table at Reid, he shook his head. "Seriously, what's your problem with me?"

"*My problem?*" Reid sputtered defensively.

"It's okay, Cyrus," Boone said, attempting to intervene.

"No, I mean it!" Cyrus clearly had enough. "You've got a chip on your shoulder. It's no secret that you don't want me here, but you've got to get past it. Neither one of us is going anywhere, so get it off your chest. What's the deal?"

It was the direct approach, Boone realized. Surprisingly few people in their profession went directly at a problem. He couldn't help wondering how this might shake out.

Reid stared blankly at the surface of the table. His hands were balled into tight fists atop the armrests of his chair, and the muscles of his jaw were corded and visible. Boone could tell that he was on the verge of simply laying it all out for them. The question was, would it make things better or worse?

When the long, uncomfortable silence stretched into an even longer and grating silence, Boone realized Reid was going to back down. He could see signs that he was withdrawing further into himself rather than letting whatever was eating at him finally bubble to the surface.

Cyrus must've sensed the same thing because he slammed his fist on the table.

Both Reid and Boone jumped. "Dammit, Reid! Spill it!" Cyrus bellowed.

Flames of anger returned to Reid's eyes as they once again settled on Cyrus. "Fine!" he declared. "I know about you and Jessica!"

The finality of the statement didn't do anything to explain things for Boone. He had no idea what Reid was referring to. Looking at the expression on Cyrus's face, it seemed that the declaration didn't clear things up for him either.

After a long moment of silence, in which Reid only glared at Cyrus as if daring him to deny the accusation, Cyrus's eyes finally narrowed slightly.

"Wait a second," Cyrus said, with a degree of suspicion. "*What exactly do you know?*"

Boone's eyes moved back and forth between the two men as if he was watching a slowly paced tennis match. Reid's stare accusing Cyrus of some unknown wrong, and Cyrus's silent response, was an oddly inconclusive non-denial, denial.

"I know about the time you've spent together, and I know about the phone calls," Reid elaborated.

The name finally clicked for Boone. *Oh, crap!* Jessica was Reid's daughter.

"*Okay,*" Cyrus said slowly, as if waiting for Reid to continue. "But what do you think you know?"

Reid took the simple question like a slap to the face. "What *do* I know? What don't I know!" He sputtered unintelligibly for a moment. "You were just flirting with our new head of Logistics, for God's sake. What do you think I know, you sonofabitch!"

Cyrus bowed his head slightly, massaging the base of his nose at the corner of his eyes. Boone knew that look. He had exactly the same headache, though he was pretty sure it was for an entirely different reason.

"Reid, your daughter is *seventeen years old*," Cyrus said, with the same reassuring calm a parent uses when trying to pacify a disaffected child.

Reid's eyebrows rose, as if the statement only proved his point.

"Have you talked with your daughter about this?" Cyrus asked.

"You're the one who should know better," he accused.

Oh, hell. Here we go.

"This is something you should be discussing with Jessica," Cyrus warned.

"I'm talking with you, *now*. I want you to stay away from her. I don't want you to talk with her—I don't want you anywhere near her!"

Cyrus took a breath and looked the man right in the eye. "Look, Reid," he started. "Jessica wanted to talk about her girlfriend."

Reid just shrugged his shoulders; the 'so what' question was clearly implied.

"No. You don't understand," Cyrus continued. "Your seventeen year old daughter needed to talk with someone about her *girlfriend*."

Girlfriend…

The implication of Cyrus's statement caught Boone off-guard. But as surprised as he was, the look on Reid's face made it clear that he'd been caught even more unprepared.

"Girlfriend," Reid said, as if tasting the word for the first time. The phrase was forcing him to alter earlier perceptions and reevaluate many assumptions. "Really?" he asked in the ghost of a voice.

Cyrus nodded. "She only talked to me about it because she was worried how you would react." Cyrus thought for a moment. "I really thought she'd told you by now. She's been worried about this for a long time."

Reid's posture deflated as he hung his head. He'd shrunken in on himself. Not only did he no longer look angry, he no longer looked like he had any emotion at all.

Finally, he looked up at Boone. "I feel like an ass," he said in a near whisper.

Then he looked at Cyrus. "All this time I had this bottled up, thinking you were messing around with my kid? She really turned to you because she didn't know how to talk to me?"

That brought a resigned shrug from Cyrus. "She knows we work together. People talk to me. She's your kid…I wanted to help."

Boone found it amusing. As far as Cyrus was concerned, it really was that simple.

"I don't know what to say." Reid cleared his throat to steady his voice. "I'm sorry. I've been shitty. You didn't deserve any of that."

Cyrus chuckled. "Just go home and talk with your daughter. Getting this off her chest will do her a world of good. I assume you're alright with her choices?"

The embarrassed smile disappeared suddenly from Reid's face. He cocked his head slightly as if considering something for the first time. "Huh," he said quietly. "Did she find herself a nice girl?"

The simple sincerity of the man's question made Boone smile. That was when he realized, not only would things be all right between Cyrus and Reid from now on, but they would also work out between Reid and his daughter.

"Yeah," Cyrus said with a grin. "She did good."

Chapter 18

Pushing his chair back from the table, Cyrus rose and collected the small stack of folders. Boone and Reid quickly followed suit. Now that the awkwardness was behind them, no one wanted to be there.

"Oh," Cyrus said, looking at Reid. "Boone needs his lighter back." It had almost slipped his mind with all that had happened. He pointed to the zippered pocket on the lower right side of Reid's tactical vest. The vest had at least a dozen pockets scattered across the front. "It's that one," he said, as he pointed.

The statement caught Reid off-guard. He'd clearly forgotten about the lighter as well.

A grin spread across the man's face. "Sorry, Cyrus," he said. "It was a good guess, but you're not even close!"

Cyrus shot him a grin of his own. "Are you sure?" was all he asked.

Reid patted his left breast pocket with confidence, the one where he'd secured Boone's treasured lighter hours earlier.

139

Suddenly his countenance shifted. He began to feel the surface of the pocket. Confused, he finally slipped open the zipper and reached inside…only to find it empty.

He looked at Cyrus, not entirely sure he understood. "How'd you do that?"

Cyrus shrugged. "I still think you should check that pocket." Again, he pointed at the lower right corner of his vest.

Curious, Reid did as requested. Pulling back the pocket's Velcro flap with an audible 'rip' of the fabric as it separated, he reached inside and retrieved the Zippo. His mouth fell open. "How in the hell did you do that?" he stammered.

Cyrus grinned and headed for the door.

Chapter 19

Memorial Tower
11:03 am

Watching Cyrus leave the room, Boone considered the unnerved look on Reid's face. Only the two of them were left in the conference room, and Boone was about to make his exit when he realized Reid still had something on his mind. Rather than question the man, he sat back on his chair and folded his hands in his lap, knowing that Reid would make his point when he was ready.

"It isn't an act, is it?" Reid finally asked. "He's just what he seems on the surface, sincere and uncomplicated."

"You mean Cyrus?" The thought made Boone chuckle aloud. "Hardly. He's anything but what he seems on the surface. There are layers upon layers to that kid. But I get your meaning. His good nature isn't just an act."

Reid shook his head, but it wasn't so much for Boone's benefit. It was more like he was in the process of rethinking everything he had believed to be true about Cyrus. "To be honest, the thought never even occurred to me," he admitted. "You fast tracked him through the system and pushed him right into the field. That kind of rapid advancement normally results in an exceptional ego. I thought he was downplaying it this whole time. If I didn't know better, I'd say he has no idea he skipped several years of mandatory training by going into the field when he did."

The corners of Boone's lips curled at Reid's realization.

"What?" Reid insisted.

"He has no idea," Boone admitted. His pride was evident in the broad smile that spanned his face. "He doesn't know that I fast tracked him, either. He has no idea that I bypassed his time on your team and moved him straight into undercover work. As far as he's aware, he followed standard training procedure."

"How is that possible?"

"Think about it," Boone reasoned. "He only knows what I tell him. I just never explained that the traditional training for work in our undercover division takes a minimum of five years."

Reid leaned on the edge of the table; his eyes were fixed on Boone, and his mouth agape. Boone could tell he had about a million things on his mind, each struggling for a voice. He cut him off before he could get started.

"You've seen him work," Boone explained. "The kid's a natural. I've never seen anyone with a greater gift for this kind of work. And I think his last op speaks for itself. Cyrus brought in Sutter and his entire crew, all by himself."

Rocking back in his chair, Reid let out a sigh. His eyes fell to the table. He clearly couldn't argue with results. "I'm just having trouble believing you threw him into the deep end of the pool like that. He's done what...? Six missions since you cut the leash and let him work solo? And he's been with us less than two years? I can't believe Monica signed off on that."

"It was a tough sell at first," Boone admitted. "But, like I said, the kid's a natural. I've never seen anyone like him. No exaggeration intended, but he may be the best field operative I've ever seen."

"Sure, one day. Once he's got more experience under his belt. You know as well as I do that there's no substitute for experience."

"That's what these last half-dozen missions have been about." Boone sat straight in his chair, his posture adding silent emphasis to his point. "Like you said, I threw him into the deep end. And not only did he prove he could swim, he proved he was a shark!"

"That's high praise coming from the man commonly regarded to be our best and brightest."

Under different circumstances, Boone would've expected Reid's comment to be laced with vitriol, but he was being sincere. Reid had always been a fiercely competitive man, but it seemed that, at least in this regard, he had no aspirations or intention to subvert Boone's unofficial title within the organization. He really was generally believed to be their best field operative.

"I'm not kidding," Boone clarified. "He's got everything I have, and more. Plus," he added, with a chuckle, "kid's got youth on his side. Truth is, there's only one more thing he needs to learn and he'll have mastered everything I can teach him."

When both of Reid's eyebrows rose in unison, his surprise was unmistakable. "*One* thing? What's that?"

Boone sat back and took a long look at the table's surface. The enthusiasm drained from him as he considered his response. "He's got to learn how to lose," he said quietly.

After a moment, his eyes shifted to meet Reid's. He saw the question before it reached the man's lips. "Every op he's run has been a success, no matter how long or high the odds were stacked against him," Boone explained. "And winning is great. There's nothing better. But, sooner or later, something always goes wrong. It doesn't matter how well you plan or how prepared you are, no one can beat the odds forever.

"Someday a mission is going to go sideways on him and he won't have a way to fix it. I'm just worried how he'll react when that day comes. He's so used to winning, so accustomed to beating the odds that the real question is, what will happen to him when he finally loses one? Will he have the resiliency to rebound and move on? Or, will he be too set on always coming out on top to accept a failure? If that's the case, a loss could destroy him. And that would be a waste of something special."

Reid sat silently for a minute, obviously letting the reality of Boone's words sink in. He was an experienced agent, working in the A.T.F. before coming to the Coalition. Boone had no doubt that he could name a dozen such cases where promising agents burned out after a mission that went sideways. It was a reality of their world, and a real danger—particularly for a young agent who had been rushed through training.

"Wait a second," Reid said finally. He grimaced, as if he had just tasted something disagreeable. "Is that why you've been feeding him these hardcore ops? Some sort of…'trial by fire'?"

"No," Boone admitted. "Unfortunately, not. So far he's just been the right man for the job. His age has been key to most operations. Particularly this last one with Sutter. People tend to let their guard down when they're working with someone so young. They see someone young and equate it to inexperience. It becomes difficult to perceive him as a threat."

Reid nodded with obvious relief. But then his look turned suspicious once more. "But you're thinking of setting him up for a fall—a test to see whether he bends or breaks." It wasn't a question so much as a statement. Reid was realizing for the first time just what kind of snake pit the other side of the company could be.

"It's been suggested."

Chapter 20

Express train out of Paris, France
8:37 pm

The train had pulled out of the station precisely on time. Paul Gladd was relieved. In his experience, the French were not the most reliable—at least when it came to maintaining a tight schedule. The overnight express train was destined for Hamburg. The Germans, on the other hand, were known for their precision, so he'd given an on-time departure fifty-fifty odds. The train had departed the Paris station at 8:25 pm, and ten minutes later had reached cruising speed. It would be a twelve hour, twenty minute non stop journey to their destination.

Removing his chauffeur's cap, Gladd tossed it to the bench seat before repositioning the wheelchair in the center of the small, four-passenger compartment. All of the bunks were in their stowed positions, folded up against the walls, leaving a bench seat along each of the two main walls. The outer wall held two tall windows, while a short counter and a sturdy sliding door leading to the hallway, occupied the opposite wall of the claustrophobic space. It had been difficult to maneuver the wheelchair through

146

the narrow doorway, though the cabin was supposedly designed with the handicapped in mind.

Gladd double-checked the door's lock, confirming it was engaged. Turning to his charge in the wheelchair and engaging the brake attached to each wheel, he released a pair of straps and removed a large, hard-shelled travel case from the back of the chair. Laying the case on the bench seat and flipping it open, he retrieved a small, broad headed hammer.

Circling to the front of the wheelchair, he considered his task. The patient was wrapped head to toe in a full body cast and bound to the chair with a Velcro seatbelt. Only the eyes, fingertips, and bare toes of the man inside the cast were visible. Gladd noticed the eyes following him as he rounded the front of the chair.

"Just speak up if you need a hand," Gladd said with a grin. His finger tapped expectantly on the hammer's long wooden handle.

"Very funny," a voice grumbled from inside the plaster shell. Irritation was plainly evident.

The entire frozen form of the man swayed slightly, then a crack formed at the shoulder of the right arm. The crack quickly spread, as a chasm opened down the outside of the arm, finally reaching the man's hand. The sleeve of the body cast fell away in several large chunks, as the process was being repeated on the opposite side.

Gladd knew the body cast had been specially designed to break in such a way. Still, he'd been told to expect his partner to require assistance when it came time to extricate him from the contraption. Apparently, his help wouldn't be needed.

Once both arms were free, the man reached up and grappled the sides of the shell surrounding his head. It took only a moment of prying and twisting before this, too, fragmented and was quickly pulled away.

Taking his first unimpeded breath of fresh air, Cyrus Cooper shook his head and sighed with apparent relief. After a moment to stretch his neck, he set about freeing his torso and legs from the remainder of the cast.

"I hope our guy isn't claustrophobic," Cyrus said, as he met Gladd's gaze.

Gladd couldn't help but chuckle. "It won't matter if he is. We brought enough tranquilizers to get Jerry Garcia stoned."

A few swift blows from his fist quickly fractured the rigid shell surrounding his hips and knees, and Cyrus finally slid free of the chair. The last of the cast clattered in chunks on the floor.

Cyrus wiggled his toes and stretched. He bent over and proceeded to unroll the cuffs of his jeans, which had been tucked back inside the cast to prevent chafing. Finally, he retrieved a pair of socks and a pair of black hiking boots from the case on the bench.

With an obvious degree of satisfaction, Cyrus went about pulling on his socks.

Gladd was puzzled by the uncharacteristic display. "What are you smiling about?" he asked.

Cyrus looked up. Although the gaze was confused at first, he soon smiled. "Well," he said, considering his words. "I guess I've never been a fan of going barefoot. Besides, there's something to be said for the simple pleasure of a fresh pair of socks."

Gladd stopped what he was doing and stared at the younger man. "You're kidding, right?"

"Ever done deep cover work?" Cyrus asked without pretense.

Gladd just shook his head. His career had been almost entirely comprised of fieldwork. He hadn't worked undercover, but he'd given a lot of thought to what it would be like to work such operations. Those guys were a different breed. The difference between undercover and deep cover was vast. Deep cover involved going under and staying there for protracted periods of time—often without outside support or even a means of contacting support. If deep cover guys had any lifeline at all, it was never within easy reach. Beyond that, Gladd didn't know how they did it. He was used to functioning as part of a team. The thought of going it alone was more than a little unsettling.

Not that he would ever admit to it.

"You spend time in some really messed up places with some even more messed up people," Cyrus explained. "The trick to getting through it is to focus on and appreciate the simple things. Like a good night sleep in your own bed, for example. Or," he held up his second sock as an object example. Flashing a broad grin, he slipped it over his foot.

Gladd shrugged. "Fair enough."

Who am I to say otherwise?

Dropping the unused hammer back in the case, Gladd retrieved a collapsed vinyl pouch and quickly expanded it into a large, five-sided container. Once formed, it was rectangular, nearly two feet long and about half as wide. It had an open top and was a little over a foot deep. Placing it on the floor, he began collecting the remnants of the body cast into a pile beside the container.

While Gladd was collecting the mess from the floor, Cyrus retrieved two small bottles from the hard-shelled case on the bench. Double-checking the unit markers on the outside of the first bottle, Cyrus removed the cap and dumped several ounces of the gelatinous fluid into the empty vinyl container on the floor. After replacing the bottle's cap, he repeated the process with the second bottle.

Gladd saw the small pools of binary chemicals begin to react as soon as they touched within the bottom of the soft-walled container. Though he'd read about the technology, this was his first chance to work with it. He didn't understand how two tiny splashes of chemicals could combine to fill the two-gallon box with solvent. But, the reaction was taking place right before his eyes.

At first, a bubbling foam spread across the bottom of the container, quickly growing in height and climbing the walls. Then, shortly after the bubbling concoction's expansion passed the halfway mark, its composition began to change. The bubbles gave way to a gooey gel. Still, the reaction continued to expand. The walls flexed under the weight of the newfound mass, becoming rigid as the density of the material inside the container continued to increase. Finally, as the box reached three quarters capacity, the gel transitioned into a fully liquid form.

Cyrus went to the window and slid aside the small vent panel. It wasn't until then that Gladd realized a mild chemical odor had filled the compartment. It wasn't caustic, but it was unusual, and who knew if it was safe to breathe. He'd never witnessed anything as unnatural as the chemical reaction before, and couldn't help wondering what sort of fumes now filled his lungs.

Cyrus must have read the concern on his face. "It's nothing to worry about," he reassured.

Crouching on one knee, Cyrus started tossing some of the larger chucks of the body cast into the now water-like chemical. The material comprising the cast began to disintegrate instantly.

"Believe it or not, this solution is completely safe," Cyrus continued. "I don't know if I would drink it, but they claim you could water flowers with it."

Piece by piece, they dropped all that remained of the body cast into the solution, destroying all evidence of Cyrus's disguise. Once they were done, Cyrus returned to the small vent below the window. It was the only part of the window that passengers could open. He gouged out the small sturdy section of screen and nodded to Gladd.

Taking the now rigid box by the two hand holds cut into opposite edges along the top rim, Gladd hefted the container. It was heavier than he expected, forcing him to lift with his knees. What had started out as a few ounces of a binary chemical was now over two gallons of a strange water-like solution. The box wasn't exactly heavy, but its semi-rigid form made it awkward to maneuver. Not a single solid remained inside the solution. The cast had been completely dissolved.

The closest thing to magic I've ever seen, he thought.

After Gladd lugged the container to the window, Cyrus released the eighteen-inch fabric tube that was folded flush along the side of the container. Dropping the end of the hose out the window vent, he released the clip that served as a primitive valve. The contents of the box began draining out the window as the train sped through the pitch-black countryside.

It took less than a minute to purge the box of the chemical solution. After that, Gladd collapsed the container and stowed it in the larger case. By that time Cyrus had folded the wheelchair and leaned it against the wall, freeing up some much-needed space in the small cabin.

Gladd removed his chauffeur's jacket, swapping it for a different coat that had been stowed inside the case. He also replaced his tie with a simple black affair that completed his disguise. Once he was done, he turned and looked at Cyrus.

"Well?" Gladd asked.

With a grin, Cyrus nodded. "You look like a conductor to me."

Cyrus turned and unlocked the cabin door. Sliding it open, he stepped aside for Gladd. "Good luck," he offered, as Gladd passed him on his way into the hall.

Assuming the role of conductor now allowed Gladd complete and unrestricted access to all parts of the train, as well as the ability to move virtually unnoticed among the passengers.

Chapter 21

Express train out of Paris, France
11:41 pm

Sitting at the tiny table in the dining car, Cyrus looked past his own reflection and watched the wilderness sweep by the window. Everything was a blur, but the full moon brought the scenery into view every time the train reached an open field or pasture.

He took the last bite of his turkey and swiss sandwich, washing it down a moment later with the remains of a flat, but flavorful root beer. The dining car was due to close at midnight, which was just as well. He'd been making use of the facility primarily to observe his fellow passengers. No one knew that he and Gladd were on the train, but he was still on the alert. Even they hadn't found out about the express run from Paris to Hamburg until a few hours before the train was scheduled to depart. And this stage of the mission would be a cakewalk compared to what would follow. There was little that could go wrong at this point. Still, he felt better getting a sense of the environment and the people who occupied it.

His partner for this part of the mission was an operative named Paul Gladd. What little he knew of the man came from a personnel file and the largely antidotal character reference that Boone provided. The file was restricted information, something Cyrus wasn't even supposed to have access to. Still, no one should be surprised. Such was the nature of his job. For the trouble he'd gone to in order to obtain it, there wasn't much in the file that helped Cyrus form an opinion of Gladd. He was an ex-Special Forces solider who'd been with the Coalition for almost five years. Prior to that, he'd served on four continents and was once awarded the Navy Cross before leaving the service. Aside from that, Boone had simply said that Gladd was a good man to have at your back if things got hairy.

That was good enough for Cyrus. This part of the op would be easy enough. Some of the CIA's digital taps and filters had managed to capture Rutger Voss's upstream communication, which had led them to Voss's associate in Paris, France. Professor Richard Ragsdale, was a longtime friend of Voss, and digital archives proved the two had kept in touch for decades. Upon being assigned the case, Cyrus began looking into archives of all the digital communication that the CIA had collected over the years, but since Ragsdale had never drawn scrutiny from the CIA or the Coalition, his background with Voss was part of the wave of white noise amassed from general internet traffic in the region over the last fifteen years. That archived information contained massive dumps of unfiltered data that was warehoused for later reference. Since it was far too much information to review in real-time, anything digital that passed through cyberspace was simply cataloged and warehoused in massive underground server farms across the planet. If at any time files relating to a person, location, or date became relevant, it was simply a matter of querying the slush pile of raw data for the relevant information.

That had been the start of Cyrus's search for a way into Voss's compound. Security at Voss's facility was tighter than most international embassies. Cyrus quickly realized that the only way he was getting inside was with an invitation, so he started searching the archive of Voss's digital data. With enough time and patience, he was certain to find something he could work with.

From the very beginning, Cyrus gained a healthy respect for Doctor Rutger Voss. The archives which constituted Voss's digital footprint—in fact, his entire digital history—dated back a full fourteen years to when the Coalition's database system had first gone online. Every email the man had sent, every web page he'd visited, was all there. But for the most part, it did Cyrus little good; from the very beginning of the archive, Voss had gone to great lengths to secure his communications with encryption, which made them unreadable.

Modern services commonly used encryption; it was finally becoming a standard practice. But fourteen years ago? It was unheard of. Most people didn't understand cryptography well enough to secure their communication in such a way back then. This evidence further supported what Cyrus suspected—Voss was paranoid to an extreme.

Realizing that the contents of Voss's email were of no use to him, Cyrus focused on what useful information he could gather from the digital data dumps. And while the contents of every email message had been obscured, their subjects and recipients always remained in plaintext, and clearly visible.

Cyrus used Voss's email history to chart who the man communicated with and how often. And with fourteen years of data to play with, patterns had soon emerged. As is common in life, Voss went through periods where he would communicate with a friend or colleague frequently for some time, only to have that relationship stagnate after a while. Looking at those relationships and taking a closer look at many of the people Voss was communicating with, Cyrus began to wonder about Voss's reputation for being paranoid and reclusive. It didn't match with the man's communication patterns. Even if Cyrus couldn't see the contents of the messages, he continued to develop a sense of the man, if only from a mile high view.

A year and a half of the most recent communication had provided Cyrus with what he needed. It was a thread of messages between Voss and Professor Richard Ragsdale at the University of Paris. Ragsdale was an American who had been living and working in France for the better part of the last decade. And, while the man's academic standing offered no hint as to his involvement with Voss, a deeper look at his personal profile brought about clarity.

Ragsdale held over two dozen patents relating to imaging technologies, and he was on the boards of three major hardware manufacturing corporations. In fact, it turned out that he only maintained a perfunctory relationship with the University—enough to keep an office on campus and remain in good academic standing. Most of his time was spent in the lab developing what was vaguely touted in some reference material as "next generation imaging technology."

One of the first things that stood out upon finding the link between Voss and Ragsdale, was that the pattern of communication had surged in recent months. Both email and Skype communication had increased tenfold. Cyrus pegged

Ragsdale as Voss's Achilles' heel. While Voss sat in an ivory tower far from the reach of even the Coalition's most advanced surveillance, the same could not be said for Ragsdale.

A team had been assigned to covertly examine Ragsdale's home, University office, and the office he kept at his off-site lab. His computers at all locations were easily exploited. Since that day, all communication between Voss and Ragsdale had been decrypted and plainly visible. Best of all, the signal intercept had proven timely.

As Cyrus suspected, Voss and Ragsdale had been collaborating on a project. With access to their correspondence, the particulars of their work became clear. Ragsdale was developing the image display component of Voss's new technology. And the first stage prototype was ready to be delivered to Voss.

Cyrus had his avenue of approach when he examined the details of the hardware exchange. Voss was paranoid. He didn't want Ragsdale making the delivery in person. Furthermore, he insisted that Voss use a cutout as the courier—someone who couldn't be directly connected to either of them. It would've been an effective surveillance countermeasure if their communication hadn't already been compromised.

Thanks to the high tech spying, Cyrus knew almost everything he needed in order to intercept the delivery. He knew that a courier, rather than a conventional freight service, would transfer the package. Beyond that, he knew that Ragsdale had arranged a single ticket aboard the overnight express between Paris and Hamburg. A ticket had also been booked on a commercial flight from Hamburg to the Isle of Kapros, the last leg of the journey.

The plan was to identify the courier when he met with Ragsdale to pick-up the package, but that hadn't gone as predicted. For some unknown reason, Ragsdale failed to meet with the courier. Boone had tracked Ragsdale the entire afternoon, but the man had never made contact with a courier.

While they were reasonably certain Ragsdale had somehow handed off the package, he'd somehow managed it without drawing the attention of the team following him.

All of this left Cyrus and Gladd on the train bound for Hamburg, knowing that their target was onboard, but with no way to identify him.

Lacking that last crucial piece of information, Cyrus had resorted to Plan B. It was more time consuming, but they were on a twelve-hour non-stop train ride. They definitely had time to burn.

Chapter 22

His finger tapping slowly on the tabletop, Cyrus stared at the empty place settings at the far end of the dining car. The gentle rocking and muffled clacking of the train over the rails pulled at his attention, trying to remind him of another train ride from long ago.

He was maybe ten years old at the time. In many ways, it was also the day that he'd been born. Aside from the slight sense of déjà vu he now felt, he had no actual memory of the train ride itself. Only waking up in the wreckage of the derailment with no idea of who he was or how he'd come to be there. It was as if whatever life he'd had before that train ride had been rebooted, and his life had started anew.

The mobile phone on the table beside Cyrus buzzed quietly and pulled him from his thoughts. The ringer had been silenced, so he was the only one likely to notice the incoming message. It was what he'd been waiting for. Without looking at the phone, he reached down and pulled a small laptop from the messenger bag at his feet. Flipping open the lid of the 12" portable, it came instantly to life. The laptop would automatically link wirelessly to his phone, and from there, gain access to the network back at Coalition Command.

Glancing over his shoulder to be sure no one was watching, Cyrus confirmed what he already knew; the dining car was virtually deserted. The single remaining patron sat behind him with her back turned, face down on the table and asleep where she'd been for more than an hour. An empty bottle of wine and a drained glass sat not far from her elbow. From time to time he'd even caught a hint of her quiet feminine snore.

Tapping the screen of his phone, the images he'd just received were transferred to his laptop. With a few taps of the keyboard, the half-dozen photos were submitted for facial recognition. It was a process that ran on the servers back at Command. His laptop was simply a control interface that allowed him to manage the process. Within seconds, the first dossiers began popping up in the corner of his screen. Each face was being matched to an identity—an extensive profile of each suspect was then assembled in real time and then pushed to his screen. The process had become so efficient that what had once taken days now took only seconds.

Cyrus opened the first profile and began reviewing its information.

Since they knew their target was on-board the train, but knew nothing more about him, Cyrus and Gladd had been forced to take a broad approach when conducting their search. Gladd had assumed the role of the train's conductor and was moving slowly from one end of the train to the other, checking each passenger in turn. But since they couldn't expect the courier to be wearing a

FedEx hat or a name tag that read, 'I'm your guy!', Gladd was on the lookout for anyone he found suspect. Then, using a high-resolution camera hidden in the frame of his glasses, he would capture a photo of each possible suspect. He would then transmit the photos to Cyrus, who would review each of them in depth. It was a labor-intensive approach, but it was their best bet.

Ten minutes later, Cyrus had finished reviewing the files relating to the images Gladd had sent. All without luck. None of them worked for a courier service or had a direct connection to Professor Ragsdale. Still, Gladd knew what he was doing. It was possible that the entire train ride was a red herring designed to throw them off the trail of the real courier. Or, maybe Ragsdale had been exceedingly crafty in selecting his courier, tasking someone so obscure they would never be able to pinpoint him or her. The ideal cutout would be a courier who had no link to Ragsdale or Voss. But, playing the odds meant the courier would have some sort of relationship with one of the men. They were civilians, after all. Neither had formal experience with tradecraft, therefor the cutout would be someone who was trusted. No mater how tangential the relationship, it seemed likely the cutout would be connected to Ragsdale or Voss in some way.

It was frustrating. Other than the fact Ragsdale was working on a special augmentation of his existing imaging technology, there wasn't anything altogether noteworthy about his contribution to Voss's project. It wasn't a secret or special design. Ragsdale had simply made hardware modifications specific to Voss's requests. Even then, those were changes that any electronics fabricator in China could've made, if provided the proper specifications. Ragsdale appeared to be working with Voss out of professional respect and personal attachment rather than any proprietary requirement. And as far as Cyrus's need for the courier, he was simply a way through the door of Voss's compound. He was an introduction that Cyrus planned to exploit.

With all of this in mind, Cyrus returned to the dossiers before him. The odds were good that the courier was among those selected by Gladd. Cyrus suspected that he needed to dig deeper into each candidate's background. Something would connect the target to Ragsdale. It was a rookie's mistake. In all likelihood, the connection would be personal.

Fifteen minutes later, Cyrus had his man. Twenty year old, Anatole Benoit. He'd been difficult to connect to Ragsdale because their lives didn't intersect directly. At least, they didn't anymore. Benoit had been a student in a history course taught by a female colleague of Ragsdale. Benoit had since dropped out of school. And, although Ragsdale was married with two children, he'd had an affair with this colleague two years prior. During that time, the woman in question had left the country for two months. While she was gone, and unbeknownst to even the faculty of the University, Ragsdale had acted as a substitute, filling in as temporary instructor for his mistress's history class while she was away.

Cyrus lost track of exactly how many degrees of separation that resulted in, but it was Ragsdale's link to Anatole Benoit. He was the cutout they were after.

Grabbing his phone, Cyrus sent a text message to Gladd specifying Benoit as the target. Gladd would collect the young man, and they would meet back at their compartment.

Flipping the lid shut on his laptop, Cyrus bent over and slid the computer into the messenger bag on the floor beside his chair. As he sat up, his eyes were met with the small dark hole of a pistol's muzzle leveled squarely at his face. It was a small caliber handgun, but that didn't make it any less deadly.

A large, steel-haired man slipped into the chair opposite Cyrus. Cyrus sat calmly back in his seat and glared at the broad shouldered figure. Then, at the sound of someone entering the car behind him, the gunman slipped the weapon beneath the table without saying a word.

"Excusé moi messieurs," the waiter said from the doorway of the car behind the silver-haired intruder. "Je dois fermer le wagon de dîner dans quelque minutes. Je suis désolé pour les inconvénients."

Cyrus heard the translation in his head, *I must close down the dining car in a few minutes. I apologize for the inconvenience.* He nodded his understanding. The waiter ducked back through the door leaving only Cyrus, the steely-haired giant, and the sleeping passenger a few tables away. Looking at the gunman before him, Cyrus realized he didn't know a word of French.

"He said we need to leave the dining car," Cyrus explained in English. "He's worried you're going to steal the silverware."

The larger man flicked a glance at the watch on his left wrist. The gun, once again raised above the table, never wavered. He nodded. "Geldbuße."

Cyrus's brow wrinkled at the comment. *Geldbuße* was German for *fine.*

"What's this about?" he asked, before he realized he'd said the words aloud. No one knew he was on this train, so the silver-haired giant couldn't be looking for him specifically.

"Get up," the man said in a flat tone. His voice was a deep baritone.

Cyrus shook his head. "I'm not going anywhere until you tell me what this is about."

The man flashed a sincere grin. "Then I will shoot you right here. It makes no difference to me." From the look in his eye, he seemed eager to do just that.

Scratching idly at the day old stubble on his jaw, Cyrus considered the man before him. "I don't get it," he admitted. "I had you figured for a professional. The way you handle the gun? You're steady like you've got experience with it. And I don't see indecision in your eyes, so I don't think you're conflicted about using it."

His eyes searched the man's face before he continued. He looked over every feature of the man's countenance before speaking. "Those qualities make me think you're a professional. But you're here...which contradicts that assessment."

The statement had the desired effect. A look of confusion clouded the gunman's eyes. It lasted only a moment, but Cyrus knew he'd scored a hit. "This is a twelve-hour train ride," Cyrus explained. "A twelve-hour train ride doesn't leave you a means of escape. You're sort of stuck here for the duration. A pro wouldn't make his move until the end of trip. That affords a reasonable chance of escape, or as might be the case, an opportunity to get rid of the body."

The final part of his statement drew a flash of recognition where the first had not. It was the vital piece of information for Cyrus. This man was here to kill him. He wasn't interested in taking a prisoner. It was a factor crucial to delivering a measured response.

"You don't even have an exit plan, do you?" Cyrus continued. He could see he was getting under the man's skin. He would see how far he could push it.

The large man's jaw was slowly moving. He was gnashing his teeth at Cyrus's words. Everything he knew so far was supposition. The only thing he knew for sure was that the man spoke English—and German.

Oh, that would work. It would be a shame to pass that one up…

Cyrus squinted his eyes and leaned slightly toward the man, even though it put him closer to the gun. "Hey," he said quietly. "Are you okay in there? You do speak English, don't you? I'm not talking to myself, am I?"

That sealed the deal. The large silver-haired German leapt to his feet. Or, at least he tried. In the tight confines of the dining car, given the close quarters, the small chairs, and the constant rhythmic motion of the train car's gentle rocking, the move was far less graceful than intended. Unfortunately for the German, Cyrus was fully prepared for it. The moment the large man began to rise, Cyrus made his move.

Cyrus had his hand on the German's gun before either of them were fully out of their seats. He parried the man's .22 off to his left as his right hand struck swiftly at the man's throat. There was an audible snap as the cartilage of the larger man's trachea crushed beneath the single brutal blow. Cyrus knew that he'd just ended the man's life.

The German fell away, toppling to the floor in a tangle of empty chairs as his hands slapped frantically at his throat. His eyes bulged, and his torso bucked. The desperate man tried in vain to draw oxygen through his crushed airway. It was a horrible way to go, Cyrus knew. Worse than bleeding out from a bullet to the gut? No one would ever know for sure, and Cyrus didn't care to ever personally weigh in on the subject. Still, there was no doubt in his mind that this man had meant to take his life. Even as he watched the man writhing on the floor in the final moments of his life, Cyrus felt no remorse. It was that simple...because it had to be. It was the key to living with the things that had to be done.

Looking at his left hand still raised in the air, Cyrus shifted himself back to the moment. He still held the German's .22 awkwardly—backward in his hand, the way he'd first grabbed it. The fleshy span of skin between his thumb and first finger was trapped beneath the released hammer of the gun. It had prevented the weapon from firing when he first shoved the gun away.

Cyrus took the gun in his free hand, pulling the hammer back and freeing his pinched flesh. A small drop of blood rose from the welt where the hammer had come to rest in his soft tissue. The gun had not fired so no attention had been drawn. That left Cyrus a narrow window of opportunity to dispose of the German's body before the waiter returned to close down the car.

Grabbing the German under the arms, Cyrus unceremoniously dragged him toward the door. The lights in the next car were dark; it had already been shut down for the night.

Sliding the heavy exterior door aside, Cyrus pulled the lifeless German into the tiny three-foot vestibule between the two train cars. The noise of the train clattering across the rails was near deafening in the small space.

Pulling the large man's legs in toward his chest, Cyrus leveraged him. Finally able to close the door, he and the still twitching body of his would-be killer were stuck in limbo between cars.

The small section of platform was dark; the only light spilled in from the tiny window to the adjoining cars on either end of the three-foot wide space. Since the next car was dark, Cyrus had little light with which to work.

Retrieving a folding knife from his pocket, its razor sharp blade snapped open in an instant. He set to work cutting a slit in the heavy, flexible rubber gasket that comprised the wall of the tiny chamber.

Since the train followed a track that would twist and turn, rise and fall, in every possible permutation, the train cars were joined in a way that allowed for such movement. The tiny platforms located between cars had hard composite floors for passengers to move about, but the walls of the small chambers needed to adjust with every move the train made as it followed the tracks. For that reason, the walls were a thick rubbery material that folded and flexed, like the baffles of an accordion—a space rigid enough to provide safety for people, but still allowing the flexibility necessary for the train to function.

Cyrus was cutting a slit in the accordion rubber wall. He kept his incision vertical. Ideally, the cut would go unnoticed for some time. There was a chance that, if he made the incision cleanly, upon inspection it would appear that the material had simply given way to the stress and wear of daily rigors. In the end, it didn't matter. Cyrus only needed his work to go unnoticed until he and Gladd were safely off the train in Hamburg.

Once the slit was cleanly cut from floor to ceiling, Cyrus pocketed the knife. Glancing back into the lit dining car, he confirmed that he was still alone. Well, almost alone. The sleeping woman still slumbered at the table at the far end of the room.

Good enough.

Parting the sides of the cut wall, Cyrus pushed his head through the opening. He was instantly slapped by the chilling wall of air rushing by the outside of the train. His eyes began to water from the onslaught. It took precious moments for him to blink away the moisture and clear his vision.

He was relieved at what he found. They were in a rural area surrounded by mostly farmland. The moon was full, leaving the landscape bathed in a cold pale glow. A telephone pole flashed by, and the thought made him cringe. He wished he'd cut the slit on the opposite side of the car, but it was too late now. A quick glance at the trackside rail bed beyond the edge of the train confirmed what he expected. It was going by in a blur, but it looked to be gravel that sloped away in a short, steep grade.

He didn't have time to waste and knew this would be the hard part. The German was *large*. First, he shifted the man as best he could into a sitting position. Bending over, Cyrus wrapped his arms around the man, grabbing low, just under his arms, and jamming his shoulder in the center of the man's chest. With a grunt, he lifted the dead man's bulk.

It was a slow, painful process just getting the German off the floor. Cyrus felt every muscle in his back and legs strain to the point where he feared something might tear. But he didn't have time to make a second attempt, and he certainly didn't have time to go back for Gladd's assistance. So, without additional options, he continued to lift.

After what felt like a lifetime, Cyrus had the man in the air. Well, as far 'in the air' as he would manage given the circumstances. The man more or less hung over Cyrus's shoulder in what would be charitably called a fireman's carry. Still, the giant's feet were off the ground and, with a little luck, Cyrus hoped he could push him through the slit in the wall without falling right along with him.

The train rocked beneath his feet, threatening to undermine his balance at any moment as the cacophony of near deafening background noise assaulted his senses. The sounds of the train blasting across the surface of the rails combined with the rush of the wind. Without insulation to suppress it, the auditory assault was dizzying. Cyrus's senses were on overload. All the while, the oxygen level in his blood was thinning…all because he needed to get rid of the body in a way that wouldn't compromise his mission.

Rolling his eyes, Cyrus gave in to the realization that there was no perfect way to accomplish the task at hand.

Why couldn't it be a midget? James Bond had been attacked by a midget assassin, hadn't he?

To hell with it!

Lowering the man's feet to the floor, Cyrus squared the back of the body to the slit in the wall. He placed the side of his boot in front of the giant's massive feet, wedging them between his own boot and the wall of the vestibule. Then, he pushed the man over hard, flinging the body like a felled tree. The head and shoulders went first and, as soon as the weight started to come off his shoulder, Cyrus immediately raised his hands and leveraged his arms to speed the body's exit from the train.

The head and shoulders of the large German disappeared as the cut expanded to allow his bulk to follow. The body picked up speed as Cyrus shoved. The lower extremities seemed almost to be sucked from the enclosure as the process was completed. This was followed instantly by a thundering, hollow *thud*.

Cyrus dropped to his knees in exhaustion. The open rush of air that had buffeted the tiny compartment disappeared the moment the body was gone and the folds of the rubber wall slapped shut once more. Only the deafening thunder of the surrounding ambient noise remained. That, and the memory of the horrible 'thud' that'd somehow managed to penetrate the background clatter.

Though he hoped he'd imagined it, Cyrus knew with certainty that the sound had been real. And while he had taken the man's life, that sound somehow seemed unfair. He realized the assassin's body had caught a passing telephone pole on its way out of the train. Even though the man was dead prior to the impact, Cyrus still felt a chill run down his spine at the thought of the harsh impact.

Pulling the door shut, Cyrus re-entered the dining car. He was out of breath and his face was dripping with perspiration. The entire ordeal felt as if it had taken an hour, though only minutes had passed. Suddenly the hours that remained before the train reached Hamburg didn't seem like such a bad thing. He could use the rest.

But who was the German? Why was he here, and how had he found him? No one knew he would be on this train. Hell, Cyrus reasoned, he'd only found out about the train a few hours before stepping aboard. On second thought, the rest of the trip might not come so easily.

Cyrus righted the chairs that had toppled when he felled the German. Then he dropped into his own seat. With a deep breath, he retrieved his phone, still in its place atop the table. He tapped out a quick message to Gladd.

> Status update?

The reply came back almost instantly.

> Package secure.

It was a relief. Whatever the German had been up to, at least it didn't have anything to do with the courier. Gladd would sit on the man until they arrived at the station in Hamburg.

Still…if the German wasn't here for the courier, Cyrus knew he must've been the target. But why? Cyrus wished he'd had a chance to get some information before killing him. Not that he'd had a choice in the matter. And since Cyrus needed to keep the train ride from becoming a bloodbath, he'd been forced to act decisively.

Still, something was wrong.

His eyes dropped back to the display of his phone. Gladd's message still read clearly, and Cyrus considered it.

It seemed like paranoid operational overkill, but why not. He picked up the phone and entered a new message.

> Alpha kilo tango one. Authenticate.

When a 'known' reply to his message was not immediately sent, Cyrus felt his pulse quicken. He pulled his messenger bag from the floor and placed it on the seat beside him. His eyes watched the phone's display closely, as if his attention would bring the desired response more quickly.

As he waited for Gladd to respond, Cyrus's mind was working through scenarios and solutions. But as much as he tried, he simply didn't have enough data with which to assemble workable scenarios. No one knew he was here, yet there was clearly evidence to the contrary. The German had meant to kill him.

What the hell is going on?

Cyrus realized that there was only one place he might find answers to his questions. Unfortunately, if Gladd was out of play, their cabin was the last place on the entire train that he should go.

Still, there was no way around it. He needed to return to their compartment; he needed to know what had happened to Paul Gladd.

The sudden buzz of the silenced phone drew Cyrus's attention. It was a new message.

> Delta whisky seven one.

Cyrus released a breath he hadn't realized he'd been holding. His eyes remained locked on the screen, as if staring at the words would somehow offer greater insight or explanation.

The code was authentication, confirming Gladd was alright. The same code ending in seven-seven would've indicated that he was under duress, so that wasn't the case. Still, that didn't explain the delay in Gladd's response. While he was sure there was a logical explanation, Cyrus couldn't help being suspicious. His eyes wandered to the exit at the rear of the dining car where he'd dragged the German's body.

He had plenty of reasons to be suspicious.

Chapter 23

Express train out of Paris, France
12:17 am

Fire lanced through Paul Gladd's body as he struggled to pull himself from the darkness. The sound of his own heartbeat rang out like rapid rifle shots in his ears, and though he struggled simply to raise his head, he found that he could not. To his shock, neither could he move his arms or legs. It wasn't like they'd been restrained—more like they were no longer attached.

Soon, he realized that it was a struggle to even breathe. He managed his next lung full of air, but only with immense effort. It was as if his body's normal functions were no longer automatic. Even drawing breath took a concerted effort.

All he knew with any certainty was that an absolute, crushing level of pain surrounded him. He felt bathed in it. It was as if every nerve ending in his body had been sanded raw and then lit on fire.

My God! Is this it? Is this how it feels to die?

When he choked on his own breath, some remaining rational part of his mind finally managed to assert itself. He realized if death were the case, the pain would soon be over. But the sense of pain without awareness of his limbs seemed reminiscent in some way. Despite himself, no matter how he struggled to hold onto the tiny bit of sanity at the back of his mind, he felt consciousness slipping away—giving in fully to darkness and agony.

Drawing another ragged breath, Gladd tried to calm himself. He was certain that he was screaming, though he couldn't hear the sound of his own voice.

Sound...

Then it registered...in the distance. It was difficult to distinguish over the thunderous crash of his own heartbeat, but there was something more out there. Something rhythmic...something familiar.

He drew another breath and focused on the unusual tones. This breath came slightly easier. Now, if he could just do something about the pain.

Focus!

The sounds... Over the racing heartbeat came a slow, steady tapping noise. But beyond that was something more. It sounded like...

Voices!

Immediately he tried to call out for help, but his breath was once again sucked away as a new level of pain struck his body, like a tsunami making landfall. It was staggering, and the darkness threatened to overtake him once more.

With a start, he sensed a blue flash where he thought his eyes should be. It was hard to be sure in the absolute darkness of the void, but with the next surge of pain came another jagged streak of muddied bluish lighting. The color flashed more vividly with

174

each crest of pain, only to fade to black like the end of an old movie when the pain level dropped back to its previous insufferable level.

That's when it occurred to him. Gladd waited for the next streak of blue, and despite the unpleasantness, it confirmed his suspicion. He was now certain he'd experienced this sensation before. Fighting with the crippling pain and his desire to understand, Gladd called desperately to the rational part of his mind once more. He didn't know what was happening, but it was somehow familiar.

Still, he couldn't place it.

There, again in the extreme distance he caught what seemed to be a hint of a voice. No—voices! Two of them. Straining, he tried to understand the words. As he struggled to comprehend, he was struck by the realization that his breathing was becoming a less deliberate exercise and more automatic.

That was something.

He focused further on the voices, realizing that they might be his only path to salvation.

Chapter 24

Express train out of Paris, France
12:17 am

Magda Keller paced slowly across the small confines of the private cabin. Her eyes were pinched, and she flexed her gloved hands into fists as she stalked. *Mongo should've reported in by now!* It had been a mistake not to send her husband, Brolin, along to eliminate the junior of the two agents. But of the two, she'd expected the senior member, Paul Gladd, to put up the greater fight. That hadn't been the case.

She and Brolin had entered the cabin, catching Gladd completely unaware. He'd had his back to the door, letting them slip silently into the room. The agent had apparently been making some adjustments to the full body cast of the man confined to the wheelchair. Still, she'd only just touched her Taser to Gladd's skin and the man went down hard. Harder, in fact, than anyone she'd ever seen. The jolt from the Taser apparently triggered some sort of epileptic fit, because the next thing she knew Gladd was sprawled across the floor, jerking and seizing. His mouth quickly began to froth with foamy bubbles, and his eyes rolled so far back in his head that he looked like a man possessed.

Though she and her husband considered themselves consummate professionals, they were both taken aback by the shocking violent display. Still, moments later, Brolin had the man trussed hand and foot, bound on the bench in the corner of the room. Gladd hadn't moved since. He only leaned against the window, his head hung so far forward that his chin nearly touched his chest. If not for the irregular rise and fall of his chest, she would've thought him dead. She'd never seen anything like it.

Magda looked at her husband. He stood in the corner, his shoulder resting casually against the wall. Though he looked apathetic, she knew better. He was as unnerved as she that Mongo was overdue in reporting in. And though both were reticent to admit it, neither wanted to risk contacting him to check his status.

Magda and Brolin Keller were a husband and wife bounty hunting team working the whole of the European Union. They specialized in the sort of 'big ticket, high value' bounties that normal hunters were wary of. They stalked the worst of the worst, such as, war criminals, gangsters, and even the wealthy sort who employed contingents of private security to protect them. If there was a price on a target's head and they were considered too dangerous for a conventional hunter, it was the sort of job Magda and Brolin focused on. Assassination jobs were out of the ordinary, but they'd still done more than their share.

'Wetwork', as it was known in the industry, wasn't Magda's preference, but it kept them busy when more legitimate work was difficult to come by. So, between bona fide jobs, they often took assignments as freelancers for different problem solving groups.

Those groups were like temporary employment agencies for mercenaries of various disciplines. And while the work wasn't Magda's first choice, she really didn't have a problem with it. That type of work was simply prone to greater complications. Moral ambiguity was required, which was not a problem. Magda could justify just about anything if the price was right.

While she and Brolin always worked together, when occasions arose and they needed a little extra muscle, they'd bring Mongo along. Mongo was six–foot-eight and had to weigh at least two seventy-five, as close as she could figure. He was big and strong, and although not terribly bright, he did what he was told—that was all Magda really needed in a subordinate.

"You're going to make me be the one to say it, aren't you?" Brolin asked in English that carried a thick German accent.

She looked at him and slowly shook her head. "No," she admitted. "I've been thinking the same. We should've heard from Mongo by now."

"Our contact suggested that these two would be trouble."

She nodded, and continued to pace. "Yes. But when he said that the young one would be the handful, we both thought he was making fun."

"Maybe not," he admitted. "I'll go check on him. His last report was from the dining cars, yes?"

She nodded. "Just make sure you—"

The small radio on the bench opposite Gladd's unconscious form came to life with a chirp. Magda spun and stared at the box as if it held the secrets to the universe. Her glance shifted to her husband who looked equally concerned.

With a growing sense of unease, she crossed the cabin and retrieved the device. When she raised the display to examine it, her husband was already looking over her shoulder.

> Status update?

With that simple message, Magda knew why Mongo hadn't reported back. They'd underestimated the younger agent.

"Scheiße!" her husband growled into his clenched fist. "Do you think Mongo's…"

"Dead?" she completed his hanging statement. She would wager money on it, though she feared that saying so aloud might invite bad fortune. Offering only a stoic stare, she simply shrugged her shoulders. Then, giving it more thought, she nodded slowly.

"Verdammt," Brolin mumbled to himself. It was his turn to pace.

"I think the agent was here securing the man in the wheelchair," she said with a degree of confidence. The man in the body cast had been unconscious when they arrived, and there was a hypodermic needle still out among the supplies Gladd had used on the patient. Additionally, the plaster cast had not fully set when they arrived. The surface of the material had still been damp to the touch. "We're not flying blind here. We have a good idea what the agent was doing when we ambushed him."

She entered a message in response and hit send:

> Package secure.

They waited for several long moments for a response. When none came, she breathed easier. But that wasn't the end of it, Magda realized. While they'd subdued Agent Gladd, their ultimate target had been the younger agent. He was the one with a price on his head. They still had to deal with him.

For some reason the idea troubled her. She now had the sense that this job was more dangerous than they'd been led to believe. They were supposed to immobilize Gladd and eliminate Agent Cooper. While they'd been warned that both men were formidable, Gladd had proven anything but, while Cooper had apparently taken out Mongo. To the best of her knowledge, no one had ever gotten the better of him—in a fair fight or otherwise. Mongo was like a guided missile. That was what made him perfect for this type of work. They needed only to point him in the proper direction and send him after a target. The man was born a killing machine.

The bad feeling she had for the assignment continued to gnaw at Magda. She wondered how her husband would react if she suggested cutting their losses and walking away. Worse yet, she wondered how their employer might respond to that decision. Theirs wasn't the sort of business where you were simply blackballed for failing to make good on a commitment. Failure invariably carried life and death consequences for the operatives involved. High-level contract killings were not to be taken lightly.

Magda's internal debate was stopped cold when the phone in her hand buzzed once again. Brolin, still pacing the small cabin, stopped in his tracks at the tiny sound.

Magda saw her husband's eyes dart to meet her own. She was now certain that he shared all of her concerns.

"What is it now?" Brolin muttered.

Reluctantly, she glanced at the display.

> Alpha kilo tango one. Authenticate.

"Scheiße!" her husband cursed once more.

Magda felt her stomach drop. Cooper was suspicious. This was a challenge code. They needed to respond properly. If they didn't, who knew how he might respond. He might abandon the train, he could summon Coalition support; or, he might even alert local authorities. She knew next to nothing about their target's employer—this…Coalition—but they'd been warned that their targets could not be allowed to call in support. Her brief encounter with the contracting party suddenly sprang back to her mind.

"If he gets on to you, expect the unexpected. He's as unpredictable as they come. Be certain that it never comes to that," the faceless man in the hat and trench coat had warned.

It had been a very brief meeting, but one Magda would not forget. In that single conversation, their client had expressed how critical it was to never underestimate their quarry. She now realized they'd done exactly that.

Brolin already had his phone out and was dialing. Their employer had provided an emergency contact number along with their final instructions when he relayed the information about the train. She now wondered if he might have foreseen these circumstances.

"Well?" she asked of her husband expectantly.

"I can't make him pick up the phone any faster," Brolin snarled. He tapped the speakerphone button so Magda could hear the phone ringing.

"Is it done?" a male voice finally answered.

"Not quite," Brolin admitted. "We've taken out the partner, but the young one has just texted some sort of challenge code. We must respond in kind."

Silence greeted them from the other end of the line. For a moment Magda wondered if their employer had severed the connection.

"What was the challenge?" the clearly irritated voice asked.

Brolin read the line of text from the screen.

"I see," the voice said flatly. "Young Cooper isn't known for following protocol. That he sent this message at all means he is suspicious. Has he identified one of your team?"

"We don't know," Magda admitted, before she realized she'd spoken the words out loud. "Mongo went after him, but now he's...missing."

"I see," the voice spoke once again, this time with some amusement. "Rest assured, your man Mongo is dead. If you complete your task and make it out of this alive, I will double the fee we agreed upon. Send this message in response: 'Delta whisky seven one'," the voice instructed.

Magda was already entering the string into the mobile phone before the voice was able to continue; hitting send, she took a deep breath.

"That code should buy you momentary breathing room," the voice clarified. "But the time it took you to contact me will have made him suspicious. That response won't hold him off for long."

Magda saw her own confusion mirrored on her husband's face. "How can you be so sure?" he asked.

"The delay in your response will have tipped him off," the voice answered frankly. "I warned you not to underestimate the young man. Now, finish the job."

"We're on it," Magda confirmed.

"Two more final points," the voice fell to a mild tone. "If you lose your nerve and decide to pull the plug on this operation, I shall use the money I offered you and put a price on your heads, as well as those of your closest living relatives. I'm entirely serious when I say that I expect results."

Magda hung her head. This operation was going to hell in a hand basket. They should've known better than to take such a contract. The money was good—*too good.*

"You hired professionals," she remained calm. Her eyes were still shut. She couldn't bear to open them. "We will see this through."

"Excellent," the voice said without even a hint of satisfaction. "Then on to my second point. Am I to understand that you have put this conversation on speakerphone?"

Shit...

"I will take your silence to indicate the affirmative," the voice continued. "And I will further assume that Agent Gladd is in the room with you right now?"

"That's right," Brolin confirmed. "But he's not really with us right now. He had some kind of seizure when we hit him with the stun gun. He's been non-responsive ever since."

The voice on the other end was silent for a few moments before finally returning. "My previous order to spare the life of Agent Gladd is hereby rescinded. Eliminate him immediately. And if you ever put me on speaker again, I will see to it that you share in his fate. Is that clear?"

Magda wanted to throw the phone against the wall. She wanted to scream. It was those cold, condescending tones that did it. If anyone deserved a bullet, it was their employer. But, a job was a job. Acting out would do no good. At this point Magda just wanted to focus on completing the mission and collecting their paycheck.

"Understood," Magda confirmed in an even frostier tone.

"Understood," Brolin agreed.

The line went dead.

The two of them were left to look at each other. "Was that fear or respect? The client seems to think this Cyrus Cooper is some sort of ghost." Brolin said in a dry voice. Their employers' words had gotten to him as well. "He's just a man. Just a boy, really. Let's finish this and go home."

She couldn't agree more. And given the circumstances, their ambitions for a subtle and covert kill were becoming less and less of a priority.

Chapter 25

Express train out of Paris, France
12:21 am

From the moment Cyrus opened the folder containing the case's information, he'd been hooked. He knew he had to be a part of it. So when the group put the mission together, Cyrus pushed hard to make things work the way he wanted. In this case, circumstances gave him a fair amount of material to work with. At least for now.

The data showed that Doctor Rutger Voss was developing a memory capture technology that he called, *Shadowlight*. According to patent applications, the technology would involve a chemical concoction as well as some sort of digital hardware that facilitated the recording of a subject's memories. Those recordings could be played back at a later time, allowing others to see and hear memories belonging to the original subject. Interestingly, Voss believed this would only be the first generation of the tech. With refinements, he stated that the technology could be extended to record not only visual memories, but sense memories as well. It would be possible to capture what a person smelled, tasted, and felt—essentially, entire experiences with absolute clarity.

If Voss could make his project work, the implications were astounding. The innovation could be used to treat any number of physical and psychological conditions. None of this, Cyrus knew, interested the Coalition. Put simply, a technology that allowed the recording and retrieval of thoughts and memories meant the end of all secrets. It would be the ultimate interrogation tool. Used in such a way, it was powerful and dangerous.

Interrogation was often used to gather sensitive information, be the target a criminal, soldier, spy, terrorist, or any other enemy combatant. When interrogation proved ineffective and the stakes were high, some believed that circumstances justified the use of torture. But with torture, just as with less invasive forms of interrogation, the information obtained was often unreliable. Was the subject lying or telling the truth? Was the interrogator simply being told what he wanted to hear? No one ever knew for sure.

Such would not be the case if Voss's technology were put to practical use. Not if the interrogator was allowed unfettered access to the mind of his subject. There would be no way to lie or mislead. The interrogator would be privy to any memory that the suspect held within.

On one hand, Cyrus saw how such a thing could be leveraged to save lives. It would yield immediate and reliable intelligence without any invasive detriment to the subject. Conversely, it was a tool that was far too easily abused. He couldn't imagine a system of checks and balances sufficient enough to police it.

Just considering the possibilities, Cyrus felt a cold pit begin to form in his gut. The more he thought about it, the more the pit grew and tore at his insides. He was with the good guys, for

God's sake, and he didn't even trust *his* people with that sort of power. What would happen if it fell into hostile hands? It was a nightmare beyond reason.

People wouldn't even be safe within their own minds.

Taking a deep breath, Cyrus centered himself. All of this was troubling, but it still wasn't the reason he'd fought to make the mission his own. He hadn't told Boone the truth about his reason for wanting this assignment. There was no question that Boone was suspicious, but to his credit, he hadn't pressed the issue. That was for the better.

If he knew the truth, Boone would've been obligated to take the information to the Red Queen, and Cyrus couldn't let that happen...for several reasons. First, he was sure that Monica would try to leverage the information in some foul way. Second, and more importantly, he wasn't willing to let anything interfere with his chance to see Natasha again. If only he knew how she would react to seeing him. The entire operation hung on her, and the way she chose to respond to his reappearance. It was that great unknown Cyrus wouldn't be able to explain to anyone's satisfaction.

Cyrus knew his mind was wandering as he made his way from one end of the train to the other. Still, it was a welcome distraction. He had an ominous feeling that something was wrong, and that Gladd was in trouble. Even though his partner had provided the proper response to the challenge code, it had taken far too long. Something wasn't right.

And if he was right about that, it meant they had another problem. If Gladd had given up the response code under duress, he would've used the duress code to let Cyrus know it. The fact that he didn't do that suggested that whoever was with Gladd knew the codes and was familiar with Coalition protocols. While that would also explain how they'd been located on this train, it didn't bode well for the overall mission.

Something was very wrong. And being stuck on a train hurtling through the European countryside at 60MPH didn't leave him a lot of tactical options or room to maneuver. Without anything he was comfortable calling a plan, he headed for their cabin at the opposite end of the train. As was often his way, he would make it up as he went along.

Chapter 26

Express train out of Paris, France
12:25 am

The world around him now spun uncontrollably. Paul Gladd finally recognized the pain and the flashes of blue light he was seeing in the darkness. In time, his memory was returning, even if his other senses were still running haywire. He'd experienced all of this once before. It had been an unfortunate experience at the wrong end of a Taser, back when he was training with the Special Operations Unit.

Special Operations Unit?

He took another breath. His memory was still spotty. The contents of his mind were inconsistent and jumbled. It was a constant struggle to keep it sorted while he worked through his current situation. He'd realized the more he focused on mental exercises, the less he suffered from the physical pain. And he was at the point where he needed to do whatever was possible to lessen the pain.

Special Operations Unit...

It was a struggle to put his thoughts back on track. He tried to recall where he'd been going with the logic...

The accident! That was the last time he'd experienced this level of agony. The class had been training with Tasers. Each student was taking a Taser hit so they would know what to expect should they encounter the device in the field. The Taser sent a 50,000 volt jolt of electricity through the human body. It wasn't supposed to injure an individual as much as incapacitate them. The blast was supposed to overload the central nervous system and temporarily immobilize a subject.

That was the case 99.99% of the time. Paul Gladd had proven to be the missing 0.01%. Whatever his rare physiological signature, the Taser blast did more than incapacitate. It was more akin to a shock and awe campaign for his neurological and central nervous system. It was essentially the most painful experience anyone could imagine.

A surge of relief coursed through his body. It was as if gathering a firm grasp on that memory somehow gave him tangible leverage over his situation. And in some ways it did. Though he still couldn't think clearly, he was finally beginning to regain cognitive control.

The blue streaks continued to pass before his eyes as he focused against the pain. And though time held no meaning, he was starting to see indications that the light show was abating. The thunder in his ears was lessening, and the flashes where his eyes should be were growing distant and less distinct. Pain levels showed signs of ebbing, and he began to feel a tired ache where his arms and legs should be.

That Goddamn Taser... Never again...

The thought made his breath catch. Something about the Taser seemed wrong. He'd made that vow once before...

So why had he...

His memory flooded back in a blast of insight. He recalled the train car and his assignment. He'd just finished securing the courier. The man was drugged and wrapped head to toe in a rapid application, full body cast. Then, the last thing he could recall was the strange sense that someone was behind him.

That was it.

At last, the room around him was beginning to emerge from the darkness. It was like having the sun spill through blacked out curtains. The light was almost nonexistent, but it was there, it was something real.

And he heard voices.

Voices? There shouldn't be voices...

Realizing suddenly that he could feel his hands and move his fingers, he wondered why he couldn't move his arms or legs. He couldn't see yet, but this was a start. Everything about his situation was troubling—even if he still wasn't entirely sure why. So was the strange sensation around his wrists. Thinking hard, that feeling also seemed familiar. He struggled to place it.

With a hard swallow, Gladd felt his heart sink. He recognized the tightness near his wrists and the numbness in the tips of his fingers. They were bound behind his back.

His mind was still scrambled but he realized he was in trouble. First the Taser, and now his hands were bound? He didn't know what the hell was going on, but he knew it wasn't going to end well.

Chapter 27

Express train out of Paris, France
12:27 am

Brolin eased his back to the window of the small cabin. The sliding door was eight feet away on the other side of the room, directly opposite him. He had his Beretta drawn and the silencer attached. The gun was held in a relaxed stance, but Magda could see her own anxiety mirrored in his icy stare.

Was their employer right? Had their delayed response caused the young agent to become suspicious? She was skeptical. Her eyes fell on Paul Gladd, bound hand and foot, now lying on the fold down bunk at the edge of the room.

Magda eased her small form against the wall. She was using the wall adjacent to the sliding door leading to the corridor. Brolin had a direct line of fire on the doorway while she could literally reach out and press her gun to the head of the young agent when he stepped into the room. All in all, they had the room's only entrance covered. Even if Cooper was suspicious, his options were severely limited.

Though they'd been ordered to kill Gladd immediately, Magda reasoned that it was far more logical to take care of Cyrus Cooper first. She couldn't imagine how the young agent could possibly get the better of them, but should worse come to worst, they could use his partner against him. The way she saw it, they were holding all the cards.

Still, something was eating at her and she was having trouble placing the source of the discomfort. It didn't help that their employer was portraying their target as some sort of avenging angel. She found it unsettling, but still wasn't buying it.

On top of everything else, Magda was harboring an increasing concern for the identity of their employer. The person behind this operation didn't have a name, but everyone in their line of work knew the reputation—cold, calculating, and shockingly well-informed. Whoever it was, it was someone with access to tier-one intelligence; contracting with independent operators throughout Europe and putting together unusual operations, like heists, assassinations, and at least one kidnapping that she knew of.

He had done a lot of contracting with operators who worked in the same circles as she and Brolin. It was a pretty tight group. Word had spread when more gregarious members of the community started taking odd jobs from a new, unseen employer. Operations were always arranged through untraceable voiceover-IP calls routed across the internet, and the voice was disguised using complicated, high-tech modulation equipment. No one even knew if their contractor was a man or a woman. Money was wired through untraceable accounts, and the jobs were always painstakingly planned. The instructions were always the same: missions had to be carried out with absolute precision and adherence to the instructions that were provided. Whoever behind the operations, word was that the plans were as foolproof as anyone had ever seen, and the supplied intelligence was always accurate.

Magda and Brolin had once thought the mysterious contractor to be a myth; an urban legend conjured amidst their community—until they were contracted for their current assignment. And though they'd been reluctant to throw in with the mysterious individual, the money being offered was simply too good to pass up.

Their reticence to contract with their employer came from additional rumors circulating in the community. While the missions their benefactor planned had been known for their craftsmanship, two operations were known to have fallen apart. According to rumor, both of the contracted teams had simply vanished following the failure of their missions…disappeared from the face of the earth.

The faceless employer became well known for that fact—the boogeyman of their profession. As a result, only the most competent, professional, and lethal operators dared work for the nameless, faceless enigma.

In a community of already scary and dangerous individuals, their employer was the only thing universally feared. Magda realized that she and Brolin now had no choice. Either Cyrus Cooper died tonight, or they did. The operation could end no other way.

But the longer they waited, the more frustrated she became. If Cooper was suspicious, he sure wasn't doing anything about it.

She wished Agent Gladd had been responsive. They could've questioned him about protocols. They could've gained insight into the young agent. The longer they waited, the more she wanted to get it over with and just go after Cooper before he came to them.

Just when Magda thought she couldn't deal with the wait any longer, a rapid knock sounded on the cabin door. Brolin responded instantly with three rapid shots from his silenced sidearm. The rounds created a triangle pattern near the center of the door in roughly the circumference of a dinner plate. The pattern was good. It ensured a solid hit even if the target wasn't standing dead center in the doorway.

Magda found herself holding her breath as she waiting for a response from the hallway. The 'thump' of a body hitting the floor, an impact on the wall, the slightest shift of the door in its track—even the return of gunfire—but there was nothing. The gentle rocking movement of the car, and the distant clatter of the rails beneath them continued uninterrupted. The smell of spent gunpowder hung in the air, but still there was no movement from beyond the door.

She watched her husband's eyes narrow on the three holes he'd created. Curious, she stepped away from the wall to get a better view for herself. Other than the occasional flash of ambient light from the hallway windows, there was no sign of movement.

Judging by the look on Brolin's face, he was equally as puzzled. He signaled her silently with a wave of his hand and stepped toward the door. She slid back against the wall beside the door, ready to pull it open along its sliding track as soon as Brolin gave her the signal.

Her husband steadied his silenced .45 and took a deep breath. Once exhaled fully, he nodded slightly. She reached out, gripping the handle with the tips of her gloved fingers. She turned the latch slowly and silently. Then, without hesitation, she stepped back, pulling the door with her and feeling it whisk across its rails into the hollow pocket inside the wall.

Everything happened so fast that she couldn't be sure of the exact order of events. The door hadn't even come to a sliding stop when she heard two rapid 'puffs' from the silenced weapon in her husband's hands. He must have found a target in the hallway even while the door was opening.

She reeled in horror as Brolin staggered backward from an impact to his torso. The two silenced gunshots she'd heard hadn't come from his gun—they'd come from the hallway. Brolin stumbled. She could see two distinct impact points where the high velocity rounds had just shredded his shirt.

Her hand tightened around the small semi-auto as she watched Brolin fall in slow motion. But there was relief. Both rounds had caught him in the upper body, square in his flak jacket. He would survive…

…Her world was shattered when a third round suddenly spat from the unseen weapon still beyond the doorframe. This shot caught Brolin square in the side of his head. Blood and brain matter splattered the cabin windows just before Brolin's body rebounded from that same surface, and slumped to the floor.

The entire series of events had taken less than two seconds; two seconds in which Magda's entire life had collapsed before her eyes. She felt her stomach drop, and then a flash from behind her eyes turned everything she viewed red with rage. She was about to step to the doorway and open fire when the tip of a handgun suppressor slid slowly into the room. The man who had killed her husband would soon follow it.

Magda didn't have to wait long. Cyrus Cooper moved slowly and cautiously, but the moment his gun wielding hand entered the room before him, Magda attacked. She lashed out, smashing his weapon and the hand holding it up against the wall. She spun to meet him, still there in the doorway, bringing her weapon to bear with her free hand, jamming it into his ribs and quickly pulling the trigger.

She was fast…Magda was shocked that Cooper had somehow reacted faster. He managed to bat the muzzle of her gun away just as another silenced round left the barrel. It happened so quickly that Cyrus landed a head-butt to Magda's face before she even realized that her bullets had missed their mark.

The room spun for Magda and she backpedaled, struggling to make sense of what just happened. She'd somehow managed to maintain a crushing grip on the gun hand of her husband's killer. But she knew that, if he were to bring the weapon up before she regained her senses, the fight, as well as her life, would be forfeit.

She blinked rapidly, forcing away the tears that followed the crushing blow to her face. Taking another step back, she retreated further into the cabin, dragging him with and hoping to keep him off balance. Cyrus came into focus for the first time. She still had his gun hand held at bay using her left hand. Magda was using the leverage of her straightened left arm to maintain that delicate balance since he easily overpowered her one-on-one. Similarly, her gun hand was pulled tight across her body as he held her wrist in the fierce grip of his own left hand. It was a stalemate—one she needed to end quickly, seeing as he had a substantial size and weight advantage.

With some confusion, she realized his full attention was not focused on breaking her grip on his gun arm. The young man was putting all of his strength into breaking the ligaments in her right wrist. She felt her gun hand go numb, and then heard the 'thud' of her weapon strike the floor. Magda was confused. The move shouldn't have been a priority. Unless—

Her eyes flared wide as the horrific idea flashed in her mind. She turned to Cyrus's gun hand. It was pushed high and wide of her, out in the air where it could do no harm. Magda's teeth ground together as she focused all of her energy on that hand. But it was too late. She watched helplessly as he simply and willfully let go of the silenced semi-automatic. It plummeted from his raised hand, but as she struggled to bring her hand up in defense, it was no good. The appendage was numb, clumsy, and useless.

Cyrus's eyes locked with hers and she witnessed the chilling certainty of his conviction. There was no anger in his gaze, no hatred—only pure focus for the task at hand.

In her peripheral vision, to her horror, Magda saw her worst fear take form. Cyrus's gun dropped from his raised right hand, only to be snatched from the air by his left when it came level with his belt buckle. There were two hushed 'puffs' and her strength disappeared in an instant.

The two shots caught Magda center mass in her body armor and sent her pounding into the wall of the cabin.

Gasping for air, Magda blinked rapidly and tried to clear her vision. She felt the brutal ache in her chest and was certain ribs had been broken. She wasn't sure if it was real or imagined, but with the suppressor attached to her attacker's gun, she thought she'd heard the sound of her own ribs cracking at the point blank impact.

As her head slumped against the wall, her husband's lifeless body fell into view. The sight brought about a gripping and exhausted sadness. And though her mind told her that the battle was not yet over—that there was still work to do—her body seemed entirely unwilling to leave her husband's side.

This was confusing. She'd never been one to shy away from a fight, yet she couldn't seem to pull herself from the floor. She turned to look upon the man who had shot her and found that even that simple movement took far too much effort. Even blinking felt clumsy…slow and sluggish.

My God, how hard did I hit my head?

She was still trying to sort through the strange sensory input when her attacker approached cautiously. He looked down at her, then squatted before her. Taking a long look into her eyes, he then placed two fingers against the side of her throat, and waited.

What the hell is he doing?

When the young agent pulled his fingers away, she could see pain in his eyes. He looked disappointed. Magda wanted to ask him what the hell he was doing, but suddenly realized that she couldn't form the words. She could think them, but she couldn't manage to voice them.

Finally, with complete and utter horror, she noticed the two fingers the man had placed against the carotid artery of her throat. They were thick with arterial blood. The reason for the cool numbness that had been present registered in her mind, as her vision began to draw dark. It wasn't so bad, she thought. After all, she would be seeing Brolin again soon, and they wouldn't have to worry about their employer any more.

Things could be worse…

Chapter 28

Kneeling before the lifeless body of the hired killer, Cyrus couldn't help his sense of disappointment. He needed to take the woman alive, but the combat instinct had been so deeply instilled in him that it was second nature. When he opened fire, he'd followed the two torso shots with a shot to the head. He'd tried to check his fire at the last moment, but the last ditch effort hadn't been enough to spare the nameless woman's life. The bullet had missed its mark as a result, but it had caught her along the edge of the throat, clearly nicking an artery. She'd bled out quickly.

Her blood was already pooled around her body and that of the partner she'd nearly landed on top of. The entire incident meant serious trouble for the mission. Cyrus was supposed to take the place of Ragsdale's courier and deliver the imaging hardware to Doctor Voss, himself. Now their train ride had become a bloodbath that would be impossible to cover up.

Cyrus found some good news when he checked on Paul Gladd. He was bound hand and foot, and resting on a bunk along the wall of the cabin. He didn't look well. His face was dripping with perspiration, and his shirt was thoroughly soaked. But as far as Cyrus could tell, his partner hadn't been physically harmed. He still had all of his fingers, and likely all of his toes. At a glance, he didn't appear to have any wounds or new bodily orifices whatsoever.

Cutting him loose, he left Gladd on the bunk to recuperate. Lastly, he checked on the unconscious man in the wheelchair. Gladd must've secured their target before being subdued by the wetwork team, Cyrus reasoned.

The thought brought Cyrus back to the pair of bodies on the floor. While he was confident that the two had been working with the large German from the dining car, he could only guess at their motivation. He searched both bodies, but just like the German, neither held any sort of clue to their identities or their mission. Also, like the German, these two clearly meant to do him in. But if that was the case, why hadn't they killed Gladd? And, from all he'd seen, this team didn't seem to have any interest in the courier. All of this, once more, led him to believe that the team had been sent after him and Gladd…only.

The questions surrounding his situation were only made more frustrating by the fact that Cyrus could only blame himself for the death of the woman. If only he'd held his last shot, there would've been an opportunity for answers. Still, extensive training for similar situations had espoused only one response. When your life is in danger, it's critical to act with decisive and deadly force. Training made such a response second nature. The theory being, when circumstances arose, there wouldn't be time for conscious decisions. As such, he'd been hardwired to operate on pure instinct.

Unfortunately, in this situation, his instincts left him with no clues and absolutely no leads.

Chapter 29

Express train out of Paris, France
4:25 am

Paul Gladd struggled to roll over. It felt like he was fighting the mother of all hangovers. His mind strained to recall what he'd been drinking the night before. He was willing to give just about anything to make whoever it was stop the constant banging downstairs. The rhythmic crashing sound manifested like someone smacking him upside the head with a large wrench, over and over and over again.

Something about the rhythm of the sequence worked its way through Gladd's addled mind, and he found himself confused. He couldn't recall drinking last night because it hadn't happened. When he moved his arms, he found that there was pain. Actually, he felt pain everywhere—through every literal inch of his body. Moving his arms also brought about an unusual raw burning sensation in the flesh around his wrists.

With a great deal of effort, Gladd pulled himself to a sitting position and looked around. He was in the lower bunk of a four-passenger train car. Mercifully, the room's lights had been dimmed. The scenery outside the windows was dark and he was confused. The particulars of his situation took a few additional moments to bubble to the surface of his mind.

Cyrus slept on the bench on the far side of the cabin. He was sitting with his eyes closed and his head tipped back against the wall. A silenced 9mm lay in his lap. A man in a wheelchair took up much of the floor space in the center of the cabin. He was wrapped head to toe in a hard-shelled cast, with the only visible parts of the man being his eyes, lips, fingertips, and toes. A quiet snoring could be heard emanating from inside.

"Feeling better?" Cyrus asked in a quiet voice.

Gladd noticed that Cyrus hadn't so much as moved when he spoke. He hadn't been sleeping after all. Though everything about his current situation was disconcerting, even if he couldn't fully recall why, Gladd found his partner's vigilance reassuring.

Throwing his legs over the side of the bunk, Gladd marveled at his renewed level of pain. It must've shown on his face.

"It might not feel like it now," Cyrus explained, "but you're doing a hell of a lot better than you were a few hours ago."

His movement had brought about a wave of nausea, and he gripped the edge of the bunk with white knuckles. "I feel like I got hit by a bus," Gladd muttered. It was all he could think to say, and he couldn't imagine that it was far from accurate.

Gladd slid from his bunk and onto rubbery legs. He leaned against the bedside for support. "What the hell happened?"

"I'm not entirely sure," Cyrus said, after a moment's consideration. "You were out cold and hogtied when I got back to the cabin. As close as I can figure, a pair of heavy hitters got the drop on you and laid you out good.

"At first I thought you were drugged, but I couldn't find anything on them that would support that. As odd as it sounds, I think they just spiked you with a Taser."

A groan escaped his lips before he could help himself. "A Taser?" Gladd rasped. "Yeah, that would explain it."

When the comment brought a bewildered expression to his partner's face, Gladd knew he had to explain. He pulled himself back up onto the bunk; it relieved some of the pain in his legs. He searched for the words to explain something he didn't want to talk about. Like a boxer with a glass jaw, the simple device was his Achilles' heel and his Waterloo all rolled into one.

"When most people take a hit from a Taser it overloads their nervous system and they drop like a log, right?" Gladd asked.

Cyrus just looked at him and waited for him to continue. Apparently, he took the question as rhetorical. Even now, Cyrus wasn't one for wasting words.

Gladd rolled his eyes, and continued, "Anyway, there's a small percentage of the population that's wired a little different than everyone else. For them, a hit from a Taser isn't just a 50,000 volt overload that causes a central nervous system reboot. For us, it's a full blown meltdown. It's more like having your body turned inside out."

Cyrus's surprise was evident by the look on his face. He took a few seconds to process the explanation. "Inside out?" he asked at last. "I'd say that looked about right. I wasn't sure you were going to make it there for a while. But at the same time, I couldn't find a damn thing wrong with you. It didn't even look like they laid a hand on you. I found the mark the Taser left, but that was it."

Setting his gun aside, Cyrus's gaze moved around slowly. Gladd knew that look. He was considering the implications of what he now knew.

"You've been through this before," Cyrus said.

Gladd nodded. He knew where this was going, but he was too tired and worn out to resist it. "Once," he explained. "About twenty years ago, give or take. It was a training exercise. Everyone had to take a hit from that damn thing so they'd have a sense of what it was like. You know, how to deal with it whether they were using it on someone, or having it used on them?"

He could see from Cyrus's grin that he knew exactly what he was talking about. The kid would've gone through the same thing, just a lot more recently.

"I'm a little surprised you were field certified after having a reaction like that," Cyrus said.

It was the point that Gladd was dreading. While he knew himself to be a damn good agent, he also knew that such a handicap was a massive liability for his teammates, as well as any operation he was a part of.

"My instructor thought the whole thing was shitty," Gladd explained. "I honestly think he was under the impression that the device malfunctioned. Whether it was that, or he just didn't want me to wash out over something like that, I don't know. But he never put it in the report, and they never bounced me for it."

Gladd fidgeted in his bunk. "I know it wasn't right, and it could've gotten you killed. I won't make any excuses for it," he explained. "I shouldn't have even been here."

With a jolt, Gladd suddenly sat fully upright. "Wait!" he gasped. "*What the hell did happen*? If they took me out, what happened to you?"

Cyrus laughed and rose from the bench. He made a motion with his hands, encouraging Gladd to calm down. Flipping the lid on the hard-shell case they'd brought aboard the train, Cyrus retrieved a bottle of Gatorade and handed it over.

"It's okay," Cyrus explained. "They sent two guys after you and one after me at the other end of the train. They were well organized and well prepared."

"You got all three of them?" Gladd tried not to sound too surprised, but it didn't work.

With a nod, Cyrus glanced at the dark blanket draped over a long object beneath the window. Gladd hadn't noticed it at first, but now saw that it was wide enough to cover a man laid out on his back.

When Cyrus saw the confused look, he explained.

"There's two of them under there. A man and a woman. This really big sonofabitch came after me in the dining car, but I was able to get rid of that body."

"Can we do the same with these?" Gladd asked.

Cyrus shook his head. "These two went down hard. It was bloody. I was able to clean the mess off the windows, but there's a hell of a mess under that blanket. Once the lights are turned on full, you can't miss it. We can't hide it like I did the other one."

Leaning back against the wall, Gladd considered the situation. He was frustrated because he knew his mind was moving slower than it should.

"I'm sorry," Gladd said finally. He realized this mess was his fault, and though he couldn't fix it, he could at least own up to it. "You were right, I should never have been allowed out in the field."

"What?" Cyrus asked defensively. "I never said that!"

"No," Gladd clarified. "That's not what I mean. I'm just saying that you're right. I should've been drummed out of fieldwork after my first experience with a Taser. At first, I was just too young and proud to admit I was vulnerable. It was stupid. I'm old enough to know better now."

"There's a difference," Cyrus offered. "You're *experienced enough* to know better now. Not old enough. Your quirky relationship with electricity notwithstanding, you're a professional, and you bring a lot of quality experience to an operation. If you ask me, it far outweighs one little problem like this. I mean, we all have our Kryptonite, don't we?"

Despite himself, Gladd couldn't help but laugh. "Still…this mess could've gotten us both killed."

Considering his words, Cyrus just shrugged. "If we wanted to play it safe, we wouldn't play with killers," he countered. "Forget about it. This never happened. Your secret's safe with me."

That brought a new, hearty laugh from Gladd. "Easier said than done. The op is blown! All of this is for nothing. And it's not like keeping it to ourselves will be an option when we head back to base with our tails between our legs."

"You're right," Cyrus agreed. "We can't keep this quiet if we pull the ripcord and head home now. But if we complete the mission, why would the brass question what happened here?"

"Great idea," Gladd remarked, adding a sarcastic roll of his eyes. When he didn't vomit from the maneuver, he was sure his health was improving. He was thinking more clearly too. That was a plus, even if it was a small one when compared to their poor circumstances. They might get off the train without the bodies being found, but it wouldn't take long before someone discovered the grisly mess. When they did, it would be front-page news. There was no way Cyrus could continue his part of the mission by replacing the courier and delivering the package once the train made headlines.

"We can still complete the mission," Cyrus elaborated. "The little one gave me the idea when she shot me." He pointed to the short stack of dead bodies beneath the blanket.

Staring for a long moment while he processed Cyrus's words, Gladd first thought he had misunderstood his partner. After a few long seconds, he finally found the words. "I'm sorry—did you say that you've been shot?"

Cyrus grinned and then pulled up the corner of his shirt to reveal a large white field dressing that was darkly stained with blood. Gladd watched—captivated, as Cyrus peeled back the dressing to show the ragged and bloody furrow that marked the lower left edge of his abdomen.

Glancing down at himself and then back at Gladd, Cyrus flashed a grin that further suggested the wound was the solution to all of their problems.

"Jesus!" Gladd leapt from the bunk, forgetting the pain, and descended on Cyrus. "Sit down, dammit! We gotta get this cleaned up!"

Raising a hand, Cyrus chuckled. "I cleaned it already. It's good enough for now. It's a through n' through, and as far as I can tell, the slug didn't fragment. The bitch was using Teflon coated rounds anyway. Apparently, they were afraid we might be wearing body armor.

"Anyway, just let it be. It can't look professionally treated for what comes next."

For Gladd's part, he found himself only able to stare at the young agent. The kid had lost his mind.

"It's going on quarter-to-five," Cyrus explained. "So we need to get you back into fighting shape as soon as possible."

Gladd's mind snapped back to their present situation. "You think there will be more hitters waiting for us when we reach Hamburg station?"

Cyrus considered it. He looked back to the long dark blanket while pondering the idea. "I doubt it," he admitted.

"Then what do you mean by *back in fighting shape?*"

"Oh," Cyrus said. "Sorry, I guess I skipped that part. I need you to beat the hell out of me before the train reaches the station."

Gladd looked at him. A big grin crossed his face. "And you think that my kicking your ass is going to save this mission?"

"Sure! See, all we need to do is—"

Holding up a hand, Gladd stopped his partner in his tracks. "No need," he said. "You had me at *kicking your ass.* Whatever you have in mind for the rest of the plan, you can count me in!"

Chapter 30

3 Days Later
The Voss Compound
11:14 am

Stepping off the elevator, Anna Voss adjusted the jacket that was draped over her forearm and crossed the copper colored ceramic tile. The building's common area was a wide, open space where her family shared a great deal of time. There were two groups of furniture, with one arranged before a large entertainment center on one end of the space. A similar group was near the other end, surrounding the hearth of a large, modern-looking fireplace. Just past the fireplace was a smaller separated area with a wide formal dining room table surrounded with heavy wooden chairs. The ceiling towered five floors above, and the entire north wall was made of glass. It overlooked a small courtyard with a circular car turn-a-bout and an elaborate decorative fountain. The late morning sun blanketed the massive glass wall, bathing the tile floor and everything else inside with radiant warmth.

Behind Anna, each of the five floors above ended at a balcony that overlooked the common area on the ground floor. A transparent glass panel topped with a thick polished steel railing fronted each balcony, leaving an unimpeded view of what went on below.

The massive glass facade on the building's north wall overlooked the small courtyard, which was surrounded by a twenty-foot stone wall. The wall circled the entire five-acre plot of land that the ultramodern building occupied. A pair of massive gates barred access to the facility via the street level, also located on the north side.

This mammoth complex was home to the Voss family, and one of the most secure locations on the island. A full security detail living on-site staffed the facility twenty-four hours a day, and they had long ago begun referring to her family home as, "The Compound." It was fitting, she thought. Yet, even though the security personnel were part of her day-to-day life, she had never really understood the need for them.

The guard standing station beside the wide automated sliding door at the building's entrance smiled as she approached.

"Will you be leaving the facility, ma'am?" he asked, as he pulled the small handheld radio from inside his tailored suit coat.

Anna nodded, offering a warm smile. "I'm meeting a couple of friends for coffee."

"I'll have your detail sent down," the guard responded, before tapping the button on the side of his radio. He made a brief transmission before Anna could dissuade him.

"That's not necessary," she countered. "Maybe just Darya? I'm only going half a block down the street. There's no need for a fuss."

The guard tucked his radio away and shook his head. He offered a reluctant, if placating smile. "Sorry, miss. Dargo's orders. You and your sister are to have at least three escorts at all times beyond the gates."

Anna's jaw dropped. "*Three?* What's happened?"

"I'm sorry, ma'am, I don't know. Those are the new orders as of 21:00 hours last night." He looked uncomfortable being the one to inform her of the change in protocol. It was common knowledge that she didn't appreciate her usual two-man detail.

"I can radio Dargo and have him come down to answer your questions, if you'd like," he offered.

Anna's mind ran with the implications of the news. Something must have happened. Dargo was overprotective to begin with, but *three* body guards? Something had obviously put him on high alert.

Her concern for the security precautions quickly took a backseat to other considerations, as she realized she would now have three very conspicuous escorts when she met with her friends. Her cheeks reddened at the thought. Such were the concerns of the twenty-year-old woman who had yet to experience life outside a 24/7, high security compound.

"So you won't let me slide, just this once? I can take Darya— I'm only going down the street for coffee," she insisted.

"Sorry, miss. It's not my call," the guard said, shaking his head.

The elevator door chimed at the back of the room and Anna turned to see three members of the security team emerge. They marched in her direction. There was some consolation; at least Darya was among them.

"Coffee with the girls?" the female security agent asked as she approached. "Or should I have the car brought up?"

"No, just coffee." Anna offered Darya a sad smile. "What's going on? What's with the extra muscle?"

"Come on," Darya said, as she stepped past the invisible sensor that activated the wide sliding glass doors. She led Anna and the pair of suited security men into the courtyard.

The morning air was brisk. Anna quickly responded by pulling on her jacket. It was especially chilly for the first few moments while they were under the building's portico. As soon as they stepped into the sunshine however, the damp chill was driven away.

Darya led the group across the wide loop of pavement. The short double lane driveway started at the pair of wide solid iron and stone gates set in the perimeter wall fifty-feet away, before sweeping around a large, ornate water fountain, to pass under the portico at the building's entrance. After that, the pavement continued, forming a loop that allowed vehicles to circle and head back to the street. Another section of asphalt swept wide to the right, leading to a fifteen-foot tall retractable garage door and the subterranean motor pool waiting beyond.

Letting the other two guards advance past them, Darya waited until the men were out of earshot. "We're not supposed to talk about it," she told Anna quietly. "Apparently, one of your father's colleagues was attacked a few days ago in Paris. They've been collaborating on a project, so it's unclear whether there is a threat to your father, his work, *or* you girls."

The news stopped Anna in her tracks. She looked Darya in the eye. "Paris? You're talking about Professor Ragsdale?"

Darya nodded. "You know him?"

"No," she said quietly, considering what she knew of the man. "But I've heard father speak of him. They go way back. Is he alright?"

"I'm sorry," Darya admitted. "I don't know anything more. And, please, don't let on that I told you this much. Dargo was specific about keeping this information to ourselves."

Anna nodded absently. Her mind was running rampant with questions and concerns over what had happen to her father's colleague. Could there be a legitimate reason for the increased security? For once, she didn't feel that Dargo, the head of her father's security team, was overreacting.

A buzzer sounded at the gate and pulled Anna's attention back to the moment. All eyes turned to the structure, including Anna, Darya, and the additional pair of bodyguards. Another security guard stepped from the small, heated shack beside the gated entrance. He quickly looked to the two men on Anna's security detail, concern evident on his face.

As the two men jogged the short distance across the drive to join the guard at the gate, Darya placed a hand on Anna's arm and stopped her where she was.

"What's going on?" Anna asked.

Darya held a hand to her ear as she listened to what was being broadcast over their security channel. Her eyes squinted in confusion as she tried to understand what was happening.

"Come on," Darya commanded. "We need to get you inside, *right now*."

Allowing herself to be led back to the building, Anna looked over her shoulder and wondered why the security team gathered around the small armored service door beside the massive front gates.

"*What the devil is going on?*" Anna insisted.

Darya refused to answer until she had Anna back inside and secure behind the facade of bulletproof glass. "There's someone at the gate insisting on being let in," she finally explained.

Anna found herself staring at the woman. There had to be more to it than that. What could the man at the gate have done to warrant such a response from security? Was he armed? Was he making threats? While dozens of questions flooded her mind, she found herself only able to look at Darya, anticipating the remainder of the story.

When Darya failed to elaborate, Anna had to bite back the scolding retort that passed through her mind. It was the woman's responsibility to be forthcoming with such details, but more than that, she was a friend. What *isn't* she saying?

"I don't get it!" Anna finally bellowed. "Is he armed?"

Darya was slow to respond, but finally shook her head. That was when Anna realized that whatever was happening had her protector deeply concerned. She wasn't being cagey—she was simply trying to process a great deal of information in a short period of time. Some part of what she knew seemed to be troubling the woman. This was unusual, because Anna had always known Darya to be shrewd and decisive.

Anna suddenly realized that she might be able to answer many of the questions on her own. She rushed to the security terminal beside the front door. The station had been abandoned when the guard was pulled from his post to see to the disturbance at the gate.

Her fingers flying across the keyboard, Anna pulled up the building's security system and then displayed the video feed from the street outside. The video, like all parts of the security in the compound, was top notch. There were three camera views showing the man leaning against the service door's frame on the sidewalk outside.

With a few additional keystrokes, Anna zoomed in and brought the stranger into crisp, clear detail. But what she saw only confused her further. Given the reaction of the security team, she'd expected the man to be brandishing a weapon or have a suicide vest strapped to his chest, bomb trigger in a raised hand. Strangely, the man didn't seem to be armed at all. He didn't even have a vehicle with him.

Anna's eyes moved from the screen and over to Darya for clarification. But Darya was talking into her radio and hadn't yet noticed what she was doing.

Adjusting the camera angle, Anna took a closer look. He was younger than she first thought. She initially mistook him as an older vagrant, but now saw that wasn't the case. He was actually rather young. He was filthy—she looked closer…and bleeding. She suddenly realized that it wasn't dirt all over his face, but bruises and cuts. He was hunched against the doorframe, not because he was a tired old man, but because he was injured and struggling to stay on his feet.

"Darya!" Anna called. "That man—you must let him in!"

Cutting off what she was relaying on the radio, Darya looked up and saw for the first time that Anna was sitting behind the security terminal. "Don't do that, Anna. Let my team deal with it. We should get you to the safe room until we know for sure what's happening."

"No," Anna insisted. "You don't understand. That man's hurt. He needs medical attention!"

When Darya advanced and tried to guide her away from the terminal, Anna took advantage of the situation and stepped around her. She rushed for the front doors but ran face-first into the thick pane of glass when the automatic mechanism failed to operate.

Staggering from the impact, Anna's hands went instinctively to her face. At first, she didn't understand why the doors had failed to open. But, then, the information hit…the building was on lockdown.

"Anna, please calm down," Darya tried to speak in a calming voice.

Not missing a beat, Anna stepped to the security panel on the wall beside the door. She tapped a few buttons on the touch-screen and pulled up a virtual numeric keypad. Twelve digits later, there was a click followed by a hiss as the front doors parted, sliding open and allowing her freedom.

Anna charged out into the courtyard even as she heard Darya stammering incoherently behind her. Anna knew her sister would be upset when she found out that the override code was no longer their personal secret, but there hadn't been an alternative.

"Wait!" Darya finally managed to yell, as she ran to keep up.

It didn't matter. She was too late to catch Anna before she reached the group of guards who had surrounded the gate's service door. Half a dozen men stood in a semi-circle facing the door with their guns drawn, as Anna charged right into the middle of their ring.

"God damn it, wait!" Darya bellowed, arriving on Anna's heels.

The security team was surprised by the intrusion, and every one of them quickly shifted their stance to direct their weapons away from her. She stood between them and the door, blocking it with her body.

"What is wrong with you," Anna scolded. "He's hurt! Let him in, damn it—he needs our help!"

Shouldering her way past them, Darya slid her gun into its holster. "Anna! You don't understand," she practically yelled at her charge. "Just because he looks hurt, doesn't mean he is! He could have a bomb strapped to him for all we know."

Anna glared at the female agent, before sweeping her accusatory gaze at the group of armed men around her. "And if he's for real? Are you going to let him bleed to death while you sort this out?"

"Honey," Darya pleaded. "We have to be careful. That means we can't make any snap decisions."

Shaking her head, Anna turned to the security panel mounted in the wall beside the door. She began tapping on the touch-screen display. Just as she brought up the section she needed, she felt arms wrap around her from behind. One of the bodyguards had grabbed her and was pulling her away from the door.

All concern for the man outside the gate being dangerous left her, as she was overcome by outrage. First, at the way they were treating the injured man, but then for the way they were treating her. She yelled and stomped down with her foot. She caught her capturer's instep with the heel of her expensive boot. The man bellowed in pain, releasing his hold.

As she spun away from the man, her elbow banged against something metal. In a flash, she realized it was a holstered sidearm. Without conscious thought, she snatched it from his waistband and backpedaled to safety.

The entire security detail responded as one, reflexively stepping back from the young woman. One or two of them actually started to raise their weapons before remembering that wasn't an option. They certainly couldn't treat her like a normal threat.

Anna, for her part, was waving the gun at the security team and moving back to the door before she even knew what she was doing.

Oh, shit…

The weight of her actions finally hit. Anna knew she'd have to deal with the consequences later. But in the meantime, there was still the man on the other side of the wall who needed medical attention.

Holding the gun in her left hand, she kept the guards at bay. She tapped quickly at the display of the security terminal. Hearing the various voices behind her urging her to put the gun down, Anna tuned them out and focused on the task at hand.

Completing the necessary sequence, Anna opened the intercom channel to the entire facility. "Gretchen, please report to the front gate immediately. We have an emergency medical situation."

Having sent the page, and knowing help was on the way, Anna tapped another key and changed the channel. She opened the channel with the intercom outside the gate.

Looking back to the security detail, Anna once more brandished the gun, warning everyone to stay away. Putting her back to the wall beside the panel, she took a deep breath.

"Hey," she said over her shoulder into the intercom. "Can you hear me out there?"

There was a long silence and Anna began to wonder if the man on the other side could hear her after all. She glanced at the screen and saw him finally raise his hunched form enough to look up and into the display.

"Are you talking to me?" the man finally asked in a shaky voice.

"Yeah," Anna said. Despite how bad he looked, he still managed to grin into the camera when he saw her. "You're not looking too good out there," she continued. The man sputtered and coughed. She realized he'd managed a weak laugh.

"I gotta be honest," he admitted. "I've had better days."

"What can I do for you? Do you need medical attention?"

"Ah," the voice stammered as if confused. "Is this Doc Voss's place?" he asked in an unsure tone.

Doc Voss? She'd never heard her father called that before. *Who is this guy?*

"Who's asking?" she asked, her voice a little more coy and playful than she intended.

She turned to see Darya scowling at her. It was as she suspected, the woman thought she was flirting with him.

Oh well…

"I have a package I was supposed to deliver to the Doc," the man explained. Already she could tell that his voice was growing hoarse. He wheezed, then slouched even more, clearly having trouble remaining upright. "I ran into some trouble on the way here."

"Oh, crap!" Darya muttered, when she heard the man's statement.

This drew Anna's attention but she didn't understand what Darya was thinking. It didn't matter at this point. She kept the gun raised, though suddenly the security team seemed less inclined to take it away from her.

"What's your name?" Anna asked.

"Cyrus," he said. The man's voice cracked. There was something more, but he mumbled the rest. He sounded like he was having trouble concentrating and she suspected he might be close to losing consciousness.

Looking back to Darya, Anna wanted to see if the name registered with her. She couldn't believe that no one had bothered to ask him his name.

Darya shook her head at Anna's questioning glance. The name didn't mean anything to her.

"It's nice to meet you, Cyrus. I'm Anna."

When Cyrus didn't respond or move, Anna got worried. He'd slumped over; only the top of his head was visible on the screen. He might've blacked out.

"Cyrus! Hey? Can you hear me?"

"Anna? *That's a pretty name.*" His response came after far too long of a silence. His words were slurred, as if he were intoxicated. She knew it was a bad sign.

"Cyrus, we're going to get you help. We have medical assistance on the way. There's just one problem, and I need your help to deal with it. Can you help me?" Her voice was rising in octaves along with her stress level. She sensed he was slipping away, and she needed to keep him with her just a little longer. She knew that the security team had a legitimate concern when it came to someone coming through the gate with a bomb strapped to their chest. Unfortunately, it was all too real of a concern these days.

"Happy to help," Cyrus slurred in a rather upbeat reply.

"This is going to sound silly, but it's important. And the sooner you do this for me, the sooner I can get you that help," she urged.

When he didn't reply, she continued.

"Cyrus, I need you to take your shirt off. Can you do that? I need you to take your shirt all the way off and drop it in the street. I know you're hurting, but this is important!"

When there was no reply and no movement, Anna felt her heart race. She wanted to release the locks and throw open the door. She'd heard Gretchen arrive a moment ago, and looked back to see that she had her emergency medical kit in hand.

"Cyrus! Can you hear me?" Anna pleaded.

"Take my shirt off?" His voice came back confused, but he acted as if no time had passed. He chuckled and pulled himself upright with great effort. He looked into the camera and made eye contact with her. "Hey? Are you hitting on me?" he mumbled, with a lopsided grin.

"No!" She couldn't help but smile. "Cyrus, come on! This is very important. I need you to take your shirt off for me!"

The man squinted into the lens of the camera as if taking a closer look at her. His grin spread into a tired smile. "Are you sure you're not hitting on me?"

She laughed. She couldn't help it. Even though she couldn't imagine feeling more on edge, somehow she found humor in the situation. "Okay," she said. "Maybe a little."

He nodded. "Thought so," he mumbled.

She watched as he pulled himself upright using the doorframe for leverage. Then he stumbled, tugged, and pulled at his button-up shirt until it finally came free. With a sputtering cough, he dropped the bloody garment in the street, and struggled to stand straight before the camera.

Anna felt Darya against her shoulder as they both looked into the computerized display. Together, they studied the man in the street clearly for the first time. His face was scraped, bloodied and bruised, but that was nothing compared to the damage that had been inflicted to his upper body. There was a large, blood-soaked bandage pulled taut across his lower abdomen, and there was massive purple bruising over most of his chest and arms.

Somehow Cyrus managed to turn around, bring his back into view. A matching saturated patch of gauze was held crudely in place on his lower back. The rest of his upper torso looked to be a web of wounds that mirrored the front.

Trying to complete his pirouette for the camera, Cyrus couldn't pull it off. He stumbled and dropped to the pavement in a heap.

Anna's eyes jumped to Darya. She saw deep-seeded concern in the woman's expression. Anna noticed that at some point everyone had lowered their guns. By then, she must have convinced the security crew that she was dealing with the situation better than they were, because no one tried to reprimand her.

"I'll get it," Darya said, as she moved to the security panel. "Guys, get out there and grab the kid. Bring him in and we'll seal the gate again. Better safe than sorry." She looked back at Gretchen. "Ready?"

Gretchen had her kit open and was already pulling out the first of the required supplies. "Ready when you are," she confirmed.

Chapter 31

The Voss Compound
5:44 pm

Pushing through the heavy steel door, Natasha entered her bedroom on the third floor of the glass and steel compound. She quickly crossed the expansive six hundred square foot space and deposited her computer bag and purse on the large mahogany desk. Without pause, she turned and made a beeline to the king size bed on the far side of the room.

Throwing herself onto the soft down comforter, she rolled onto her back and closed her eyes. It was a relief to be home. What was supposed to have been a weeklong trip to the Falkland Islands had turned into a grueling three-week stay. Thankfully, the extra time had been worth the effort. She'd been there to oversee the work that a small private lab was doing for her father. Synthesizing a stable version of the protein-based tagging enzyme had proven more difficult than either of them had originally expected. A great deal of trial and error had occurred before a stable base solution was devised.

More than anything, she was curious what had transpired while she was away. Nearly a week ago, the size of her five-man security detail more than doubled when Dargo dispatched seven additional men to babysit her for the remainder of her visit. Dargo never spared any expense in regard to her safety, but that was extreme. He'd been looking out for her for as long as she could remember; still, such a hike in security was unprecedented.

Out of concern, she'd contacted her father and asked what had happened back at home. Not surprisingly, he downplayed the increased security, saying that it was prudent given the general state of world affairs. He'd been frustratingly vague, and she knew better. There was something she wasn't being told. But a follow-up call to her sister had proven equally fruitless, and she had quickly understood that she wouldn't get a straight answer until she returned home.

Now that she was here, Natasha was confident that she could get to the bottom of the matter. Oddly, she wasn't concern about security or the safety of her family. Like her father, she had complete faith in Dargo and his people; she just wanted to know what the hell was going on. Dargo's security team was large enough to constitute a small army. She'd had armed guards under foot her entire life, regardless of the fact that—as far as she knew—there had never been an event necessitating their presence.

The knock chime sounded at her door. With a sigh, she pulled herself upright and called, "Come in!"

The computerized system controlling the door responded to her voice, causing the door to slide open with a quiet, pneumatic hiss. Her younger sister, Anna, stepped across the threshold before the door automatically whisked shut.

Anna smiled, obviously sharing Natasha's gratitude for finally returning home. The two of them were close. Natasha's extended trip had been an inconvenience for her as well.

"Welcome home!" Anna trumpeted, as she bounded across the massive bedroom.

She landed on the bed beside Natasha with a wistful laugh. "At least tell me the trip was worthwhile," Anna urged.

Natasha smiled and offered a weary nod. "It took some time, but they did it. Father is happy."

"Great! I've missed you at practice. Gretchen's been filling in, but—ah…she's not as young as she used to be."

"She's only thirty-six!" Natasha countered.

Anna rolled her eyes. "That's practically a dinosaur when it comes to tennis. She's having trouble keeping up."

Natasha laughed. Anna'd been competing on the professional tennis circuit for the past three years. Gretchen's responsibilities as medical doctor for the facility were secondary. Primarily, she served as Anna's professional trainer and coach. They practiced six days a week on a regulation size tennis court located on one of the basement levels of the building. Gretchen had been a professional tennis player herself, years earlier.

"You could just say that you missed me," Natasha muttered with a weary shake of her head.

"You know I did," Anna laughed.

With her body giving in to exhaustion, Natasha grabbed one of the pillows from the head of the bed. She curled up in a ball with her head on the pillow, facing her sister who sat cross-legged at the edge.

"You look wrecked," Anna observed.

Stifling a yawn, Natasha smiled. "I don't know if I'll be able to stay awake until dinner. I can barely keep my eyes open."

"Hey!" Natasha said, her eyes brightening. "Did you ever figure out what caused the red alert around here? Dargo had a dozen of his guys with me in the Falklands. That's more than King Borden travels with, for God's sake!"

King August Casper Borden, II was the ruling monarch of the Isle of Kapros. He was also a close friend of the family, so Natasha and Anna had unique insight into the royal family's security.

"Whatever's going on," Anna explained, "everyone's been tight lipped. But it's safe to say that it has something to do with the guy in the infirmary."

Natasha's eyes were falling past half-mast; she was only moments away from slipping into sleep while her sister spoke. After a few beats, Anna's words reached her conscious mind, and Natasha's eyes widened.

"I'm sorry—what? What did you just say?" she sputtered.

Rolling her eyes, Anna repeated herself. "Nobody's talking. But I'm sure it has something to do with the guy in medical."

A mischievous smile spread across Anna's face. "You haven't seen him? He's actually really cute!"

Natasha propped herself on an elbow and squinted at her sister. "Wait a minute. Start over—and remember that I've been out of the country for the last three weeks!"

Anna proceeded to tell the story of how the man in their infirmary had arrived at the front gate. She explained how security overreacted and how he was finally allowed access. She concluded the story by explaining that the guy had been unconscious for the better part of the last three days.

The two of them were now sitting face-to-face on the bed, Anna having just concluded her story. "I don't get it," Natasha reasoned. "Nothing interesting ever happens around this place. Then I leave for a little while and holy hell breaks loose?"

"Did I mention that he's super cute?" Anna beamed. There was an unmistakable brightness in her eyes that spoke volumes.

Natasha laughed. "Several times! I'm more concerned with the part of the story where you pulled a gun on Darya."

Anna shrugged. "You didn't see him," she offered. "All kidding aside, he was in *really* bad shape. He looked like he might drop dead right there in the street. And the way things were going, security was going to let him because they were afraid to bring him inside."

Natasha sighed. Weighing the choices in her mind, she gave in to her curiosity. Sleep could wait. She crawled to the edge of the bed and slipped back into her shoes.

"What are you doing?" Anna asked.

"You've got me interested," she admitted. "I want to take a peek at your Prince Charming!"

With a girlish giggle, Anna rolled to the edge of the bed and hit the floor in a mad dash to catch up with her older sister.

The bedrooms for the entire family were located on the third floor. They took the elevator down one level, which was home to the kitchen as well as the infirmary.

Reaching the doors to the medical area, Anna held her finger to her lips. She looked around and seemed suspicious. "That's odd," she whispered. "Dargo's had two guards posted here ever since Cyrus was brought up. I wonder why he let them go?"

Natasha shrugged, peeking through the small window set inside the swinging double doors of the infirmary. The lights were dim and the room was cloaked in shadows. One of the three main beds had been wheeled to the center of the room. She could see the vague outline of a figure laying in it. A collection of medical devices flanked the bed near the man's pillow. Even from across the room she could tell that some of the equipment monitored his vitals.

Slowly, they pushed through the swinging doors and slipped into the room. Though she was silent, Natasha could sense her sister right at her heels. As they entered, the quiet 'thump' and 'hiss' of the medical equipment became audible.

As she stepped to the foot of the bed and stared at the unconscious figure lying helpless, Natasha felt her heart seize in her chest. Her knees threatened to buckle and, for a few moments, the entire room went silent as the dull clatter of equipment was muted by her mind's inability to interpret what she saw. With lips quivering silently, she felt the floor shift under her feet.

She suddenly felt Anna's hand on her arm. "Tash, are you alright?" she pleaded in a harsh whisper. "You don't look so good."

Natasha turned and locked eyes with her sister. She struggled to reconcile the story Anna had relayed back in her bedroom. "This is who you brought in from outside the gate?"

Anna nodded. Her lack of understanding was evident in her eyes.

Natasha felt her sister take her by the hand. "Come on. We need to get out of here. You look like you need to sit down—and we don't want to get caught in here," Anna said.

In a trance, Natasha let her sister lead her from the room. As they reached the doorway, she stole one more glance over her shoulder and confirmed that the figure in the bed was exactly who she thought.

What in God's name is Jonny doing here?

Chapter 32

Watching from the shadows in the corner of the room, Dargo remained silent watching the two girls sneak into the infirmary. They had no business there, but at the same time he could hardly blame them. The young man's arrival was the most unusual thing to happen around there in a long time. He'd worked hard to keep it that way.

He chose not to interrupt their sojourn. The kid had been unconscious since he'd been brought through the gate. Even so, with his restraints he didn't pose an immediate risk to anyone. Still, the fact that the girls had snuck in at all was a bit disconcerting.

Dargo watched as the sisters stepped closer to the bed. But when Natasha took a look at the young man, her demeanor changed. Her hand shot to her mouth and she looked as if she might collapse. Dargo couldn't understand her reaction. The boy was badly banged up, but Natasha was made of sterner stuff. He was surprised to see her react in such a way.

Even more surprising, it took Anna several attempts to regain her sister's attention. Anna hadn't reacted to the young man's injuries in such a way. The nature of Natasha's unusual response nearly caused Dargo to step from the shadows. He only stopped himself at the last moment. There was more to be gained from silent observation, than loud interrogation. Natasha had never been entirely forthcoming when it came to personal matters, which is something Dargo already knew. And whatever was wrong now seemed to be deeply personal.

Though it was difficult, Dargo remained silent. Two minutes later, he watched Anna lead her sister from the room. It was difficult to tell in the poor lighting, but Dargo was almost certain that he saw tears running down Natasha's face.

Chapter 33

The Voss Compound
Time: Unknown

Opening his eyes, Cyrus found himself in a dimly lit infirmary. He lay in a bed that had been wheeled to the center of the large space, several machines pulsing quietly at his side. His heart rate, blood pressure, and other vitals were displayed on screens among the equipment.

The simple act of turning his head caused a sharp pain to spike through his skull, and the meager contents of his stomach to roil in protest. He closed his eyes as the room spun and the pain radiated across the back of his neck and down his spine. When he tried to raise a hand to steady himself, he found that he could not. Braving his vision once more, fearfully, he cracked opened his eyes. He found his wrists strapped to the rails of the hospital bed.

Confused, he looked around the sterile room. Memories of what had happened outside the gates of the Voss compound flooded back, and he suddenly had a good idea of exactly where he was.

At least, he hoped that he knew.

His suspicion was further supported when a figure stepped from the shadows—a large man, easily six and a half feet tall with wide shoulders. Cyrus guessed him to be in his mid-fifties. He had short, silver-gray hair, a square face, and a strong jawline. The two-day-old stubble on his face was also gray.

The man advanced into better light with slow, deliberate steps. When he stopped, he stood silently at the end of the bed and regarded Cyrus with penetrating dark eyes. He was a bear of a man. He looked far more formidable in person than Cyrus had expected. His name was Ian Dargoslav, and he was the head of Doctor Voss's security team. Dargoslav was more commonly known simply as Dargo, according to the reports Cyrus had read.

While Dargo regarded him silently, Cyrus took a few moments to consider his situation. If things had worked according to his plan, he was now inside the infirmary of Voss's secure installation. The hint of a disapproving scowl evident in Dargo's expression definitely supported that theory. According to all that Cyrus had read, Dargo was near fanatical about limiting outsider's access to the compound. In the last fifteen years, few had ventured beyond the installation's front gates.

Looking down at his restrained hands, Cyrus pulled at the straps. "Is this really necessary?" He asked. "*Where am I?*"

Appraising him for another quiet moment, Dargo turned and walked a few paces away. He pulled a small radio from inside his suit coat and tapped the transmit button. "He is awake and coherent," was all that he said before slipping the radio once more into a pocket.

The man spoke English, but his voice was heavily accented with Russian. Not to the point where he was difficult to understand, but enough that it was clear English was not his first, or preferred language. That was a relief to Cyrus since, while he was familiar with Russian and German, he wasn't fluent in either. Though the Isle of Kapros's official language was English, its proximity to Norway and Sweden meant that both languages were well represented within the nation's borders.

A couple of minutes later, a tall thin woman pushed through the swinging double-doors. Her long, dark hair was a striking contrast to the white linen lab coat she wore. According to her file, Cyrus knew she was in her mid-thirties, and that serving as the compound's medical doctor was only Gretchen Gamble's ancillary responsibility. Approaching the bed, she examined the displays beside Cyrus before making eye contact.

"My name is Gretchen," she said, in a detached, professional manner. "How are you feeling?"

"Where am I?" Cyrus asked, rather than offer an answer.

Before responding, Gretchen shot a look over to Dargo. He scowled, but then nodded his approval with a seemingly reluctant distaste.

"You're in the infirmary at Doctor Voss's family estate," she explained. "Tell me, are you in any pain?"

"Are you American?" Cyrus asked. His confusion was obvious on his face.

"Yes," she smiled for the first time. "I'm the staff medic and personal—"

From a few feet behind her, Dargo cleared his throat. It was an obvious signal that she was revealing more than was appropriate. Cyrus realized that Dargo's professionalism was everything he'd read it to be. The man didn't miss a beat. No intelligence would be gained from her while he was around.

"American—yes," she corrected herself, somewhat uncomfortably.

The squeak of the doors alerted them to a new arrival. Cyrus looked up to see Doctor Rutger Voss for the first time. He was a compact man, perhaps five-foot-six or seven, weighing no more than one hundred and forty pounds. He had a thin face, with a head that was bald on top and a fringe of gray circling just above the ears. Like Gretchen, Voss also wore a white lab coat.

Just before Voss reached Cyrus's bedside, Dargo flipped a series of light switches on the wall. The overhead lights blinked on full force, driving every bit of shadow from the room.

Stabbing pain shot through Cyrus's head as the light stabbed at his eyes. His first reaction, to shadow his face with his hands, was defeated by the restraints still wrapped around his wrists. He couldn't help the gasp that escaped his mouth, as his eyelids slammed shut. He turned his head and fought the urge to vomit.

Voss reacted swiftly. Though Cyrus couldn't see him, he heard his voice for the first time.

"Dargo!" Voss chastised. "That's not necessary! Please turn off half the lights. You know the young man has a severe concussion!"

From behind closed eyelids, Cyrus saw the blazing light dim. Thankfully, his stomach reacted favorably and calmed to some degree. The stabbing pain, however, continued to shoot back and forth through his head, like a televised tennis match running on fast-forward.

He took a few deep breaths, but was still reluctant to open his eyes for fear of being sick. Suddenly, he felt a numbing sensation in his jaw. The sensation spread across his face and then through his head. It felt like he'd slowly submerged his skull in a bucket of cool water. It was an odd sensation, but strangely comforting.

Upon opening his eyes, Cyrus saw Gretchen pulling a syringe from the side of the IV bag that hung near his head. He wanted to ask what she'd done, but found himself momentarily unable to gather the words. The sudden reprieve from the unrelenting pain was refreshing. Even as he watched her step back from the IV stand, he felt the injection working its magic. Some measure of comfort began to reach his extremities for the first time since waking.

"Don't worry," Gretchen said, as if seeing the concern in his eyes. "It's only something for the pain. You have a concussion, several deep lacerations, and deep tissue bruising to most of your torso. And that's saying nothing of the gunshot wound to your abdomen. I'm afraid this pain medication is going to be your close friend for some time," she concluded.

Despite the clinical way she'd recited his injuries, Cyrus recognized an almost maternal sympathy in her eyes. That fit with what he knew of her. Though Dargo had stopped her from explaining it, aside from being the facilities ad hoc doctor, she was also a professional tennis coach for Voss's youngest daughter, Anna. According to the files, Gretchen and Anna had a close relationship. In some small ways, it seemed that Gretchen filled the role of Anna's mother, a woman who had died shortly after Anna was born.

"Thank you," Cyrus said finally. "That helps a great deal."

"Surprisingly," Gretchen continued, "those may not be your biggest problems. That gunshot wound had become badly infected. You're lucky to be alive. To be honest, I'm not sure how you survived as long as you did."

"I was worried about the infection," Cyrus admitted. "I broke into a veterinary office outside of Copenhagen and helped myself to some antibiotics."

A hint of a smile crossed Gretchen's face. "Yes, we found the drugs among your belongings. You do realize those antibiotics were intended for dogs, don't you?"

Cyrus offered a slightly embarrassed smile. "I figured that, if they were good enough for dogs, they were good enough for me." Then, he thought better of his condition. "Then again, I'm not feeling so hot. Should I have looked for something used on horses?"

Gretchen burst out laughing. Voss joined in from his position behind her. The only one among them who was not amused, was Dargo; he remained stone faced and wary.

Voss wheeled a high office stool to the side of the bed, and climbed onto it. "All of this begs the question," he asked rather frankly, "Why go to all the trouble? You were attacked—shot, actually. Why not go to the authorities?"

Cyrus took a long look at the man before responding. "You're Doctor Voss?" he asked in a quiet voice.

The man nodded, smiling warmly. "Rutger Voss," he said, and offered his hand.

Instinctively, Cyrus went to shake, but was held fast by the thick leather restraints.

Voss scowled and looked at the bindings as if seeing them for the first time. Then, he looked to Dargo. "I don't think these are necessary. Please release the young man."

Dargo didn't move.

"Dargo," Voss urged. "Please release him. He's clearly no threat—certainly not in his current condition."

Dargo simply shook his head, his expression cold and unchanging, silently refusing the request. Clearly Dargo took security far more seriously than Voss. It was surprising given the lengths Voss had gone to, securing his family in a compound the way that he had. Cyrus filed the information away for future reference.

"I'm sorry," Voss said; his face red with embarrassment. "It's his job to protect me from myself. Why don't you tell us what happened? I'm sure once everything has been explained, even Dargo will have no problem *releasing you from your bindings.*"

His last words were barbed with sarcasm and spoken over his shoulder in Dargo's general direction. Cyrus found himself already liking the small man with the comforting demeanor.

"It's understandable," Cyrus conceded. "Something's going on and I'm not sure what it is. Your man is right to play it safe. Someone already tried to kill me, and I'm afraid they might try again."

This was the next stage of the plan, and the reason he'd had Paul Gladd beat the living hell out of him just before getting off the train in Hamburg, Germany. Cyrus needed Voss to believe that someone was after him, and that the only place he would be safe was inside the walls of the high security compound. That would give Cyrus prolonged access to the facility and aid his infiltration.

The gunshot wound had been accidental, a parting gift from the female assassin on the train. The rest of the injuries were all the work of Paul Gladd, at Cyrus's request. Even Gladd had been reluctant to offer up the level of beating that Cyrus insisted upon. But in the end, Cyrus had gotten exactly what he needed; complete with a concussion and more abrasions and contusions than he could easily count. The infection had been a bonus. Though the bullet had passed through his abdomen without striking any vital organs, it had managed to offer up a nasty infection. Cyrus really had broken into a veterinary clinic to find treatment as he claimed.

Cyrus needed to be offered sanctuary, and in order to get Dargo to go along with it, he knew he would need to convince Voss that there were life or death consequences in refusing him. He had already seen Dargo overrule his employer when it came to matters of security. He had to put Voss in a situation where he would not allow Dargo to countermand him.

"After I was attacked on the train," Cyrus explained. "I called Professor Ragsdale back at the university. Since I was delivering a package for him, I needed to know how to proceed. But I couldn't reach Ragsdale at first. When I finally got a hold of someone close to him, I was told that he'd been mugged and was in the hospital.

"My friend didn't know what happened, but he said that Ragsdale was in really bad shape. It didn't take a genius to realize that what happened to the Professor was likely related to what had just happened to me. So I had to make a decision. I had to figure out what to do with the package that I was supposed to deliver to you."

"And you decided to fulfill your task and complete the delivery?" Voss seemed surprised at that decision. "Why not go to the authorities?"

Here we go…

Shifting in his half reclined position, Cyrus hinted that he was reluctant to answer the question. He took a few moments to consider his words before responding. "Ragsdale gets himself into trouble from time to time," he finally said.

Cyrus was trying to be vague, hoping to seem as if he were being diplomatic regarding Ragsdale. He really didn't know how much Voss knew about Ragsdale's proclivities.

"You're referring to his gambling?" Voss asked.

Cyrus met his eyes. "Yes," he said with relief. "I wasn't sure if what happened to Ragsdale was the result of trouble he'd gotten himself into over a gambling debt. And when I realized that I was pulled into whatever mess he'd started, I knew I could be getting myself into even more trouble by going to the police."

From the look on Voss's face, Cyrus could tell he was processing the line of thought. Dargo's face, however, betrayed nothing. He simply watched Cyrus with cold, dispassionate eyes.

"To be honest," Cyrus said, somewhat sheepishly, "I didn't know if bringing the package to you here would get me out of trouble, or just put me in deeper. But I didn't think I had a choice. I didn't have anywhere else to go."

He looked down at his hands, strapped to the rails of the bed, and then back at Voss. "I appreciate the medical attention and all, but I'm still not sure I made the right choice," he said flatly.

Voss watched Cyrus's eyes for a few moments, and Cyrus could see the wheels working inside his mind. Finally, his expression softened, and he smiled warmly. "Dargo," Voss said without taking his eyes off Cyrus. "Free the young man, please. Now."

It was subtle, but Cyrus saw the slight narrowing of Dargo's eyes. He wasn't happy about the decision. Still, he must not have had any counter argument because he stepped forward and began removing the restraints.

"I need a phone," Cyrus said to Voss. "I want to check on Professor Ragsdale. Maybe he can tell me what's going on."

The sad expression on Voss's face surprised Cyrus. "I'm afraid that won't be necessary," he said quietly. "Richard has been in a coma since his attack. An associate at the hospital will alert me as soon as there is news regarding his prognosis."

Cyrus was confused by Voss's statement. Any type of coma was news to him.

"Richard and I attended University together," he explained. "We are very close. His daughter contacted me as soon as she heard what had happened.

"I don't know who did this or why," he continued. "But you did the right thing, bringing the package here. Richard would've wanted you to do that. And you're safe here while we sort this out."

While Cyrus considered Voss's words, he scratched at his jaw absently. Suddenly his eyes widened. Sitting straight up in the bed, he brought both hands to his face. Several days' worth of stubble had accumulated.

His eyes shot to Gretchen who was sitting quietly to the side. Then, he looked back at Voss. "My God," he muttered. "How long have I been here?"

"You've been unconscious since you were brought through the gate four days ago." Gretchen said.

Chapter 34

Sitting on the edge of the hospital bed wearing a heavy cotton robe, Cyrus waited for Gretchen to return with a wheelchair. He'd spent the last eight days in bed, and desperately wanted to stretch his legs. Still, Gretchen had explained that his injuries were severe and that he shouldn't expect to be on his feet right away. It would take some time for his body to regain its strength. She'd insisted he use the wheelchair, at least while he was taken to his temporary quarters and shown around the facility.

The use of a wheelchair wasn't a concern for Cyrus. Truth be told, he was just glad to be free of the catheter. He'd never experienced that particular unpleasantness before and hoped he would never suffer the indignity again. Removal had been bad enough. He was just thankful he'd been unconscious when it was inserted. More than anything, right now, he just wanted to take a shower. He hadn't bathed since the night before boarding the train in Paris, and he could barely tolerate his own presence. Though he knew Dargo had issued an order that only security personnel and Gretchen be allowed access to him while in medical, he doubted anyone could've tolerated his scent, regardless.

The doors to the infirmary squeaked open; Gretchen entered pushing an elaborate wheelchair. It had a sleek, high-tech look and was made of lightweight aluminum. A battery pack hung from the back of the chair, and he could see small motors attached to the large primary wheels. A small joystick was attached to the right armrest.

He offered a quiet whistle at the sight. "You folks don't skimp on anything, do you?"

Gretchen smiled. "Nothing but the best from Doctor Voss." She leaned toward him and offered a mock conspiratorial whisper. "It's okay. Between you and me, he can afford it."

Cyrus laughed. She'd made the statement loud enough so that the security guard stationed at the door would overhear. Interestingly, the man didn't so much as bat an eyelash at the statement, or their conversation. Voss's men were very well trained.

Gretchen had warmed to him during their time together. It was a good sign. He hoped to win over the rest of Voss's family along the way. A deep-seeded uneasiness reminded him that one, more than the others, would present a particular challenge.

Accepting her offered hand, Cyrus slid from the edge of the bed and onto his feet. His legs were weaker than he expected. He grudgingly turned and lowered himself into the wheelchair more quickly than he'd hoped. Stretching his legs would have to wait.

"As you know, your infection has proven surprisingly resilient," Gretchen explained. "I've had trouble getting the antibiotics to make headway. But the new course of treatment is finally showing some progress. We have Doctor Voss's friend at the Mayo Clinic to thank for that. He suggested an experimental drug, which Doctor Voss had flown in just for you. Whoever shot you must've laced the bullet with something nasty."

A poisoned bullet? That was a new one in Cyrus's book. He'd never heard of such a thing, and he'd examined the ammo that the assassins had been using, too. The rounds were coated in Teflon, increasing their odds of penetrating body armor. He'd been under the impression that the infection was the result of his body's exposure to the Teflon, or the inadequate attempts he'd made to clean the wound. After fleeing the train and making his way to Voss's compound via improvised transportation, he wouldn't have had an opportunity to look into it even if it *had* occurred to him. At the time, staying off the grid while making his way to the compound had been his only priority.

It seemed the assassin's bullet had nearly completed its task after all.

"But we have a problem," Gretchen continued. "I'll be out of the country for the next few days, so I'll be leaving your care to my understudy." She smiled. "Don't worry, you'll be in capable hands. The infection is under control. It's really only a matter of monitoring your vitals and administering the antibiotic shots twice a day. I'll be leaving pain medication for you to take as needed."

Though she didn't say it, Cyrus realized the woman's primary responsibility was taking precedence over his care. A tennis tournament was coming up in the United States, and Gretchen would be making arrangements in advance of Anna's participation. According to his research, it was standard practice.

"No problem," Cyrus smiled. "I appreciate all that you've done. You saved my life."

Gretchen explained the simple procedures for operating and recharging the wheelchair. She also mentioned that one of the security team would be assigned to escort him at all times. Though this statement didn't surprise him, it wasn't what he wanted to hear.

When the doors to the lab squeaked again, Cyrus tapped the chair's joystick and spun around to face the newcomer. He was greeted by Anna's beguiling smile.

"Cyrus Cooper, this is Anna Voss," Gretchen introduced.

Cyrus shook Anna's offered hand. "I think we've already met, haven't we?" he asked with some trepidation.

Anna laughed. "Then, you do remember? We weren't sure that would be the case. You were in bad shape that day at the gate. It's nice to meet you, Cyrus."

Gretchen stepped forward. "Anna will be showing you to your accommodations," she explained. "And this is Mister Wagner." She motioned to the burly dark-suited security guard standing post beside the door. "He's been assigned to escort you for the remainder of the afternoon."

"It's nice to meet you, Mister Wagner," Cyrus said. Wagner met his eye, but offered only a slight nod in acknowledgment.

"Don't take it personally," Anna explained. "Dargo's very strict when it comes to the discipline of his men. They're not supposed to even interact with *us* on a personal level." She turned her head and spoke loudly over her shoulder. "*They're supposed to act like robots!*"

Cyrus laughed. Anna looked back at him and offered a sly smile, before continuing. "All kidding aside, they're all good men and very good at what they do. They keep us safe. Can I show you to your room?"

"Please! You wouldn't believe how badly I want to take a shower."

Taking hold of the handles on the back of the wheelchair, Anna began pushing him toward the door. "Believe me," she said quietly. "Anyone in the same room with you shares your pain." Though he couldn't see it, a tight smile crossed her face.

"Tell me about it," he responded. "I feel like I haven't bathed in a month. And you wouldn't believe where they start sticking needles and tubes when you pass out in this place."

She burst out laughing.

"I'm not kidding," he continued. "I'm going to have nightmares…"

Chapter 35

Anna wheeled Cyrus down the hall and into the elevator; they rode up one level to the third floor. From there, she pushed him down the main corridor and around the corner. As they passed other closed doors, she explained that the bedrooms belonged to family members. After turning another corner, they entered a slightly narrower hallway with doors running along only one wall. Letting him know they'd reached the guest rooms, Anna gave a little laugh. It seemed humorous that they had guest rooms at all, she thought, since no one was ever allowed to visit the facility.

Reaching the far end of the hall, Anna stopped at the last door. She showed Cyrus the touch-sensitive display at the edge of the doorframe.

"It's all pretty self-explanatory," she said; but explained, nonetheless. "You press here to open the door. If the door is locked, the 'open' button will have been replaced with a 'knock' button. You can knock on the door the old fashioned way, but the rooms have heavy soundproofing for privacy. Odds are that no one will hear you. So tap the 'knock' button, and a chime will sound inside the room. The person on the inside can open the door from anywhere with a voice command."

His eyes lit up. "That's really cool!"

"It is," she smiled. "There are a few more tricks to keep in mind. Say, it's your room and you locked it while you're out. When you come back, the button will display the 'knock' option. But you don't need that, right? Because it's your room, and no one is in there to let you in? Just place your finger on the button and swipe down across the screen."

She did what she was explaining, and the display changed to show a numeric keypad. "Just enter your personal code to unlock the door." She tapped in the code of 1-2-3-4-5-6-7-8 to demonstrate, and the door hissed as it slid, disappearing into a pocket in the wall.

"You can set the code to whatever you want," she continued. "But keep in mind that security can override it if they need to."

She noticed Mister Wagner glaring at her, and offered him a shrug and a smile. These weren't exactly state secrets.

"Nothing but the best," Cyrus muttered quietly to himself as Anna pushed him into the room.

Cyrus's room wasn't nearly as large as the bedrooms belonging to family members, but Anna knew Cyrus would have no way of knowing that. All the same, she could tell he was impressed by the accommodations. A shortage of space had never been an issue inside the compound.

The room was approximately two hundred and fifty square feet, and slightly rectangular. There was a queen size bed with a pair of large oak dressers along the wall to the left, and a good sized matching oak desk, complete with a laptop computer along the center of the back wall. The right side of the room was occupied by a large couch and matching pair of chairs that were arranged around a flat panel television hanging on the wall between a pair of tall speakers. The walls were a warm copper color, and the carpet was Berber in a rich earthy tone. There were two doors on the back wall, one on either side of the desk. One led to a richly appointed bathroom; the other, a large walk-in closet.

Pushing Cyrus's chair to the grouping of furniture by the entertainment center, Anna parked it before dropping herself into the chair opposite him. "All of your clothes were thrashed," she explained. "They've been disposed of. The only things salvageable were your boots. We had someone get you a change of clothes. If you're happy with them, we can send out for more. We pulled your sizes from your old stuff before they were burned."

Though she didn't want to tell him, she and Natasha had done the shopping themselves the previous day. She doubted he would care much that they'd been the ones to select his more personal items, but for some reason the thought made her uncomfortable.

She reflected on how strangely Natasha had been acting since first seeing Cyrus at the compound. Something about his appearance had deeply affected her. And though she'd tried, Anna hadn't been able to convince her sister to talk about whatever it was. She was clearly upset; still, when she asked, Natasha claimed not to know him and refused to discuss the matter.

She'd been distant and moody ever since—a countenance that was entirely foreign to her, and Anna was concerned. And though she wasn't willing to talk, Anna had made numerous attempts at conversation over the course of the last several days.

Anna had almost given up until the day before when she ran into Natasha in the hall. Anna was on her way to the motor pool. When she explained that she was going to the mall and planned to pick up a fresh set of clothes for Cyrus, Natasha offered to come along. After the moodiness Natasha displayed over the last several days, Anna hoped it was a sign that her sister's foul disposition was finally lifting. Still, they'd shopped silently together with a four-person security detail in tow. Every attempt Anna made at conversation was met with simple shrugs or one-word responses.

It wasn't until they started selecting clothes that Anna began to get a hint of insight into the situation. When Anna selected a pair of jeans in the right size, Natasha took a long look at them as if she had something to say. When Anna asked what was wrong with the jeans, Natasha mumbled that they were the wrong brand and pointed to a different series of shelves.

It was strange, but Anna shook her head and they'd moved on. Anna quickly selected a couple of t-shirts and then set out to find a hoodie to go with them. But when she came back, she found that her sister had replaced the two shirts with a different pair. When she asked what was wrong with the shirts she'd selected, Natasha seemed even more uncomfortable and simply shrugged. When Anna finally forced the issue, Natasha stated simply that she didn't like the tags in the back of the collar of the first two, and had chosen a pair of shirts without the scratchy tags.

Anna was floored. She'd never seen her sister act so strangely. But what upset her most was, that whatever was bothering her beloved sister, she wouldn't share it.

When they continued to shop, the pieces of her sister's discomfort finally fell into place. While selecting socks, Anna asked her which ones to purchase, crew cut or ankle? *Crew*, Natasha quickly answered. When they reached the underwear, she asked, boxers or briefs? *Boxers*, Natasha responded immediately, and handed her the proper size.

That had cinched it. At that point she was certain—despite claims to the contrary—Natasha knew Cyrus. And knew him well. For days Anna had been hard pressed to get anything more than grunts and grimaces from her sister, but now she was answering personal questions without thought.

Anna knew something was going on, but she needed a way to figure it out. She knew that, whatever it was, Natasha was struggling with it. But if Natasha knew Cyrus, why wouldn't she admit it? What was the secret?

As messed up as the situation was, Anna realized that her sister wouldn't act so strangely without good reason. So as much as she wanted to confront Cyrus, Anna understood that a direct approach wasn't an option.

Cyrus's eyebrows arched. "I'm sorry, did you say that you *burned* my clothes?"

She nodded. "What can I say? Our security is very thorough. Besides, your stuff was history. It was covered in blood and God knows what else."

Glancing over his shoulder, Cyrus eyed Mister Wagner who was standing beside the door to the hallway. Anna guessed that he was thinking their security procedures leaned close to the side of paranoia, and she really couldn't blame him.

"I left an iPod in the desk for you. You can use the laptop to access the music that Tash and I have shared on the network. If you want something more, you can just download it. The laptop's signed into my account. Help yourself."

"Tash?" Cyrus asked. His confusion was evident.

"I'm sorry," she smiled. "My older sister, *Natasha*." She watched his eyes for any hint of recognition that the name might stir. When there wasn't any, she only grew more interested.

On to plan B…

"I'm sure you'll meet her later. Anyway, our music libraries are shared on the Wi-Fi. You'll be able to pull it up on the laptop."

"Thanks," Cyrus said, with a warm smile. "That's very generous."

She shrugged. "Believe me, you'll need it. It seems you're a prisoner here, just as much as the rest of us. You'll need the distraction if you're going to save your sanity!"

Walking to the door, she continued, "So the clean clothes are over there, and we can finish the tour when you're smelling more…human," she laughed.

"Thanks," he grinned.

"Oh, and Gretchen said that your dressings will need to be changed after you get cleaned up. Have Mister Wagner take you back to medical when you're done showering."

Chapter 36

The Voss Compound
9:50 am

Once Anna left, Cyrus took a closer look at his room. It was his first chance to stretch his legs after being bound to a bed for more than a week. He found himself lightheaded and weak, but even the short walk around the surprising well-appointed room was invigorating. The guard standing inside his door, however, was more than a little disconcerting. Mister Wagner didn't watch him, exactly, he mostly just stood like a living gargoyle; his eyes unmoving. If not for the rise and fall of the man's chest, he could've passed for a mannequin. While off-putting, this also told of Wagner's professionalism. Cyrus knew that standing station while maintaining a detached and unassuming profile didn't come without a great deal of experience.

The set of clothes Anna had referred to surprised Cyrus. Not only were they precisely his size, but they were just his taste as well. He didn't know what to make of that. Pondering that oddity, he walked into the bathroom where he stopped in shock. If this was the bathroom of the guest quarters, he wondered what main rooms had to offer.

The floors were a rich textured tile, and the wide counter was made of highly polished marble that held a pair of sinks. There was an extra-large standing shower, with semi-transparent etched glass doors, in addition to a spacious Whirlpool tub. The toilet was in a small water closet, and there was a large armoire stocked with towels, toilet paper, and all sorts of miscellaneous bathroom sundries.

Slipping from his robe, he tossed it to the floor on the other side of the room. He turned on the shower's faucet and was impressed by the water pressure that virtually blasted from the jets. Letting the water reach temperature, he went to the tall, freestanding cabinet and retrieved a towel. Sorting through the cabinet, he found a bathmat. He was on the mend, and the last thing he needed was to slip and break his neck on his way out of the shower.

Just before he stepped into the shower, he noticed the array of grooming supplies laid out at the end of the sink. There was an electric razor, a pair of disposable razors, a can of shaving cream, several small bottles of aftershave, as well as a toothbrush and several small tubes of toothpaste. Shaking his head in disbelief at the first-class accommodations, he stepped under the powerful water jets.

Anna calls this *being a prisoner?*

Chapter 37

The Voss Compound
10:16 am

Cyrus walked out of the bathroom with a towel wrapped around his waist. He'd taken the hottest shower his body could tolerate. It would've been longer, but he'd been forced to cut it short; weakness in his legs and biting pain from his gunshot wound were quick to remind him that he was still on the mend. Gretchen was right, the infection was worse than he expected. Not only was he more fatigued than he would've imagined, but the wound wasn't healing as it should.

Dargo's man, Mister Wagner, was still at his position by the door. Though, to his credit, he didn't even look at Cyrus when he entered the room. The level of professionalism Dargo instilled in his men once again struck Cyrus as impressive. Unfortunately, that same professionalism would become a problem for him in the near future.

Throwing the towel aside, Cyrus began dressing in the clothes that were left on the end of his bed. He couldn't believe that all of his old stuff had been disposed of. Was that Dargo being hypervigilant, or was it just that the clothes were truly a total loss? Cyrus couldn't be sure. The plan was for him to make his way from the train station in Hamburg to Voss's compound by improvising travel and staying off the grid. It was a slow way to move, but it had made sense after what happened on the train, and because Cyrus needed Voss to believe that his life was very much in danger. Taking such precautions went a long way toward substantiating his story. Cyrus and Gladd had left the train, abandoning the dead bodies in their cabin, stacked like cordwood. There would certainly be an investigation. Even if the train line managed to keep the incident quiet, someone with Dargo's resources would learn of it quickly enough. At some point he would link the bodies found on the Paris train to the attack Cyrus had survived.

All of that would strengthen Cyrus's cover story, supporting his role as a courier for Professor Richard Ragsdale, tasked with delivering the prototype imaging equipment to Doctor Voss. Voss now believed, as far as Cyrus knew, that his life was in danger. As such, Voss felt inclined to provide sanctuary for Cyrus—at least until he was healthy again and could make it on his own.

Everything had been well planned. Even Ragsdale's medical emergency was part of the plan—though his coma was an unexpected improvisation. In truth, the man was safe and sound in a safe house somewhere in Paris. Boone had seen to that part of the operation. Boone would stay with Ragsdale until the mission was over. That was important, because if Ragsdale ever got word to Voss, the entire mission would be blown. Boone would ensure that never happened.

The only deviation from the plan had been the infection left by the assassin's bullet. Cyrus had originally counted the combat wound as fortunate. The original plan had called for Paul Gladd to stab him, in addition to delivering the physical beating. Cyrus needed legitimate wounds and injuries in order to sell his situation and gain access to Voss's secure installation. Getting shot hadn't been part of the plan, but it worked out for the better.

All except for the infection. As unlikely as it seemed, the assassins must've coated their ammunition with some sort of toxin. That was unusual. He planned to look into the practice as soon as he could get access to a secure internet terminal; or even better, access to the Coalition's network.

After crudely taping a couple of large gauze pads over the wounds on his abdomen, Cyrus pulled on a t-shirt and headed for the door.

"I'm all set," he said to Mister Wagner. "I guess you're supposed to take me to medical now."

Chapter 38

Wagner led Cyrus to the infirmary, one floor below. Along the way, Cyrus marveled at the scope of Voss's operation. It was one thing to read about it on paper and quite another to see the facility in person. The installation was impressive. Each floor ended at a wide balcony that overlooked the building's entrance and the common area on the first floor. Each balcony also offered a breathtaking view overlooking the city beyond the wall of the compound.

The building's front face was a glass and steel facade stretching from ground level to the fifth floor high above. The glass was treated with a high-tech anti-glare semi-opaque solution, Cyrus knew. The morning sun shone through, filling the surrounding area with a pleasant warm radiance. But there was no harsh glare. And as clouds passed overhead, the tint of the glass seemed to shift in accordance with the strength of the sunlight. Recalling surveillance photos shot from street level, Cyrus thought about the way the glass appeared to have a mirror finish when viewed from the outside. It was likely that the adaptive window tinting worked in conjunction with the external mirror finish that kept the building's interior safe from prying eyes. Such technology didn't come cheap. Certainly not when it covered the entire face of such a massive structure.

Cyrus also knew that the glass was resistant to not only small arms fire, but it had also been designed to repel more aggressive attacks, such as explosives from smaller rockets and RPGs. There was no doubt about it, Voss's work had to be profitable. His home was proof of it.

Before stepping away from the second floor railing, Cyrus looked down into the common area. It was unoccupied for the moment, but Anna had asked him to meet her there later for lunch. She hinted that they would have something to discuss by that time.

The way she'd said it had seemed odd. Something about the statement still concerned him.

Mister Wagner cleared his throat, drawing Cyrus's attention back to the moment. "Yeah, I'm coming," he muttered, following him to their destination.

Still giving Anna's statement thought, Cyrus followed Wagner into the medical area. The morning was passing quickly and, since they were meeting for lunch, he figured it was only a matter of time before he found out what she was up to.

Cyrus was expecting to see Gretchen, but when Wagner stepped out of the way, Cyrus was stopped cold in his tracks. Natasha was arranging a series of medical supplies on the wheeled cart beside the bed. He watched silently as she continued.

After a few moments, her actions slowed, as she became aware of the new presence in the room. Her eyes rose and met

Cyrus's stare. With a silent sputter, Cyrus released the breath he was holding.

This was it, the moment of truth.

He'd reached the point where his mission could still come crashing down around his ears. It was all up to Natasha and how she reacted to his surprise appearance.

The silence between them seemed to stretch forever. It was uncomfortable and refreshing, all at the same time. He hadn't seen her in almost three years, but in that time she hadn't changed a bit. She was every bit as breathtaking as she'd been the first time they'd met. Seeing her again brought back every sensation he'd experienced that first time, and he was shocked at how quickly his mind jumped back in time; the memories he'd walled away came rushing back.

She looked just like she had the first time they'd met. The thought kept running through his mind and left him speechless.

No, he thought, *it was more than that…*

She looked *just* like she had the first time they met! Exactly the same. *How could that be a coincidence?* Her long blonde hair was pulled up in a ponytail, and she wore the same short-lensed, black-framed glasses that she'd been wearing that spring day. He recalled them distinctly, because his first thought was that they made her look both smart and sexy.

Taking her in, he realized she was now wearing a white lab coat, just as she'd been that day in the university chemistry lab. The sense of déjà vu was unmistakable, and more off-putting than he could've anticipated. But as he moved past his shock, he saw her expression change too.

There was indecision in her eyes rather than the surprise that he'd expected. Of course, he realized there was some logic to that. He'd been laid up in the infirmary for more than a week. It was entirely likely that she already knew he was here.

So the real questions became: Who had she told about him...and what had she said? The fact that there was only one guard with them, and that he'd just been given private quarters were telling. He hadn't been locked up or kicked out of the installation entirely.

There was no question that Natasha knew enough to compromise his operation.

Glancing over his shoulder, Cyrus looked at Mister Wagner. He'd taken up a position at the entrance to the infirmary. He wasn't within immediate earshot, but he was close enough to overhear them if they weren't discrete.

Meeting her eye again, Cyrus looked for some hint of Natasha's intentions. He was troubled by the cool detachment he saw there. It wasn't what he expected from someone he'd once been intimate with. Then again, that was a large part of the problem.

The seconds ticked by; it seemed like an eternity while he waited for her to make her intentions known. He was sure that she didn't know why he was here, but she seemed to grasp the fact that they stood at an impasse. She now had the power to burn him, or play it cool and see how things worked out.

Cyrus could only wonder how much of the Natasha he once knew was still there. Would she give him a chance to explain, or would she shut him down and turn him away? She'd always been a passionate and headstrong woman, and he knew with absolute certainty that her decision could easily go either way.

Cyrus opened his mouth to speak but stopped short when her look sharpened almost imperceptibly. She shook her head ever so slightly, warning him off. It was as if she'd made a last minute decision of her own.

Finally, she offered a halfhearted smile. "I'm Natasha," she said quietly. "And, you are?"

It was all Cyrus could do not to wheeze a sigh of relief.

"Cyrus—Cyrus Cooper," he managed to say. She hadn't offered her hand at the introduction, so he offered his. He could see reluctance in her eyes. Her decision to give him this reprieve had been a tough call, and she wasn't entirely confident in her choice.

"Cyrus Cooper? That's an interesting name. You don't strike me as a Cyrus."

Very subtle, he thought.

"You're not the first person to say that," he offered with a sincere smile. "I've been told that a more common name, like John, would fit me better."

She made no reply for several seconds, nor did her expression change. Finally, a small smile turned up the corner of her lips. "Maybe Jonny," she offered. "I could see you with a name like Jonny."

"*Jonny* Cooper?"

"Ugg, no," she decided, with a sour expression. "You're right. That doesn't work at all. I guess you're better off with Cyrus."

He smiled. That sounded more like the Natasha he'd once known. It was the first sense so far that he might be breaking the ice. It felt as though she'd thrown him a lifeline. He hoped that was the case.

"Gretchen tells me you've got a nasty infection that needs some attention. Why don't you have a seat and let me take a look at it?"

Pulling himself up onto the side of the raised bed, Cyrus slid his shirt off over his head. Natasha looked at the crude bandage over his abdomen and then glared at him. "Is this a joke?" she protested.

He shrugged. "I just needed to keep my shirt clean long enough to come down here."

She shook her head. Then, without any attempt at gentleness, she ripped the bandage from his flesh. The fresh tape tore at his sensitive skin. When he yipped at the unexpected move, her glare only intensified.

Rolling her eyes, Natasha looked to Mister Wagner. "Would you mind giving us some privacy?" she asked. "If he's going to carry on like this, it's going to be embarrassing."

"I'm sorry, ma'am," Wagner said flatly. "My orders are to stay in the room with him at all times."

Natasha blew out a breath and thought for a moment. "Does that include trips to the restroom?" she asked.

"Ah...no, ma'am,"

"So you'll concede that he needs to be offered some minimal level of personal space, then?"

"Ah...I suppose that's the case."

She nodded with satisfaction. "Then please consider this one such situation. Besides, I want the privacy because I'm the one who's embarrassed—even if he's not."

Cyrus felt his brow furrow as he considered her comment. He wasn't sure how to interpret the statement. She had either defended him or slighted him, and he wasn't sure which.

The guard pondered her argument.

"Fine. I'll be just outside," he agreed.

As soon as Wagner was gone, Natasha looked Cyrus in the eye. "Keep your voice down," she warned. "There are still security cameras."

"Got it," he whispered.

She took a long look, then broke away and went to the wheeled cart. Pulling on a pair of surgical gloves, she poured hydrogen peroxide on a thick cotton pad. A work light was attached to the cart by an articulated arm. Taking the pad in a pair of forceps, she lowered the light and shined it on Cyrus's wound. Slowly and meticulously, she began cleaning away the clotted blood and questionable tissue.

"What are you doing here?" she whispered while she worked.

"It's a long story," he mumbled. "But it's important. Is there someplace where we can talk without having to do it like this?"

She stopped and glared at him. "What makes you think I even want to talk with you?"

Ouch.

"Come on, Tash, this is important," he insisted.

She stared at him.

"This entire place is wired," she said finally, turning her attention back to his wound. "And Dargo's got his eye on you. He's suspicious of everyone, but he seems to have taken a particular dislike to you. Talk about being under the spotlight. I don't see any way around that."

Natasha repositioned the light at a different angle and studied her work. "It looks like this is healing well enough," she observed. "But this is deep. You're going to have a nasty scar."

She applied antibacterial gel to a sterile cotton pad and then taped it in place. "Gretchen said you had a second wound on your back?" she said absently, as she motioned for him to turn.

Cyrus complied and braced himself for the moment when she tore the second improvised bandage away. To his surprise, she peeled it away gently and with great care.

From the corner of his eye, he saw her toss the sticky pad into the nearby trash can that was marked with a biohazard symbol. He heard the creaking arm of the articulated lamp as she swung it to take a closer look at his back. She began scraping at his tender flesh with a clean hydrogen peroxide soaked pad. "Yeah, this one looks nasty too," she observed. "Really deep…"

Abruptly, she stopped poking and prodding at his flesh. Cyrus heard the creaking of the light's arm as she adjusted it several times in rapid succession. Finally, she stepped back and glared at him.

"Cyrus!" she stammered. "Have you been shot?"

He offered her a weak smile. "I told you it was complicated," he whispered. "Find us a way to talk in private. *Please?*"

Chapter 39

The Voss Compound
4:23 pm

Cyrus was sitting on a sofa reading a paperback novel in the common area when Rutger Voss seemingly appeared out of nowhere. Cyrus looked up in surprise, the quick movement sending a shot a pain blasting through his side.

"I'm sorry to startle you," Voss said. "Do you mind if I sit?"

"Please," Cyrus encouraged, setting the book aside.

Voss took a seat in one of the adjacent over-stuffed armchairs. After a long, contemplative look, he spoke, "Natasha tells me that you're not taking the pain medication. Are you alright?"

"Absolutely," Cyrus responded without hesitation. "I'm just not a fan of drugs—prescription or otherwise. A little pain now and then, doesn't hurt." He smiled at his own play on words. "And anything is better than veterinary drugs."

It brought a chuckle from Voss. "Under normal circumstances that would be commendable, but I would like to remind you of the fact that you've been shot. I think that, under the circumstances, the use of prescription pain relief is understandable."

"You're right. And if the pain becomes too unpleasant, I'll talk to Natasha about it. Probably before bed, if I'm going to have any chance at a good night's sleep."

"That's good," Voss smiled. "As long as you're comfortable. I must admit, I feel more than a little responsible for your predicament."

Cyrus didn't understand. The look on his face must've made that clear enough to Voss, because he explained.

"You were delivering Professor Ragsdale's equipment when you were accosted," Voss said. "You were delivering it to me, so I share at least some responsibility for what happened to you."

Cyrus shrugged, and then shook his head. He'd given the matter a great deal of thought and knew exactly how he might handle this conversation. "I'm not sure that what happened had anything to do with you," he countered. "Ragsdale has a gambling habit. It seems likely that the people who came after me were doing it to leverage him. I can't say for sure, but you know—you hear rumors."

Voss considered the scenario, and nodded. "It's possible. But, as you see from the level of security here, I'm not without my own concerns when it comes to safety."

That brought a heartfelt laugh from Cyrus, which resulted in him wincing and clutching his side in order to steady himself against the surge of pain. "You certainly have enough security," he admitted, once he had his breathing back under control. "And they don't seem to appreciate my presence. I feel like I'm under a microscope."

Voss sat back further in his chair and offered a reluctant sigh. "Yes, Dargo's men take their work very seriously. What they lack in warmth, they make up for in professionalism. But you're right—it can be off-putting. I don't want you to be uncomfortable in my home."

"I appreciate that," Cyrus said. "But I think I should be going, just the same."

This brought an uncomfortable look from Voss. One that Cyrus wasn't sure how to interpret.

"What is it?" he asked.

Taking a moment to consider his words, Voss leaned forward, perching on the edge of his seat.

"The truth is," he began. "I'm not sure it's safe for you to leave at the moment. The people who attacked you on the train— I'm not confident that they were after Richard's prototype. There's a greater chance that they learned you were on your way here, and that's why you were attacked."

Considering Voss's words, Cyrus wasn't sure what to make of them. "What are you saying? What have I gotten myself mixed up in?"

"Nothing illegal," Voss said with great seriousness. "That I can promise you. In fact, my work focuses on medical technology. Unfortunately, my research is considered to be of great monetary value to pharmaceutical firms. Some of them have proven willing to do very underhanded, and often illegal things, to gain access to my research. I fear that the attack on you was one such example of this."

Cyrus hung his head and considered his options. At least, he put on a good show of it. He was working hard to put himself into a situation where he could leverage Voss to his own advantage. In spite of what he claimed, leaving the compound was the furthest thing from his objective. But if he played his cards right, not only would he be allowed to stay in the building, he might free himself of the omnipresent second shadow he had in Mister Wagner.

"So, you're saying that I can't leave." It was a statement rather than a question.

"No," Voss said with a warm, disarming smile. "Not at all. You are free to leave whenever you wish. I am, however, suggesting that it's in your best interest to stay here for a short while. My people can offer you protection. In fact, I feel obligated to offer you this protection.

"Plus, you're still recovering from your injuries. I'm told you will need antibiotic injections for at least several more days. In truth, I would feel better if you were near the watchful eye of medical attention should any complications arise."

Cyrus considered his words. "What about your security guys? They seem keyed up when I'm around. Is that going to be a problem? To be honest, they're extremely unnerving. Being watched constantly is making my skin crawl."

Voss chuckled. "Not to worry. If you choose to stay, you'll be relieved of your escort. There are parts of the building that are restricted, but you'll be allowed full access to the unrestricted areas."

Cyrus smiled. "I suppose you're right. My life expectancy seems better if I stay here for the time being. I appreciate your hospitality."

"Not at all. It truly is the least I can do!"

Voss pulled himself from the chair and prepared to take his leave. Cyrus had accomplished most of what he wanted but decided to press his luck just a little further.

"I didn't think to ask," Cyrus said, in an offhanded manner. "Did Ragsdale's hardware make it through undamaged? I took a beating on the ride here, but so did the device. I didn't get a chance to inspect it before I arrived at your door. I hope nothing was damaged too badly along the way."

With a grin, Voss looked Cyrus in the eye. "The prototype arrived in significantly better condition than you did, I'm afraid. Given the choice, I would've wished it the other way around."

Cyrus laughed. "That's ok. I can heal. From what Ragsdale explained, that prototype was one of a kind. It wouldn't heal if it was damaged."

"You're right about that," Voss admitted. "I have high hopes for its integration with my new procedure."

"Ragsdale was very vague about the purpose of the prototype, and to be honest, I didn't press the issue. But he did say that you were involved in some kind of memory related research. He said it was one of the reasons that the prototype needed to be delivered in person."

Voss looked confused at the statement. "I don't understand. Are you familiar with neuroscience?"

Cyrus bit at the corner of his lip and did his best to look uncomfortable, even reluctant with what he was about to share. He took a few seconds before answering, and even then he shot a quick glance over his shoulder before making his reply.

"No," he said finally. "Nothing like that. I've just got this memory *thing*." His words were spoken quietly, as if he was reluctant to admit them. "An *eidetic* memory," he explained.

A crease formed on Voss's forehead as his eyebrows arched. "Truly?" he muttered in an equally conspiratorial voice. "Are you serious? How accurate is your recall?"

Cyrus shrugged. "Accurate? Is there a way to measure it?"

"Oh, most definitely!" he said with great exuberance. "But we can get to that later. Generally speaking though, how reliable has it proven to be in your daily life?"

Again Cyrus shrugged. "It's hard to say. I don't know what it's like not to have it."

He considered the question for a few moments before continuing. "I know it always made school a breeze. I never understood why others had trouble with tests—or even studying. It was never a problem for me. I just read something once, and I know it.

"It took me years of school before I realized that I retained things differently than everyone else. But once I figured it out, I found that I could relate to people easier. To be honest, it made my early years very awkward. I think that's why I'm still not comfortable talking about it."

Voss nodded absently. "Understandable," he muttered, almost to himself. "You know, since you'll be staying with us, I wonder if you would mind working with me on a few experiments?"

Cyrus shifted uncomfortably in his seat. He was about to say something but then thought better of it. Remaining silent, he looked off into the distance, and tried to find the right words.

"Oh, no!" Voss said defensively. "Don't worry, it's nothing invasive! And nothing that you would be uncomfortable with, I can assure you. The thing is, I'm working on a project that will one day be used in the treatment of Alzheimer's patients and people with cognitive impairments. I specialize in cognitive research. Memory, in particular.

"I've worked with a number of people with exceptional memory abilities over the years. And every opportunity to gain additional insight has proven enlightening. The level of recall you're describing is exceptional. I was just suggesting running you through a series of diagnostic tests and, if you're inclined, perhaps a couple of MRI's and CT scans."

Voss sat back in the chair. "Please don't misunderstand. You're under no obligation. But this must be what Professor Ragsdale was hinting at when he suggested that you were the best man for the job.

"Please, give it some thought," Voss encouraged. "We can talk tomorrow if you like. Either way, I will speak with Dargo. You'll be free of your security escort, and you will be given a tour of the building and access to the unrestricted areas."

Voss pulled himself from his chair once more and offered a sincere smile. With a concerted effort, Cyrus climbed from the couch. He shook Voss's hand and grinned. "Again, I appreciate your hospitality," he said. "And if putting me through a couple of memory games and brain scans will help you with your Alzheimer's research, you can count me in."

Voss's face lit up at the prospect. It actually made Cyrus feel good to think he might help him with such a noble endeavor. In fact, seeing the man speak so passionately about his work, Cyrus had trouble understanding how the work Voss was referring to, and the research the Coalition was so concerned about, could possibly be one and the same.

Cyrus had worked deep cover missions many times before. Each time, he knew exactly where he stood. It was always clear who the enemy was. But when he looked at Voss, he wasn't seeing anything other than a driven scientist, a loving father, and a man who believed in taking responsibility for his actions.

On the positive side, Cyrus knew he'd be losing his security escort. And while the facility was being monitored around the clock, this was still a major move in the right direction. It would give him freedom of movement. Without that, he had nothing. And Voss would literally be inviting him into his secure lab in order to run the tests they'd discussed. That was a major win.

But for all of the progress he was making, he still wasn't satisfied. All of those objectives were secondary to his personal reasons for taking this mission. He needed to talk with Natasha. He'd disappeared on her three years earlier and never gone back. An explanation was long overdue. The only thing he knew for sure was that she wasn't going to make it easy for him. Some things weren't easy to forgive, and she'd never been the forgiving type to begin with.

Chapter 40

Though she was accustomed to the long international flights, Gretchen Stone still appreciated the accommodations of Doctor Voss's private jet. The luxurious cabin turned what would normally have been a 14-hour commercial flight into a very dependable 12-hour commute, all held in the quiet and comfort of plush leather upholstered chairs, and with easy access to every amenity imaginable.

Still, when she boarded the jet at King Borden's private airfield on the northern coast of the Isle of Kapros, the idea of the long flight was anything but appealing. To that end, she'd popped an Ambien, and the next thing she knew, the pilot was announcing that they were on approach for Atlanta's Hartsfield-Jackson International Airport.

As was always the case, Dargo's security team had her itinerary down to a science. The aircraft had no sooner rolled to a stop before a private hangar at the outskirts of the airfield when a pair of dark SUV's glided into position. Gretchen's visit to

Atlanta included an attachment of six armed security escorts. In addition to that, two more men would remain behind with the aircraft at all times. She was having trouble understanding the sudden increase in security presence, particularly for her. If there was a threat, it stood to reason that Voss would want additional protection surrounding his girls. It seemed odd that such substantial security considerations were extended to her. Under normal circumstances, a single armed guard would've accompanied her—two men if Dargo were feeling particularly paranoid.

Pushing the security concerns aside, Gretchen stepped from the jet's narrow staircase and onto the sweltering tarmac. One of her guards quickly ushered her in the direction of a waiting SUV. It was just as well—even with autumn setting in, the temperature in Atlanta was unpleasantly warm when compared to the lower sixties she'd left back home.

It took only a few moments for the security team to assume their positions. There were three men in the vehicle with her and three more in a following truck. She knew it would be a short ride since the offices of Fairfax and Clauegh were located near the airport.

Gretchen was excited when Anna had come to her the previous morning. She had finally announced her decision to participate in the celebrity tennis tour. Gretchen had been trying to convince her to participate for more than a month, and was disappointed by Anna's unusually noncommittal receptiveness to the idea.

Though Anna refused to admit it, Gretchen knew that her reluctance stemmed from the fact that her one time friend, Stanna Yavonavich was among the tournament's charter participants. The two were once very close, competing together for three seasons before suffering a falling out. Since Anna was reluctant to discuss the cause of the problem, Gretchen had been stuck without a way to help settle the young woman's troubled mind. Worst of all, she knew that if Anna declined to participate in the charity tour, she would inevitably regret the decision.

Without enough information to resolve Anna's problem, Gretchen could only urge her to consider the positive effects that the promotion would have, as well as the money that it would raise for charity. It was a weak game plan, Gretchen knew. Anna's mind was never easily influenced. For weeks, all subtle encouragement had fallen on deaf ears. Whatever troubled her young charge was not going away on its own.

All of that had led to Gretchen's almost literal sense of shock when Anna tracked her down in the infirmary first thing that morning and asked if it was too late to register for the tournament. Gretchen had been so surprised, she had immediately phoned Lee Fairfax in Atlanta, to see if Anna could still make registration.

In her haste, Gretchen had neglected to consider the fact that Atlanta was in a time zone seven hours behind her own. She woke Lee in the middle of the night. Generously, he'd explained that, while their signup period had technically ended, he would be happy to backdate Anna's registration paperwork if it meant they could add her name to the prestigious list of participants.

Unfortunately, due to the poor timing and the already closed deadline, there were registration formalities that needed to be dealt with as quickly as possible. Hours later, Gretchen was on board Voss's private jet en route to Atlanta to finalize registration and resolve an issue with Anna's visa following her last visit to the U.S.

Everything had happened so quickly, Gretchen realized that she had never gotten a good explanation for Anna's change of heart. It was likely that she'd just come to her senses and realized how much her participation would benefit the charity. Still, Gretchen couldn't shake the feeling that Anna's motivations were somehow more complicated. The last minute decision was unusual, even for someone like Anna, whose impulses were often dictated more by the heart than by the mind.

The SUV pulled up to the curb along a quiet section of a downtown city street. Gretchen watched through the dark tinted glass as the security team went through their threat assessment routine and secured the area. Moments later, one of the guards opened the door for her and helped her step down from the rear door of the large vehicle. Another guard already stood fifteen yards ahead with the door of the four-story office building held wide.

While the rest of the armed team escorted her inside, one of them remained at the street level door. As it had been explained to her, he would watch the vehicles and main entrance while remaining in contact with the rest of the team via wireless headset. The remaining five men surrounded Gretchen and escorted her to the elevator, which they took to the fourth floor. Exiting there, one of the men peeled off from the group and remained at the elevators.

The building was a warren of offices and suites belonging to lawyers, doctors, and other professional services. Gretchen followed the lead of her detail, as they navigated several interlinking hallways until reaching the solid oak door marked simply, *Fairfax and Clauegh*. She followed two of her guards through the entryway, suddenly realizing that they'd lost two members of the team along the way. As it was explained to her, those men would be taking up strategic points along their route through the building.

It still seemed like overkill, as far as she was concerned. It was a lot of fuss for what was only a quick visit to the office of the tournament coordinator before making the long flight back home.

Both remaining guards led the way into the small reception area. There was a counter that partially obscured a computer terminal and displayed some pamphlets, flyers, and brochures that likely contained information specific to events that the small firm was managing. A cramped sitting area to the right contained five nondescript chairs and a coffee table with an assortment of magazines. A small water cooler stood as a visual demarcation between the waiting area and the reception desk.

The guards looked around cautiously. The fact that no one was there to greet them was disconcerting, and Gretchen could tell that it had raised their hackles.

A moment later, a young woman in a long skirt and white silk blouse emerged from one of the two office doorways in the wall behind the counter. She had long, dirty blonde hair pulled up in the back, and she wore glasses with stylish, modern, minimalist frames.

"I'm sorry," the woman said with a warm smile. "I didn't hear you come in!"

She slipped behind the reception counter and set aside the clipboard she was carrying. "You must be Miss Stone, here to see Mister Fairfax?"

"That's right," Gretchen said with a nod. "I'm sorry to drop in on such short notice."

"Oh, it's no problem at all," the receptionist drawled in a sweet southern accent.

The security guard stepped forward. "I beg your pardon, ma'am," he said, with the slightest hint of a smile. "But I need to have a quick look around."

She nodded. "Oh, sure. Help yourself. It's just the two offices back there, anyway. We're a small outfit. Mister Fairfax is in the restroom, just off his office. He won't be but a few minutes. Mister Clauegh is out of the office this afternoon."

The guard passed behind the counter and disappeared into the first of the two offices. A moment later, he reemerged before ducking into the second. There must not have been much to see because, in both cases, he'd been gone for only a few seconds. Gretchen was surprised to see the guard, Mister Hines, offer an appraising glance at the secretary before he rounded the counter. It was the first sign of humanity she'd seen in one of Dargo's men, and she very nearly felt the need to compliment him. The security team around the Voss compound was so disciplined and efficient that she'd long ago begun considering them to be emotionless robots. The momentary crack she'd witnessed in Mister Hines's veneer, however sexist, was at least human.

"You're welcome to wait for Mister Fairfax in his office, if you like," the secretary smiled and pointed to the appropriate door.

Looking from the secretary to the pair of rigid security guards, Gretchen decided she wouldn't mind waiting for Fairfax in his office, after all. The stiff demeanor of her detail countered the spunky warmth radiating from the receptionist. It reminded

Gretchen of opposing weather fronts, and suddenly a few moments alone seemed preferable.

Stepping into Fairfax's office, she found the furnishings sparse. It had been nearly two years since her last visit to the exact same room and, as far as she could tell, not a single thing had changed. The old wood desk looked like it might've come into Fairfax's possession via a second hand office surplus supply. But the two small armchairs that faced the desk may have influenced that suspicion. They were equally old, worn, and mismatched.

While the furnishings had a venerable, eclectic feel to them, Fairfax's workspace was tidy and well organized. The top of his desk held a small laptop computer, a lamp, and an assortment of neatly arranged office supplies, such as a tape dispenser, paperclip holder, and mug full of pens and pencils. Aside from that, there was only a short stack of neatly arranged file folders on the end of a bureau running along the wall behind his chair. There were no family photos or mementoes of past vacations or adventures. Fairfax's workspace reflected the bland efficiency that Gretchen had come to expect from the man's personality. He was a good-natured, likable man, but he wasn't at all interesting.

She paced the silent office and waited for Fairfax to return. There was a light shining from beneath a door on one wall. She presumed that to be the restroom the receptionist had referred to. Not finding anything of interest to occupy her attention in the office's sparse furnishings, Gretchen finally took a seat in one of the chairs facing Fairfax's desk. In an effort to occupy herself, she retrieved her mobile phone from her purse. Setting the bag at her feet, she began tapping the phone's touch screen and scrolling through her email.

The minutes ticked by with Gretchen sitting in silence. Dealing with her email had taken no time at all. After which, she'd checked her Facebook page and commented on posts left by several friends. Once finished, she tried to sit quietly. It wasn't long before she became troubled that Fairfax had not yet arrived. The man was typically very punctual. She tried to remind herself that he'd gone to great lengths to work her into his schedule at the last minute, but the longer she sat, the more she was consumed by the growing sense that something was wrong.

Gretchen eyed the dim light emanating from beneath the door to the restroom. Then she realized that it might not be a lavatory at all. It could be a closet or a short passage to the adjoining office. Deciding she had waited long enough, Gretchen finally rose from the chair. Nearing the closed door, she listened intently for any indication of habitation beyond.

There was none.

Reluctantly, she raised her hand and rapped her knuckles against the door. "Hello?" she asked, in such a timid voice that she surprised even herself. If it was the restroom, and she was disturbing the man, she would be mortified.

But when no response came, her curiosity grew. Gretchen knocked more aggressively, her fist striking the solid wood surface with a clatter as the door rattled against its frame. "Mister Fairfax? Are you there?"

When still more silence greeted her ears, Gretchen's next thought was to ask her security detail to check on the man. Thinking better of it, she realized that was about the only thing that could make a profoundly awkward situation even more unpleasant. So, taking a deep breath, she tried the doorknob herself…and found it unlocked. Puzzled, and not knowing what to make of the unlocked door, she slowly pushed across the threshold. If the door was unlocked, that certainly ruled out the likelihood of it being a restroom, she reasoned.

Stepping in, Gretchen realized that the small space was, in fact, a restroom. Thankfully, it was empty. There was a toilet on one wall, and a small counter with a sink on the opposite. Looking at the light fixture over the sink, she realized why the room was so poorly illuminated. Three of the four bulbs in the fixture over the sink were burnt out.

With a shake of her head, Gretchen turned and headed for the door. This didn't explain where Mister Fairfax had gone, but it had settled an anxiety that was growing inside her. Turning back for the door, she stopped mid-stride. Looking over her shoulder, Gretchen regarded the light fixture; the bulbs were exposed as part of its design. Something about them had caught her eye.

Stepping to the sink, Gretchen took a closer look at the extinguished bulbs. Each of the three burnt out globes was marked by a pair of small dark smudges. Puzzled, she reached up, standing on her tiptoes, and twisted one of them. It instantly blinked back to blinding life. With a furrowed brow, she moved on to the next two, turning each of them only slightly before they, too, proved to be functional.

Rocking back on her heels, Gretchen was perplexed. Who would purposely turn out most of the lights in the small room? Other than a level of personal shyness that would qualify one for a lifetime of therapy, it made no sense. Could Fairfax be trying to save money on the electric bill? It didn't seem likely.

Dusting her hand on the side of her skirt, Gretchen turned once more for the door. Her vision was spotted with floating orb-shaped blind spots thanks to her close proximity to the bulbs as they'd blinked on. She fluttered her eyelids in an attempt to clear the distortion.

Stopping short of the door once more, Gretchen looked down at her right hand. Her fingertips felt sticky. She hadn't noticed it until she'd tried to dust them on her thigh. Now, looking closer, she could tell that the pads of her fingers were smeared with some kind of tacky substance.

Blinking away the small orbs that still danced at the center of her focus, Gretchen stared more closely at her hand. The tips of her fingers were dark with some kind of damp residue. She turned back toward the light and felt her heartbeat quicken. The substance was blood. She must have cut her finger on one of the bulbs.

That would explain why the lights had been turned out.

Running the water from the sink's tap, Gretchen washed the blood from her fingers. Glancing in the mirror, she noticed that she'd smeared some of it on her skirt at some point along the way.

That figures…

But when she wiped her hands dry, she was surprised to find no injury of any kind. Stepping back half a pace, she considered the mirror over the sink. It made no sense. If she wasn't cut, where had the blood come from?

Her senses went instantly on alert. Suddenly Fairfax's disappearance seemed a great deal more than an inconvenience. Gretchen realized that she needed to notify her security detail immediately. And, while there was likely a logical explanation for what she'd discovered, she would leave it for them to sort out.

Passing quickly into Fairfax's office, Gretchen walked through the empty room and rushed into the reception area. Her mouth was already sputtering unintelligible words when she froze mid-stride and felt the hair on the back of her neck rise to attention. The reception area was empty. Both members of her security detail were gone, and so was the receptionist.

"Hello?" Gretchen called in a voice that was so full of anxiety that she was hard pressed to recognize it as her own. "Is anyone there?"

It wasn't like there was anywhere for the three of them to go in the tiny office suite, so rushing to the main entrance, Gretchen threw open the hallway door.

A vast, silent, empty corridor awaited. Somewhere in the distance she could hear the muffled whistle of the building's ventilation system forcing cool air through the structure. Aside from that, it was eerily quiet.

She stumbled into the hallway on rubbery legs, her mind still trying to make sense of the situation. The disappearance of her security detail had her more spooked than anything. Dargo's men were first rate. There wasn't a man among them who would abandon his post—let alone the entire team.

Spinning around, Gretchen knew with absolute certainty that something was unquestionably wrong. She would barricade herself in Fairfax's office until she understood what was happening.

Marching back to the doorway of the Fairfax and Clauegh office suite, a scuff on the wall caught her eye. She drew closer and tried to rationalize the strange mark on the painted plaster. There was a short, deep divot in the wall that was perhaps an inch and a half wide. It tapered to a point on both edges but flared to almost a quarter of an inch in width at its center.

Looking down at her feet, Gretchen noticed two small dots marking the dense weave of the hallway's carpeting. Kneeling closer, she instantly recognized the spots for what they were: Drops of blood decorated the carpet's thick pile.

Her eyes shot higher up the wall, returning to the strange indentation. She suddenly realized the gouge for what it was—the location of a knife strike.

Gretchen's eyes scanned the length of the hallway, as she backpedaled toward the open door of the Fairfax and Clauegh offices. She stumbled across the threshold and promptly slammed the door shut. It only took a second to secure the lock as well as the deadbolt.

Her eyes flashed around the outer office, finding nothing to help barricade the door. Stepping to the reception counter, she looked for anything that might be of use; anything she could use as a weapon. What she saw made her blood run cold. Sitting on the receptionist's chair was a blonde wig and a pair of dark framed glasses. Her stomach churned; the sweet southern receptionist wasn't who she'd claimed to be.

Grabbing one of the chairs, Gretchen returned to the front door. She wedged it under the door handle as best she could. It wasn't like the chair would stop anyone who could defeat the lock, but at that point, she figured every little bit helped.

Surveying the room and deciding she'd done everything possible, Gretchen returned to Fairfax's office. There, she closed the door only to find that it had no lock. As with the front door, she took one of the visitor's chairs and wedged its back under the door handle. Finally, she spun, searching for her purse.

Already running on a terror fueled adrenaline rush, Gretchen's heart rate redlined when she couldn't find her handbag. A dreadful whimper escaped her throat, as she circled the desk in desperation. Seeing her purse on the floor behind Fairfax's desk, she lunged, skidding across the coarse carpet and scraping her knees. Flipping open the clasp, she dumped the bag's contents into a pile. Without wasting a second, she snatched her mobile phone from the mix of useless objects.

There was nothing complicated to remember at that point. She tapped the number nine and hit send. It was part of a security protocol she knew backwards and forwards. She'd never expected to need it, but Dargo had prepared every member of the Voss family for similar eventualities. An endless two seconds later, she heard the remote end of the line ring.

"This is Triad," the voice said simply.

"This is Hummingbird," Gretchen sputtered. "My team is gone—there's no one left! I need help!"

There was a momentary pause before the man's voice returned, calm and professional, despite the frantic nature of her situation. "Need to confirm, Hummingbird. You're six man detail is down?"

"They're gone! Just gone! I—I don't even know where!"

"Understood. I have your location," the voice said smoothly. The man went on to describe in exact detail not only the address where she was currently located, but also her floor and her position in the building. She wasn't sure how he knew all of the details, but everything he asked her to confirm had been completely accurate.

"Is there an immediate threat to your person?" the man asked in conclusion.

Gretchen's mind was still reeling from all of the locational data the man had been able to gather from the other side of the planet. "I'm sorry?" she mumbled. She realized her adrenaline surge was wearing off, and her mind was starting to feel sluggish. It was becoming slow to respond to her body's requests. *Or was it the other way around?*

"Is your aggressor present?" the man insisted.

"No," Gretchen said firmly. "I've barricaded myself inside an office. I'm okay for the moment, but I don't know for how long. I—I don't even know what happened to the guards!"

"Please stand by, ma'am," the voice said in a calm, reassuring tone. "I've re-tasked your transport detail. They're en route from the airfield as we speak…ETA is four and a half minutes. I'll remain on the line with you until they arrive."

With a wheezing sigh, Gretchen finally eased off of her aching knees and sat against the base of the credenza behind Fairfax's desk. She took a deep breath and worked to calm herself. As the revving of her own heartbeat began to slow, its thundering rhythm receded from her ears, and the room's ominous silence returned. Only the electric buzz of the reignited bulbs in the bathroom disturbed the quiet.

Sitting there on the floor, Gretchen's eyes returned to the light that spilled from the half-open bathroom door. Her eyes pinched as she focused on what she was seeing. Something about it wasn't right, and it took deliberate concentration to cut through her fear in order to see it.

She could hear the voice on the other end of the phone line speaking in the distance, as she pulled herself to her feet. Almost in a trance, Gretchen set the phone aside and moved slowly toward the bathroom door. It was the light coming from the small room—that was what didn't fit. It had grown a bit dim once again. It had been much brighter after she'd screwed the remaining bulbs back into place.

Confounded for an explanation, Gretchen pulled the door slowly open. She was right. This time only two of the four bulbs were lit; the two in the center. The bulb on each end of the short lighting ballast had once again gone dark.

Confused, she padded silently into the room and stared up at the lights. With a shake of her head, she leaned forward over the sink and reached for one of the darkened bulbs. Just as her fingertips reached the warm glass, her toes shot out from under her. Gretchen crashed down, her ribs slammed against the hard edge of the counter. Her elbows impacted next, hitting the unyielding porcelain of the sink. For as much as both strikes hurt, at least they saved her from smashing her face before bouncing and landing on the cold linoleum floor.

Gretchen's eyes rolled listlessly, as her body struggled with the onslaught of overwhelming pain and disorientation. After a few moments—she would never know for sure how many—her eyes finally focused, and she found herself lying on her side. Shifting only slightly, the pain returned with renewed intensity.

Focusing her eyes again, she noticed the muddy streaks on the floor in front of her, representing the location of her feet when she'd slipped. She raised her head slightly to get a better view. That brought the dark puddle into sight.

With a gasp, Gretchen vaulted herself up into a sitting position. She crawled backward until she struck the wall beside the toilet. The dark pool of blood on the floor was immediately recognizable. It had formed directly beneath the sink. The logic of the scenario made her stomach burn. Clamping her eyes shut, she wished with all her heart that this was just a dream—that this would be the part where she would wake up, safe in her own bed.

When she opened her eyes once more and the cold linoleum and dark pool remained, Gretchen knew there was no way around it. Taking a deep breath, she steeled herself and reached out. Wrapping the tips of her fingers around the cabinet door, she pulled it quickly open.

A whimper finally made its escape from somewhere deep inside her, and the tears spouted from her eyes. Slowly, and without taking her gaze off the contents of the cabinet, she scooted away from it, and the horror it contained. When she felt her back once again touch the far wall of the small room, she pulled her legs up close to her chest and hugged them tightly in her arms. Tears streamed down her face as she sat unblinking, staring at the twisted, folded, bloodied body of Lee Fairfax—his body jammed savagely into the cabinet beneath the sink.

Chapter 41

Anna raced down the staircase, circling the wide concrete flights as fast as her feet could carry her. Each strike of her running shoes echoed up the starkly unadorned walls of the emergency stairway. With a leap, she landed on the second floor platform. Without hesitation, she turned left and rushed down the next flight.

Just as she burst from the stairwell entrance, she heard the *bing* of the elevator announcing its arrival. She skidded to a stop in front of the elevator doors just as they began to slide open. Running her hands through her long hair and struggling to calm her breath, Anna made an effort to look as if she'd been waiting for some time.

"Very funny!" Natasha laughed, as she stepped off the lift. "You're lucky you didn't break your neck." She threw her arm around her sister, and pulled her close, both of them were laughing. "Tell me again why we had to race?"

Anna let out an exasperated sight. "It's a little thing called *fun*. You were familiar with it, once upon a time!"

She wheezed as her sister tightened the hug. "Very funny, smart ass!"

Though she was laughing, Anna was serious about the comment. They'd had a long talk earlier in the afternoon, and some of Natasha's admissions had truly shocked her. Partly because she couldn't believe there was an entire area of her sister's life that she'd known nothing about, and partly because of the unusual circumstances that had now arrived at their door.

Anna thought the drama surrounding Cyrus's arrival was thrilling enough. But while there was finally some excitement in the building, Natasha had seemed anything but curious. Rather than rally with enthusiasm for the recent intrigue, the more that happened, the more Natasha grew quiet and withdrawn.

Though she knew her sister well, better than anyone actually, Anna had never seen Natasha's mood fall to such an extreme. Though, there was precedent. When she'd gone away to college, she'd left as a spirited and carefree girl. But when she had returned, dropping out less than a year later, a dour and serious young woman had replaced the sister she'd known. Something had happened while she was away. Whatever it was, it had been enough not only to convince her normally self-assured sister that she didn't want to return to school, but it had also changed her overall disposition from a wide-eyed, carefree person, to a grounded adult who took the world much too seriously.

At the time, Anna gave her sister the space she needed. Then, she provided moral support when Natasha decided against returning to school. And though she always intended to get around to addressing the cause of her metamorphosis…in time,

Anna had chosen the path of least resistance and let the subject drop. Her sister was home, and she'd once more found a balance as well as a way to be happy. She wasn't the same person who had left a year earlier, but at least the sister she loved was back. At some point, that had become enough.

But now Cyrus was here—presumably someone none of them had ever met before. But that didn't match what Anna saw in her sister's eyes when she looked at the would-be stranger. And it didn't track with the sudden pall that had fallen over Natasha's demeanor since his arrival. While Natasha didn't admit to knowing the stranger, Anna was becoming certain that there was some sort of recognition between them.

One thing was painfully clear—Natasha had been irritable and frustrated from the very moment she'd first seen Cyrus lying unconscious in medical. But it was the times when Natasha thought no one was looking that truly fascinated Anna. It was the way she looked at Cyrus in those brief moments. She let her guard down when she felt sure that no one could see her. There was something different in those moments—something Anna couldn't quite define. Was it caring? Concern? Suspicion? Heartache? Whatever it was, it was deep-seeded and visceral. And it pained her.

It would be so much easier if you would just explain it to me, Anna thought, as they entered the open dining area at the end of the common space on the building's ground floor.

Her father was already in his chair at the head of the table. Anna flashed him a smile and slid into her seat to his left. Likewise, Natasha assumed her normal position opposite her sister, at her father's right.

"Good evening, girls," Voss said. "How was your afternoon?"

"Uneventful," Anna offered in a sarcastic tone.

"Fine," Natasha said simply.

Voss smiled. "Excellent!"

Anna glared at him. "Only you would take *uneventful* as a positive assessment," she grumbled.

"You're young," he smiled. "Someday you'll find that the uneventful days are the ones you cherish most."

Seeing two additional place settings, Anna perked up. "We're having guests?" The hope in her voice was unmistakable.

Finishing a sip of wine, Voss nodded. "Cyrus and Dargo will be joining us," he said, as if it were the most natural thing in the world.

"What?" Natasha sputtered. Somehow she'd managed to fit an entire protest into a single word.

Anna, for her part, was grinning so widely that she held a napkin to her face in order to mask it. It was an interesting turn of events, and one that might yet pry some answers from her reluctant sibling.

As far as Dargo's presence at the table, Anna found that far more interesting. He never ate with them—and not for lack of invitation. Dargo had been with the family for decades. He was such a constant presence in their daily lives that she and Natasha felt that he was more like a quiet uncle, rather than their head of security.

Then again, if Cyrus was joining them, it was likely in spite of protests from Dargo. Dargo would insist on keeping a personal eye on their guest under such circumstances.

It didn't matter. Based on the look in Natasha's eyes, sparks were going to fly one way or another.

"Ah! Cyrus, thank you for joining us," Voss said, as Cyrus suddenly appeared and approached the table. Not surprisingly, Dargo was close on his heel.

"No problem," Cyrus said, offering a warm smile to all three of the Voss's at the table. "I appreciate your hospitality. Most of all, I'm glad to be out of your infirmary...no offense."

Anna laughed, and so did her father. Natasha offered only a weak smile and focused primarily on her empty plate.

Cyrus looked at the two empty seats and was trying to decide where to sit when Dargo made the decision for him. Without a word, Dargo pointed to the empty spot beside Anna. Cyrus's brow rose at the odd gesture, but he offered only the tiniest of shrugs before rounding the table and taking a seat.

A quick glance at the table confirmed Anna's suspicion. She was the only one to notice the odd interaction play out between Cyrus and Dargo. Anna knew it meant that she would have an unobstructed view of her sister, just as Natasha had an unobstructed view of Cyrus. It was an ideal configuration for an impromptu social experiment.

When Cyrus had first arrived, Anna thought he was interesting, even attractive. He was certainly the first bit of excitement to come into the building in...*forever*. So, from the beginning, she had hopes that he might have cause to stay a while. It seemed like a long shot, but she wondered where things might lead.

But she saw her silly schoolgirl fantasies for what they were the night she brought Natasha to see him in the medical bay. Natasha hadn't needed to say anything; judging by her reaction, Anna knew that there was some kind of connection there. At that moment, Anna had realized that her relationship with the young man would never be what she'd first hoped. Instead, she would devote herself to uncovering the cause of the complex reaction she'd witnessed in Natasha's eyes that first moment in the infirmary.

The silence surrounding the table was thick and unpleasant, so Anna took it upon herself to fix it.

"I didn't think to ask, what's for dinner?" she shot a quizzical glance at her father.

"Ah!" he chuckled. "In honor of our young friend," he said, tipping his glass toward Cyrus, "we're having good, old-fashioned American cooking!"

As if on cue, two servers emerged from doors at the back of the room, each pushing a wheeled aluminum cart, and began filling the plates.

Anna watched in rapt fascination as a meal their cook had never before prepared was quickly assembled before them. Each plate contained a gigantic cheeseburger on a toasted sesame seed bun, complete with a side of thick French fries and a pickle spear. Next, a large bowl of Texas chili was placed beside each plate. Finally, on the last pass, the servers circled the table and placed a frosted beer stein and a bottle of some strange microbrew in front of each plate.

Cyrus watched the presentation by the kitchen staff with a grin on his face. Once the meal was assembled, there was no question that her father took great pride in the eclectic rally of American cuisine. He eyed Cyrus nervously, waiting for some sign of whether the meal met with this approval.

"This is amazing," Cyrus said finally, offering up a sincere laugh. "A truly first-class spread, Doctor Voss! I'm honored by your generosity."

"Please, call me Rutger," Voss said, with a proud smile. "I'm so glad you like it!"

When he looked around the table, Anna saw a rare twinkle in her father's eye as he beamed with pride. She realized that this dinner was very important to him, and she found it odd. She wondered how he would feel if he knew that Cyrus had a secret. Because, while Anna knew that Cyrus was here to deliver something to her father, the longer she thought about it, the more certain she felt that there was far more to unearth.

Natasha hadn't offered much of a reaction to the odd display of food. She seemed so intently focused on the place setting in front of her that someone could've set the chandelier on fire and it wouldn't have garnered her attention.

While Natasha had stepped out in some small corner of her mind, Anna noted that her sister wasn't the only one who was failing to take the evening in stride. Dargo sat stiffly in his chair with his hands folded in his lap. He was paying greater attention to everything in the room, rather than the food.

Anna knew Dargo well enough to know he wasn't comfortable having Cyrus at the table. It was a safe bet that he wanted Cyrus tossed outside the gate or locked in his room for the remainder of his stay. It was a good thing her father had taken a liking to him, or that might have ended up being the case. Still, it seemed an extreme reaction, even for Dargo. His hackles were up, and they were only having dinner.

"While I greatly enjoy these meals," Voss said, after they'd all begun eating. "The truth is that we don't take enough time to dine together, or enjoy one another's company."

He took a moment to look at each person at the table. "Tonight we needed to take time due to special circumstances," he continued. "I know you girls have both spoken with Cyrus briefly, but I wanted to sit down together as a group so we could become better acquainted. For obvious reasons, Cyrus will be staying with us until his recovery is complete. But beyond that, he has agreed to aid me in my research. As such, he will be staying with us for the foreseeable future."

Anna grinned. That explained why Dargo was more on edge than usual. But looking across the table at her sister, she saw Natasha's previous vacant stare immediately replaced by one of concern. Anna watched her gaze shift momentarily to Cyrus, before it fell on her.

Natasha reached out abruptly and picked up the stein of dark beer. Tipping the mug back, she drank, and didn't stop until it was empty. Without any acknowledgment, she placed the empty mug back in its original place and returned her gaze once more to the center of her plate.

An uncomfortable silence fell over the table, so Anna cleared her throat. "It seems like my wish for a little excitement has finally been granted," she said, with a not so subtle laugh.

"You could be more correct than you know," Voss explained. "The truth is that someone attacked Mister Cooper—" he stopped himself. "I'm sorry—Cyrus—on his way here with Professor Ragsdale's prototype. Those responsible may have been after Richard's work as a way of collecting on some outstanding debt, or they may have been after it in connection with my studies. Either way, Dargo's team will be stepping up security until we better understand what has happened."

"Will this affect my charity tournament in November?" Anna asked with concern.

Natasha's eyes finally rose and shifted to her father. Anna knew that her sister had a vested interest in the tournament, as well. While Anna would be the one competing, Natasha was her training partner. They trained and practiced together six days a week. Natasha wanted to see Anna compete every bit as much as Anna wanted to participate.

"We'll have to wait and see," Voss said reluctantly.

Both girls instantly set upon him in a verbal onslaught—the likes of which no father could ever defend against.

"Wait—Wait—Wait!" Voss raised his voice. "We simply don't have enough data with which to make an educated decision at this time," he said, as if clinical analysis would support his point of view. "Gretchen is already in Atlanta making final arrangements. If all goes well, you're registered and ready to compete.

"In the meantime, we must remain patient and give Dargo's team time to gather evidence and sort out what happened to Richard, and young Cyrus, here."

Anna found her mind overcome with a litany of reasons why she should be allowed to compete in November, regardless of the state of Dargo's investigation. Completely gone from her mind was the rational fact that, only 36 hours previous, she'd been entirely noncommittal about participating in the event.

She would force the issue with her father, hopefully snapping Natasha from her funk in the process. Even as she drew breath for the argument that would be her opening salvo, she stopped when Dargo placed a finger at his ear. He spoke for the first time since taking a seat at the table.

"Say again, Talbet?" Dargo said, in his baritone Russian accent.

Whatever was being relayed to him though his earpiece, Anna knew it wasn't good news. She watched Dargo's eyes darken as he listened to information transmitted from the security center on the fifth floor. Her heart grew cold when Dargo's gaze shifted, slowly circling the table. For a moment, he stopped on the empty chair at the end of the table, and Anna was suddenly terrified that something was wrong with Gretchen. She was the only member of their extended family who was not present.

"Understood," Dargo responded finally. "Scramble our American assets to provide support for Fuller and Stills. I want Hummingbird back on board and in the air *immediately*."

He listened as a response came back over his earpiece. "Da. Double guards on the front gate and rotate shifts every three hours until further notice."

The big man slid out of his chair and buttoned his suit coat. "Gretchen's team was attacked in Atlanta," Dargo stated simply to Voss. "She is unharmed, but I have men missing and need to attend to the matter. Gretchen will be airborne and on her way back within thirty minutes."

Without another word, the gruff Russian stalked from the room on his way to the elevator. Anna knew that he would quarterback the situation from the security office on the fifth floor.

Suddenly, all of her wishes for thrills and excitement seemed foolish and simple. They were now getting more than she'd bargained for, and she was terrified for her friend. Her eyes fell on Cyrus as her mind searched for answers. First, he'd been attacked, and now Gretchen. It couldn't be a coincidence.

Chapter 42

After dinner, Cyrus returned to his room. The compound was in an uproar. What little he knew of the inciting incident was sketchy at best. There had been some sort of attack on Gretchen while she was attending a business meeting in the United States. Apparently, there were casualties, but Gretchen wasn't among them. She was on her way back to the island aboard Voss's private jet. At the same time, Dargo had left with a small contingent of men to launch a thorough investigation of the crime scene.

The entire scenario bothered Cyrus, but without all of the details, he couldn't put his finger on the part that was causing concern. Still, it was a kerfuffle with security, and something he could leverage. Step one was to lower his own visibility. He'd returned to his room and stayed there for some time.

After things had a chance to calm down, he decided to test the limits of his newfound freedom. No one had given him a tour of the facility yet, so if he was stopped by security he could legitimately feign ignorance. Hopefully, it would be enough for him to get away with a little trespassing.

He set out to explore the compound. Many of the doors were locked, requiring a keycard in order to access restricted areas. He soon understood that security had little reason to hassle him since the building was so compartmentalized that he couldn't accidentally wander into an off-limits area. Few outsiders were allowed into the building in the first place. Those who were, would've been cleared for the appropriate access zones.

When he'd first read the mission brief back at Coalition Command, Cyrus had nearly overlooked Natasha's involvement in the case. Back when he'd known her, she was attending school and using her mother's maiden name rather than the surname of Voss. It wasn't until he'd read the full name of Voss's late wife that he put things together and realized that Voss's daughter, Natasha, was the same Natasha Schroeder he'd known at school. Since that moment, he'd been able to think of little else.

According to his mission parameters, he should've been looking for a way to communicate with the outside. He'd walked into the installation knowing that would be an uphill battle. Given the level of security, he wasn't disappointed. Still, while his mission objectives dictated what he should be doing, those parameters had absolutely nothing to do with his actual goals.

Though she'd made it clear that she had no desire to speak with him, Cyrus only wanted to find Natasha. She was the reason he'd taken the mission in the first place. She was his primary objective, regardless of mission parameters.

But after nearly forty-five minutes of searching the open areas of the compound, he hadn't found her. His search included two stops at her room, at which point he could only ring the doorbell and hope she would answer.

When plan A; checking her room, and, plan B; scouring the common areas of the building, both failed, Cyrus resorted to plan C. That led him straight to Anna's door. He'd noticed the way she'd looked at him very early on and worried about complicating matters. She seemed like a sweet girl, she just didn't know what it was that she didn't know.

Things were already more complicated than he would like, but he had to press on.

He glanced at his watch and hoped he wouldn't be waking her. The hour had grown later than he expected. In retrospect, he realized he should've started with Anna. There was a good chance she would know where her sister was, and it would've saved a lot of time.

Without wasting another moment, he tapped the button on the panel beside the room's double sliding doors. He was expecting, at best, to hear Anna ask who was there. To his surprise, the doors slid open with only a quiet hiss of the pneumatic mechanism.

"Come in, before security gives you a hard time," Anna's voice came from just inside the doorway.

Stepping into the room, Cyrus heard the doors slide shut behind him. He was surprised by the size of the room. It was large and open, broken into zones, with a bed and set of dressers in one corner, a group of furniture and an entertainment center in another area, and a large display cabinet filled with trophies and awards taking up its own space. Even then, there was a tremendous amount of open floor left to move about.

"You're up late," Anna observed. She motioned for him to come further into the room.

"It's sort of hard to sleep with what happened at dinner. Is there any news about Gretchen? Is she okay?" his voice was somber.

"She's on her way back now. She's okay, but she's really shaken up. Beyond that, I don't know much more. Dargo's gone to investigate. He's on his way to the States right now."

She motioned him over to the grouping of chairs near the entertainment center. He took a seat in one of the over-stuffed armchairs, and sighed. "Dargo seems pretty hardcore," he offered.

She laughed. "You could say that. He takes his job seriously. He takes the security of my entire family *very* seriously.

"It's odd," she continued. "First, you were attacked, and now Gretchen…someone clearly has an agenda. But for the life of me, I can't figure out what that might be."

He nodded. "I'll admit, I'm extremely interested to find out what happened to Gretchen. What she saw, who she saw, and what exactly happened. I want to know if there is a connection to what happened to me."

She smiled. "That's understandable. You were nearly killed."

He considered her statement. "There's that," he admitted. "But Gretchen patched me up. I'm not sure I would've made it without her care. I owe her a debt that I can't repay."

"What happened to you, anyway?" Anna asked. The question poured out of her mouth so fast, and was delivered so bluntly, that Cyrus knew she'd been thinking it for a good, long time.

"I mean…on your way here with the device for my father," she elaborated. "At the gate when you arrived, you were in worse shape than I've ever seen anyone in my entire life. I heard that it happened on a train… But what *exactly* happened?"

Cyrus considered the question. He could feel his disposition darkening as he replayed the fictitious version of the scenario in his mind—the version that supported his cover story. "A man and a woman cornered me in my sleeper car. At first, I figured they were just a couple traveling together like couples do. But there was something different about them. They just looked…wrong—carried themselves *differently*. I think that's what tipped me off.

"The next thing I knew, one was pulling a gun," he explained. "Everything after that was a blur. I don't think they expected me to fight back. When I did, they were as surprised by the situation as I was."

"And you got shot," she said, in an effort to coax the story along. Cyrus had drifted off in his thoughts, reliving the real experience in his mind.

Cyrus shook his head. "I don't remember getting shot." His eyes rose to meet hers. "There was at least one gun—maybe two. One of them had a knife at some point. It all happened in one of those little sleeper cars, so it was close quarters. My memory is sort of a jumble."

Anna didn't interrupt. She just waited, giving him time to fill in the gaps in the story as he saw fit. It was the right way to draw information from someone, and he was impressed by her patient skill.

"I killed them," he said quietly. "I killed them both."

She waited, giving him more time to speak, but he said nothing.

"How do you feel about that?" she asked, in a calming, sensitive voice.

After a long moment, his eyes once more raised to meet hers. "I'm sorry? What was that?"

"I asked how you feel about the fact that you killed the man and the woman. I can't imagine that taking the life of another person is easy to deal with."

He shrugged. The truth was that he hadn't given it a moment's thought since. In his line of work, you didn't dare. Doubt could eat you alive. You trust your instincts and refuse to second guess yourself. In this case, it wasn't hard. "I probably don't feel as bad as I should, in that case," he said matter-of-factly. "They tried to kill me—almost succeeded in the end, actually. I can't say that I'm losing any sleep over that part, to be honest."

He was silent for a long while, then he looked at her again. "Do you think that makes me a bad person?"

His cover story being what it was, much of his conversation with her was more honest than he would ever admit. Especially the part about killing his would-be assassins. In a life or death fight, he wasn't willing to risk being on the losing side.

"I think that makes you a very practical person," she said, sending him a sincere smile. "It sounds like just the right attitude to get you through the experience."

After that, she grew silent. She seemed to be contemplating the things he'd said. The stillness of the room stretched on for some time, but Cyrus was surprised to find that the silence was neither uncomfortable nor troubling. He didn't feel like she was judging him. She just wanted to know him better—to understand what was going on around her. And he could respect that.

But judging by the darkness that had fallen across her face, he knew that something new troubled her. If she felt as comfortable talking with him as he had with her, she was now considering the pros and cons of sharing it with him. Not sure how to proceed, he simply waited for her to make up her mind.

It was nearly a full minute before Anna spoke again. When she did, Cyrus could see tears threatening to form in the corners of her eyes. "Thank you for sharing that with me," she said quietly. "I'm sure it wasn't easy."

"You're easy to talk to," he said, and offered his best reassuring smile. "If you've got something on your mind, I'd like to return the favor."

His statement had the effect of breaking the emotional dam that was Anna's disposition. Tears erupted from her eyes, and her body shook with silent sobs.

Cyrus's eyes bulged at the shocking transition as she crumpled before him. He knew she was approaching a precipice where she would either say what was on her mind, or she would push the troubling thoughts away…and him along with them. The aggressive step she'd taken over that figurative threshold had been powerful and quick, and it caught him off guard.

Moving quickly from the armchair, Cyrus dropped onto the couch and put his arms around her. She buried her face in his shoulder and sobbed for several minutes before starting to put together a coherent string of words. Once she was able, it seemed the waterworks had offered some cathartic purge, clearing away whatever emotional blockage was keeping her from voicing what was on her mind.

After a few additional minutes of sniffling and wiping the tears from her puffy red face and runny nose, Anna was ready to talk.

"I think that what happened to Gretchen was my fault," she said, in a scratchy voice.

Cyrus smiled and shook his head. The idea was foolish. "It couldn't possibly be your fault," he offered. "We don't even know what happened yet."

"I don't need to know what happened," she explained. "Gretchen wouldn't have been there if it wasn't for me. She went to Atlanta because I sent her. She was there because I told her I wanted to be in that stupid tournament."

"Okay," Cyrus said. He was beginning to understand her logic, or at least her line of thought. "So you're thinking that, if you'd never decided to participate in the tournament, Gretchen would never have gone to Atlanta and would never have been in danger?"

Anna nodded.

It was linear logic, he reasoned. But the events of life seldom follow a linear process. "Consider this," he began. "For the sake of argument, say Gretchen was targeted the same way I was. If that's the case, then it didn't matter if she went to Atlanta yesterday, today, or in a month. If she went to the U.K., or even the mainland here at some point, it's likely that the very same thing would've happened to her.

"If she was targeted, you asking her to go somewhere or do something didn't get her in that bind. Whoever is behind it did it for a very specific reason. The attack must serve some sort of purpose. And in all honesty, whatever's going on, I don't think it has anything to do with your decision to participate in a tennis tournament."

Anna listened to everything he said, and he could see her thinking it through. Slowly, the light returned to her eyes. Finally, she offered a small nod and a slight smile. Wiping the last residual tears away, she squeezed his arm.

"You make a good point," she said quietly. "And I think you're a pretty good listener, too."

Cyrus laughed.

"Plus," she continued, "I don't see how anyone could possibly have known I was joining the tournament at the last minute. Gretchen had to pull strings to get me in, actually. That's why she had to fly out so abruptly."

Her statement stopped Cyrus's warm and fuzzy moment dead in its tracks. This was new information, and it was troubling. "How last minute?"

"Ah," she stammered, looking away in embarrassment.

"What?"

She took a deep breath and finally met his eyes. "Okay," she explained. "I hadn't actually planned to participate in the tournament. I was kind of looking forward to some down time. But when you showed up, you caused a big upset around here. I mean *big*.

"Once they finally brought you inside the gate, they realized how bad you were hurt, and you were taken to the infirmary. You were unconscious down there *for days*. Anyway, right after all the drama, Natasha came back from a trip to some God forsaken lab somewhere. I was telling her the story of everything that happened while she was away. And why not? It was the first interesting thing to happen around here in *forever*.

"So, I took Tash down to the infirmary so she could see what all the fuss was about. Only the reaction she had when she saw you wasn't at all what I expected. In fact, I've never seen anything like it from her. It was only made worse by the fact that she wouldn't tell me what the hell it was all about. She just told me to keep quiet and don't tell anyone that she'd seen you."

By this point, Cyrus was sitting on the edge of the couch with his elbows on his knees and his face in his hands. For all the ways he'd considered first seeing Natasha again, he could never have imagined the way things had actually transpired.

"How does all of this relate to Gretchen ending up in Georgia?" he finally asked, talking into his hands.

Anna puffed out a breath before continuing. "Tash wouldn't tell me what was going on, but she kept an eye on you while you were unconscious. I mean, she didn't think anyone noticed, but I'm her sister. She can't hide that kind of thing from me. So, while I knew something was up, she wouldn't talk about it. Then you finally woke up. I thought she would be over the moon!

"But she wasn't. That's when she really got moody. There was an entire day where I couldn't get more than one word answers out of her. She'd pretty much just checked out. It was like her mind was somewhere else.

"So, what could I do? I knew there was something there. I knew that you two knew each other, and she obviously had feelings for you—whatever they might be. So I thought I would help her along a little bit."

Not understanding where the long story was going, Cyrus finally pulled his face from his hands. He didn't want to know what happened next, but he needed to... He needed to understand. There was something more going on, and he needed to get a handle on it. Even though he'd used the attack on the train as a cover, that attack had taken place nonetheless. At the time, he wasn't sure if it had anything to do with Voss or his own past work. But now there'd been an attack on Gretchen, equally odd from what he could tell so far, and the only thing that connected the two events was their mutual relation to Voss.

"I understand that you're confused and worried about your sister," Cyrus said, with as much sympathy as he could muster. "But what does this have to do with Gretchen?"

"Gretchen deals with all of our medical issues here," Anna explained. "But that's a lot of responsibility to put on one person, so she has an assistant—an understudy. When Gretchen is otherwise occupied, her understudy takes care of the infirmary."

Cyrus groaned, as he understood what she was getting at. "And Natasha is Gretchen's understudy," he concluded.

She nodded. "Once you were stable, you just needed daily antibiotic shots, and your bandages changed. That was something Tash could do in her sleep. So I figured that, if I could get Gretchen out of the picture for a day or two, it would put you and Tash in the same room a couple of times a day. Maybe whatever it was that had her so upset would finally get resolved. I mean, be honest, you may have delivered that prototype for my father, but that's not the real reason you're here, is it?"

He couldn't contain the proud smile that he offered Anna. She'd put together a great deal. She hadn't compromised his mission, but she'd figure out what the spymasters back at the Coalition couldn't. She was putting together his past relationship with Natasha, and she was keeping it on the down-low.

"So you signed up for the tennis tournament at the last minute knowing that Gretchen would have to fly to the States in order to finalize everything. All so you could put Natasha and me in the same room?"

"Well, you have to remember that I did this while you were still on lockdown. You were confined to the infirmary. I didn't anticipate whatever magic you worked on my father to get yourself the run of the place. I figured I would need to get creative if you were going to get the time with her that you'd clearly gone to so much trouble and pain, to afford."

Cyrus thought about all Anna had done and her motivations for it. "You're a good sister, Anna," he said, giving her hand a squeeze. "And a good friend. Thank you."

She smiled back weakly.

"I can't see how you could be in any way responsible for whatever happened to Gretchen, though. Like you said, she went out there at the drop of a hat. The question that comes to mind is, given that odd situation, who would even have known she would be there? Whatever happened, it couldn't have had much planning. Even Gretchen didn't know she would be visiting Atlanta until, what…an hour or two before she stepped on board a private jet? That's pretty suspicious, if you ask me."

Cyrus considered the situation further. "You know," he said, with a hint of enthusiasm. "Would it be possible for you to put together a list of anyone who knew about Gretchen's outgoing flight?"

"You mean, just between the two of us?"

He nodded. "At least for now. Something doesn't smell right. And if there is a connection between what happened to Gretchen and what happened to me, I might be able to find it."

"I don't see why not," she muttered, already giving the matter some thought. "There would be the people in the building, but we would need to consider anyone who knew that the jet was being prepared. It's hangared at the King's private airfield. Let me give it some thought. I should be able to pull a list together."

"Perfect," Cyrus grinned. "Then maybe we can get some answers."

"Ah…on another note," he said somewhat sheepishly. "I realize Natasha doesn't want to talk to me, but I really do need to see her."

"Did you try her room?"

"Twice. She didn't answer."

Anna cringed. She picked up the phone from the table at the end of the couch and dialed an extension. After letting the line ring for nearly a minute, she placed the phone back in the cradle.

"I don't think she was blowing you off," Anna said with trepidation. "I don't think she's even in the building."

That was the last thing Cyrus had expected to hear. "Not in the building? What about the lockdown? No one in or out until Dargo gets back with some answers—that's what he said. Are you saying she talked her way out of that? Would they let her leave, even with a security detail?"

Slowly and nervously, Anna shook her head. "Dargo's lockdown's aren't as effective as he thinks. If Tash has left the building, she did it without anyone knowing…and without a security escort."

Chapter 43

The Voss Compound
11:13 pm

With concern for her sister growing, Anna led Cyrus down the hall to the door of Natasha's room. She didn't waste time knocking. That she was gone had become a virtual certainty in her mind. Natasha had been acting strangely over the last week, and when she was stressed, she liked to get away from the compound and everyone in it. Unfortunately, given that Gretchen had just been attacked in the U.S., it didn't seem like a good time for her to be off on her own. And since sending security after her would only add to a growing list of problems, Anna was willing to let Cyrus go after her.

Punching the access code into the touch screen lock on the door, Anna shot a quick look toward each end of the hallway before grabbing Cyrus's elbow and stepping into the room.

"What's wrong?" Cyrus asked, as the doors hissed shut behind them.

"I would rather no one noticed us coming here," she explained. "It would only draw more attention. Are you sure you can find her and bring her back?"

Cyrus nodded. He looked like he had a reply, but whatever it was he kept it to himself. "Why are we here?"

He looked around the wide bedroom suite for the first time. She watched his eyes as he took it all in. Like her own room, Natasha's was expansive and separated into smaller areas by the way the furniture was arranged. The main difference in the case of Natasha's room was that there was no wasted space as there had been in Anna's suite. A large section of the room along the right wall was dedicated to a small painting studio. A wide easel and two smaller stands, along with a stool and a pair of small tables covered with assorted, half-used supplies.

Anna saw the surprise on Cyrus's face and wondered what he knew about her hobby. She knew that Natasha had dabbled with sketches and painting before going away to school, but she hadn't been serious about it until she returned home to stay. It raised more questions about the portion of her life that Natasha had shared with Cyrus. He hadn't said as much, but Anna was becoming more and more confident that their paths had crossed, perhaps romantically, in the brief period of time that Natasha had spent away at school. It was likely that her unscheduled return even had something to do with Cyrus. It might at least explain Natasha's rigid response to his unexpected appearance.

When Anna looked again, Cyrus was examining the group of musical instruments and gear that was off to the side of the small artist's nook. He seemed to have a special interest in the small stack of amps and the pair of guitars that stood on stands beside the speakers. One guitar held his attention in particular. It was purple with airbrushed red and black claw marks across the body.

Though Anna was in a hurry, she suspected that the instrument had triggered a memory, because there was a faraway look in his eyes as he ran his fingers down the neck of the guitar.

"She still plays?" Cyrus asked without looking up.

"Only by herself. I've asked her to play for me, but she won't. I've walked in a couple of times and caught her when she didn't see me. She's good. I don't understand her reluctance."

Strangely, Cyrus nodded as though what she was describing made perfect sense. Then he stood up, took a long look at the third guitar stand, this one empty, before finally turning to move on.

"You were going to tell me why we're here?" Cyrus urged.

"Right!" She crossed the room.

Anna led him to the wide doorway at the back of the room, and flipped a light switch as she entered the massive walk-in closet.

"When father took over the building, he had most of it gutted and renovated to his own specifications. He wanted his lab and office set up on the fourth floor—with the kitchen and medical set up on two. For the most part, the third floor required the least structural work. When the building was the French consulate, the third floor was mostly personal quarters. It stayed living space, but was reworked; part of the original configuration remained because the rear wall didn't need modification. Tash's room still has one of the original walls from back in the old days," Anna explained.

She moved to the back wall of the spacious closet and began shifting a section of hanging clothes. She pushed the hangers aside, revealing the oak paneling that was part of the ornate built-in shelving and hanger system.

"When the closet shelves were installed," Anna explained, "they just bolted the wood paneling to the existing walls. It was years before we made the discovery, but one day we found *this*!"

Placing both of her palms against the large oak panel, she pushed. It took a moment, and she had to leverage all of her weight in a prolonged shoving motion, but finally there came an audible 'click'. She stepped back as a section popped free revealing a dark cleft in the wall. She pulled the hatch open, a three-foot by three-foot section of the surface swung toward her on unseen hinges, revealing a hidden door.

"How in the hell did you two find this?" Cyrus marveled.

Anna just shrugged. "We think that most of the closet was a holdover from one of the suites back in the embassy days. This door leads to a passage that runs behind the bedrooms on this floor. There's a narrow stairwell that goes down to the basement levels. There, you'll find a tunnel that leads beyond the outer wall."

Cyrus rubbed his eyes. The shocked look was plainly obvious on his face. "It must've been some sort of emergency escape route for the French ambassador. It's not unheard of. Still, I can't believe this wasn't found when the building was reconfigured."

Anna grinned sheepishly. "We've used it to sneak out on our own over the years. If Tash was feeling pent up and needed to get out by herself, this is how she did it."

"Which means that she's out there, unprotected, when someone is clearly targeting people close to your father."

Anna didn't know what to say. She only nodded.

Cyrus took a long look at Anna, then offered a tired smile. "Don't worry," he said. "I'll find her and bring her back."

With that, he took a flashlight from the shelf and stepped into the darkness of the secret passage. He gave Anna a wave, and waited for her to close the door behind him.

After that, Anna knew that all she could do was wait and hope for the best. It seemed unlikely that anyone would be watching for Natasha to appear on the outside. Then again, it seemed even less likely that anyone would follow Gretchen to the United States…yet there she'd been attacked and was lucky to be alive.

Anna wasn't sure why, but she had faith in Cyrus. Though he hadn't said as much, she could see the concern in his eyes. She had confidence that he would find Natasha and talk her into returning. Hopefully…before anything bad could happen.

Chapter 44

As soon as the hidden door closed behind him, Cyrus flipped the switch on the flashlight. He found himself in a four-foot wide hallway with walls made of stacked cinderblock. A thick layer of dust covered the floor, providing him with an easy view of a well-worn trail of small footprints leading off into the distance.

Cyrus followed the hall for nearly thirty yards before an opening appeared on his right. There, he discovered the platform of a narrow staircase that stretched both up and down from his perch on the third floor. Since Anna mentioned that the passage exited the facility via a tunnel through one of the lower levels, he headed down. But, even as he descended the twisting spiral staircase, he wondered what he might find if he explored the upper levels. It seemed an unlikely way to gain access to Voss's secure lab, but it was a thought. It would require a massive oversight on the part of the construction crew to allow this sort of rear access to the high security lab. At the same time, it was likely that the very *same* construction crew had overlooked the hidden hallway and tunnel system in the first place.

Filing those ideas away for future reference, he reached the bottom of the staircase. Since he'd passed the platforms leading to other floors, he suspected he'd reached one of the subbasement levels. At least there was no question as to which direction to go; with the tunnel leading off in only one direction, he followed the only path available to him.

It was a safe bet that the tunnel was subterranean; the temperature had dropped nearly twenty degrees since he entered the cavern. He was walking down the center of what was essentially a concrete pipe, about eight feet in diameter. As with the hallway above, he could see the small footprints left in the chalky dust on the ground.

Cyrus followed the underground pipe for hundreds of yards— a distance that left no question that he'd passed beyond the outer wall of the compound. For the first time, he began to wonder where the tunnel might exit. Wherever it came out, it was likely to be a location that was controlled, and not open to the public. If the tunnel's exit were obvious, there was no way it would've remained hidden for so long.

He walked the tunnel for several minutes. At one point, the path had taken a ninety-degree turn to the right, after which the slope dropped and took him at least thirty feet deeper. Finally, another ninety-degree turn brought him to the foot of a wide steel ladder that was bolted into the face of a smooth concrete wall. The top of the ladder disappeared though a wide circular hole in the ceiling about ten feet over head.

Again, lacking any choice of direction, Cyrus began to climb. Every rung reminded him that his existing injuries were nowhere near healed. Still, he pressed on. The ladder went much higher than he expected. After passing through the ceiling of the chamber, he found himself in a narrow vertical shaft. It was fifty feet or more of climbing before he reached the top and emerged through the floor of a small room with a rough, textured concrete floor and matching walls. The room was tight; eight feet square at most, with the ladder emerging from the very center of the floor. The top of the ladder extended about five feet beyond the floor, making for a safe and easy dismount. Cyrus simply climbed to the top, then stepped off onto the firm footing of the eight-foot square room.

Shining his light around, he noticed a large hook beside the sturdy steel door on one wall. Three keys hung from the hook, each had its own key ring. Taking a closer look, he was puzzled to find that all three keys were exactly the same.

He tried the heavy steel door's release lever and found that it wouldn't budge. The purpose of the keys became clear. Pulling one from the hook, he inserted it into the lock and turned. The locks heavy mechanism spun easily, the lock disengaging with a deep *thunk*.

Pushing the door open only far enough to slide from the room, Cyrus stepped into the moonlit darkness and found himself on the roof of a commercial building several blocks away from the Voss compound. The building's roof was covered in gravel. Here and there, patches of tarpaper substrate peeked through. At the far end of the roof, standing on powerful support legs, was a massive water retention tank.

Walking to the edge of the roof, Cyrus took in the city two stories below. It was going on midnight so everything was blanketed in the peaceful calm that came after the majority of the population had retired indoors for the evening. Still, the city around him was awash with scattered lights. Light came from street lamps, distant windows, the occasional passing car—the city slumbered, but there was still enough activity to keep Cyrus mindful and cautious of what could be hiding in the surrounding shadows.

At one corner of the roof, he found another ladder leading to the alley below. A tall, chain-link fence surrounded the foot of the ladder. The fence's gate was unlocked, so he lifted the latch and stepped into the silent alley beyond.

A moment later, and he was standing on the curb of a wide city street. Sidewalks paralleled every lane within sight. It was the city's downtown district. One and two story buildings lined the streets, some separated by small alleys. Rivven Rock was the capital city of the Isle of Kapros, and was by far its largest city. Still, by comparable population standards, the city was quite small. The Isle of Kapros, as a whole, boasted a population of less than five million people. The island nation itself had a landmass nearly equivalent to the large island of Hawaii. But with its proximity to Norway, its climate couldn't have been more different.

Aligning the city's visible landmarks in his mind, Cyrus considered his options. If Natasha was out there somewhere, there were only so many places she could go given the time of night. How many places would be open at this hour? Of course, she could've gone to visit a friend, in which case he had absolutely no chance of finding her. Though he was certain, if Anna knew of such a friend, she would've pointed him in that direction to begin with.

Walking across the deserted street, Cyrus headed for the only open business in sight. It was a twenty-four hour gas station, which was also deserted. If not for the bright lights shining from the attached convenience store, Cyrus would've assumed that it was closed.

His conversation with the station attendant lasted less than three minutes. By the time he walked away, Cyrus had a good idea where he would find Natasha. There was a bar just a few blocks away. According to the clerk, it had live music and was open late into the night.

She would be there. He was certain of it.

Cyrus walked through the empty city streets. The cold night air quickly saturated his body. The temperature was only a few degrees above freezing and, given his clandestine exit from the compound, taking a coat hadn't been an option. By the time he rounded the corner and saw the entrance to the dive bar, it was a welcomed sight.

The exterior of the one story building was sturdy, but rundown. It was clad in old, discolored siding that looked more at home in some rural neighborhood rather than in the heart of the city's downtown. Even the bar's sign, which called the establishment simply, *The Cuban*, looked like it hadn't seen a fresh coat of paint in decades. But for all that it lacked, the place was packed with people. The surrounding parking lot was filled to capacity with no obvious spaces to spare.

As Cyrus approached the front door, he passed a row of parked motorcycles. Some were new but many were old, classic Harleys. There were even a pair of beautifully restored Indians parked along the curb. A half dozen leather and denim clad bikers stood around a burning trash barrel near the door. They smoked cigarettes and eyed Cyrus with suspicion.

Cyrus didn't say a word, but he felt the group's eyes on him as he stepped into the dimly lit, tightly packed space. Old school rock boomed from an ancient jukebox in the corner. A large stage was set up at the far end of the room; it was covered with speakers and instruments, but no performers. Apparently, the band was between sets.

Cyrus scanned the room as he threaded his way through the shoulder-to-shoulder crowd and over to the bar. There must have been two hundred and fifty people packed into the place—a space that should've held just over a hundred on its best day. He could barely hear the canned music playing over the din of humanity.

Finally reaching his destination, Cyrus pushed in between two large bikers who were just taking their drinks from the bartender. Cyrus took advantage of the opportunity and ordered a beer from a tall blonde in a very tiny tank top.

While he waited, Cyrus glanced up and down the long counter, hoping to catch a glimpse of Natasha among the thundering mass of people. While he wasn't sure of her current habits, he knew she'd never been much of a drinker. A crowd like this would've been near the top of her list of things to avoid under normal circumstances, too. But she did love live music. When the gas station attendant mentioned a local bar with a live band, Cyrus was sure that this would be the place. But now, as he looked around, he was feeling considerably less confident.

The bartender returned with Cyrus's beer. He handed her a ten and told her to keep the change. She shot him an exhausted, but appreciative smile, as she stepped away from the bar. He was overpaying for the beer, but he figured she more than deserved the tip given the number of people she had to deal with. Plus, if worse came to worst, he would double back and ask her if she'd seen Natasha.

Taking a long pull from the beer bottle, Cyrus ambled off, pushing his way through the crowd and scouting the room. The place was so jam-packed, he couldn't understand why people would choose to spend their night in such a way. Then again, what he saw likely constituted the nightlife 'scene' in the small city. These people were just taking what they could get. It seemed like a profitable business opportunity just waiting to be seized.

A reverberating screech bellowed from the speakers that were spread around the perimeter of the room. It became instantly apparent that someone, somewhere, had just picked up a microphone. The bubbling white noise of the horde reduced by half in response.

"Alright folks," the disembodied male voice called above the clamor. "Thank you for waiting while we wet our whistles and took care of some personal business."

The rest of the throng finally began to settle.

"Are you ready for some more rock-and-roll?" the man continued. "Cause we've got a little something special for you tonight. We're lucky to have a local talent with us, and she's agreed to sit in for a couple of sets."

As soon as Cyrus heard the announcer refer to their guest as a *she*, his mind instantly flashed back to the empty guitar stand in Natasha's room. His heart skipped a beat. There was only one thing that Natasha loved more than listening to live music, and that was playing it herself.

She wouldn't be crazy enough to get on stage with all that was happening, he found himself wondering. It would mean standing in front of a crowd of hundreds, possibly with a target on her chest.

The announcer continued his spiel, but the guest musician must have stepped out on stage just as her name was announced, because that part of the commentary became inaudible over the whooping and cheering. From where Cyrus stood, he couldn't even see the stage. He was at the wrong angle and there was a fifty-foot wide wall of humanity between him and the raised platform.

But when the signature guitar solo launched the intro to a cover of AC/DC's *You Shook Me All Night Long,* Cyrus no longer needed to see the stage in order to know who was playing lead guitar.

Shit!

The crowd erupted with shouts, whistles and applause, as the drums rumbled and the rest of the band kicked into high gear. The band's singer didn't sound anything like either Bon Scott or Brian Johnson, but that didn't matter. The room was going crazy.

Bull's-eye or not, Natasha was on stage. Even after all these years, there was something about the sound of her guitar that was unmistakable. He began working his way in the direction of the stage. Cyrus's mind had moved into heightened threat assessment mode. It was no small feat to move quickly through a room full of mostly drunken people who were now making a point of bumping into and bouncing off one another.

It was impossible to pick out a threat against a backdrop of pure chaos. Cyrus did the best he could, and felt some relief when he finally reached the rightmost corner of the stage. He took up a position where he could keep Natasha in his eye line while maintaining a sweeping view of the remaining floor.

After the first few minutes, when nothing catastrophic had transpired, Cyrus's nerves settled by a matter of degrees. He still felt like she was a Prairie dog sticking her head out of a hole on the first day of hunting season, but he knew *he'd* been lucky to find her. What were the odds that someone else might track her to this random location as well?

Chapter 45

The band went on to perform more than a half-dozen additional songs from groups like Godsmack, Monster Magnet, George Thorogood, and Buckcherry. Through it all, Cyrus was nothing short of astounded. Not only was the band good, but Natasha's work on lead guitar was electrifying. She found a way to bring her own sound to everything she played. And while she'd played during their time together at school, she'd never sounded anything like this.

The only thing preventing him from being swept away by her performance was the near overwhelming sense that such a public display was tempting disaster. The rational part of his mind warred with the instinctual. There was no reason to think that anyone would be looking for her in some dive bar in the middle of the night. Even her personal security detail believed she was locked away behind the walls of the Voss family fortress. All the same, Cyrus couldn't fight the sense that something was already going wrong.

Looking back at the unwashed mass of people, it wasn't hard to understand what was triggering his sixth sense. The audience was largely comprised of haggard and suspicious looking bar patrons. But they weren't a threat. As far as they were concerned, the band was a smash hit. They belted out crowd-pleasing favorites that were seasoned with a unique and entertaining new twist.

Though Natasha wasn't playing to the crowd, there was no question that she would prove to be a rising star. She had the audience eating out of her hand. While the rest of the band had the quintessential throwback heavy metal look: long hair, dark clothes, and lots of tattoos—Natasha was dressed simply in a white tank top, black jeans, and knee high boots. Her long blonde hair fell forward to cover her face at the opening of every song. Cyrus knew that wasn't an accident. She'd suffered from terrible stage fright when he had known her, and while her appearance on stage here impressed him, he could see that it wasn't as easy as she made it seem. She pulled her hair back from her face at the end of each song, just long enough to briefly breathe in the audience and prepare for the next piece.

Cyrus marveled at how jaw-droppingly gorgeous she was standing on that stage. Bathed in the pulsing rhythm and lights, she was showing the world a hint of the remarkable woman he'd once fallen for. For the first time since arriving at the Voss compound, he was able to put the feelings of guilt out of his mind. Seeing her up there, doing what she loved, finally made seeing her feel real. She was doing alright for herself. She didn't need him, and leaving really had been the best thing he could've done for her.

Natasha had fought crippling stage fright since before they had met. The disability was made that much more cruel by the fact that she wanted nothing more than to play in a rock band. But every time she'd tried to perform before even a small group of friends, she'd choked. A few bad experiences had proven crushing and, no matter how much support or encouragement Cyrus had offered, she had never been able to work through that fear.

But none of that mattered now. She'd found her way without him. She was doing what she loved. Even if he could see that she was terrified to be standing up there, she was doing it, and she was amazing!

Looking back over the audience, Cyrus knew he wasn't the only one to think as much. The room was going absolutely insane. And, even though he didn't think it was possible, it looked like more people had packed into the building over the past half hour. His little corner at the right of the stage was cramped. It seemed like the crowd had become a single living mass that moved with the pulse of the music. Since he was on the leading edge of that wave, he had to keep them from grinding him against the edge of the three-foot high platform. With what had to be two hundred or more people in constant motion, that was a trick easier said than done.

Shooting a glance over his shoulder, Cyrus tried to keep sight of the front door. The building was now well over capacity, and *standing room only* had become a literal description for the event. Someone couldn't fall over, even if they wanted to. He was pretty sure there wasn't any easy way to get to the exit in an emergency, and that made him uneasy. Part of his basic operating procedure was to know the exits and know how to get to them fast. He had neither ability here, and began to wonder if that was the cause of his nagging discomfort.

The cause of that grating, nagging feeling of concern suddenly became apparent when Cyrus saw a man pull himself up onto the far end of the distant bar counter. It was a clumsy effort given the density of the audience, so the move had quickly caught his eye. Given the preoccupation of the crowd, only the bartenders seemed to notice the man's bold action. But Cyrus did, and he knew the man was trouble even before he saw him pull his coat aside to reveal the compact MP5 submachine gun. It was slung from his shoulder by a strap he'd used to conceal the weapon inside his coat.

Cyrus knew that a machine gun in such densely packed confines would turn the place into a slaughterhouse. Unfortunately, he was unarmed and, therefore had to focus on his number one priority. Vaulting onto the short stage, he crossed half of it in four long strides before launching into a flying dive. In doing so, he managed to clip the lead singer with his shoulder, sending the man spiraling across the stage. Cyrus's flying tackle caught Natasha high in the body. The two of them went crashing off the back of the platform, tangled in the power cord of her guitar.

The moment Cyrus and Natasha slipped from the rear of the stage, the first volley of automatic gunfire peppered the spot where Natasha had been standing. The music had stopped abruptly with Cyrus's violent appearance on stage. The gunshots sent the remaining band members scurrying for cover, and the bar's sound system screeched with feedback from the discarded instruments and microphones. Moments later, the audience began its fevered reaction.

Even though the shooter had taken a high position, standing on the bar at the back of the room, it was a long shot for a weapon designed for close quarters like the MP5. The shooter's first rounds had struck their intended location; however, missing their target. But with his advantage gone, the shooter began to fire more rapidly, peppering the stage with a wide spray of lead. In the process, several members of the crowd closest to the stage—those slow to react and in the wrong place at the wrong time—took lethal fire and were cut down where they stood.

The shooter was not deterred. As the terrified crowd succumbed to their survival instincts, he forged on. The man in the long coat moved smoothly down the length of the bar's surface, dropping his spent magazine as he went. His eyes scanned the stage and surrounding area as his hands moved across the weapon with practiced precision. The automated stage light show continued unimpeded, so the entire end of the room remained awash in flickering, flashing, multi-color strobes that helped to confound his deadly vision.

Slapping a fresh magazine home, the gunman raised his weapon and sprayed the ceiling mounted lighting rig. One end of the bar broke free and fell; the stage was submerged into shadows as a resulting electrical short blew out breakers.

The blackout brought renewed screams from those fleeing the destruction. Half the crowd had already found its way out the main exit, while still more had made use of a narrow emergency exit near the restrooms down a nearby hallway.

As soon as the room dropped into darkness, Cyrus tipped his head over the edge of the stage. The shooter had been peppering the platform with random gunfire in an attempt to hit them where they'd taken cover. The platform's thick plywood deck, combined with the oblique angle of the shooter's assault, had resulted in little critical damage to their barricade.

Cyrus could see the shooter standing halfway down the length of the bar. He was silhouetted in the light from the neon beer signs behind the counter; it was a shame, Cyrus thought, if he had a gun, the man would've made an easy target. But, as it was, he was entirely unarmed. Having spent the last week in an infirmary under close guard, there had been no way to smuggle a gun into the compound. And after he'd left in a rush tonight, there'd been no opportunity to acquire one.

A new commotion at the front door drew Cyrus's attention. People continued to pour out, thankfully forgotten by the shooter. Someone was fighting the stampede, and making his way into the building. At first, Cyrus wasn't sure what was happening, but then two gunshots came from the doorway and the crowd parted, as if they were the Red Sea and the new gunman was Moses, himself.

As soon as the second killer walked fully into the room, the mad dash for the parking lot and beyond, resumed. Moses paid the fleeing patrons no mind. He simply looked to his partner, who still stood on the counter. When his partner shook his head, Moses didn't look happy. He ground his teeth and holstered his sidearm. A moment later, he withdrew his own MP5 from beneath his long coat and waved the other man toward the stage.

Cyrus was accustomed to walking into dangerous situations unarmed. It was one of the many hazards of undercover work. But it was also something he didn't spend much time worrying about. Dangerous situations typically meant that, while he didn't have a weapon, he was often surrounded by people who did. The trick was not getting hung up on being unarmed yourself. You concentrate on the fastest and easiest means of acquiring a weapon in any given environment.

In this case, there was a good chance of a gun being hidden behind the bar. The fact that the shooter was located between Cyrus and the bar made that option less than ideal. That left taking a gun from one of the shooters. It wasn't ideal either, but it wasn't impossible. It was only made more complicated by the appearance of Moses.

The man on the bar jumped down and inched toward the stage. Moses was covering him from a distance. Cyrus dropped back behind the platform. The room was growing steadily quieter as the audience was allowed to flee the building unimpeded. He at least had the cover of darkness thanks to the blown breakers.

For the first time since forcing her bodily from the stage, Cyrus's eyes found Natasha's. They were wide, terrified, and full of questions. But to her credit, she didn't say a word. She was likely too scared to break the silence, which was good. Giving away their position at the moment would prove fatal.

Cyrus smiled with confident reassurance, and squeezed her hand. "It'll be okay," he whispered.

Looking around them, they were still in a loose tangle of wires and cables that fed the stage. Part of the drum set had fallen off the back of the platform, probably as the band took cover in the wake of the gunfire. The lead singer, a long-haired twenty-something, laying about eight feet away, looked like he was on the verge of either a panic or an asthma attack. Looking close, Cyrus guessed asthma since he was sweating profusely and looked terrible. On the upside, it didn't seem like he was on the verge of doing something irrational.

The bassist was actually three feet under the stage with his arms wrapped tight around one of the two-by-four structural supports. He had his head tucked up against his body and was trembling. It was hard to tell in the murky darkness, but Cyrus guessed the kid was alright—just shell-shocked by what was happening.

The drummer sat flat on his butt, right behind Natasha. Shirtless and covered in sweat, blood ran from the corner of his eye. If Cyrus had to guess, the guy hadn't noticed the minor injury yet. He was in shock. He just sat there on the hard tile floor with a drumstick raised in each hand and a blank look on his face.

Cyrus and Natasha were tangled in the cable from her guitar. Carefully and quietly, he pulled at it and extricated himself from her prone, motionless form. Her eyes followed him the entire time. It was a good sign. She was responsive and had maintained her composure. That would be vital for what was to follow.

With a minimum of effort, Cyrus slid into place directly before the drummer. The kid failed to react. His eyes didn't even flicker; he was virtually catatonic.

Rising on his knees, Cyrus glanced over the stage. The first gunman was advancing slowly from the right. He would be on them in a matter of seconds. Cyrus knew he needed to act quickly or the man would simply walk onto the stage, look down at them, and finish what he came here to do.

Glancing back at the drummer, Cyrus grinned as a plan formed. "Mind if I borrow these?" he asked, sliding the drumsticks from the young man's unmoving hands.

"Is that still plugged into the sound system?" Cyrus pointed to the guitar that was twisted uncomfortably by the strap across Natasha's shoulder and hip.

She nodded and whispered, "That's why I'm trying not to move. One little shiver and I'm liable to send feedback through the speakers."

"What about the blackout? Didn't that kill the speakers?"

She pointed to the small LED light on the body of her guitar. "There's a battery backup somewhere," she whispered. "Breakers blow a lot around here. They run part of the gear on battery to keep it from killing the show. At least, a few of the speakers are still live."

That brought a smile to Cyrus's face. "Good. When I give you the signal, I need you to go Zakk Wylde on these guys," he said, giving her a wink.

Her brow furrowed. She shot an awkward glance over her shoulder, and he knew she was picturing what perils lay beyond the stage. A smile crossed her face and her eyes burned with a new light. "You got it."

Cyrus took a quick peek over the lip of the stage to gauge the vector of the approaching gunman. He shifted his position to compensate, moving four feet further toward the far end of the stage. The last of the bystanders had just left the building, and it was time to make his move. He heard the creaking of the wooden stairs on the opposite end of the platform, as the gunman climbed to the deck.

Waiting for the sound of three slow footfalls, Cyrus peered over the edge of the stage, still cloaked in darkness, and confirmed the position of his target. The gunman was only yards away. Without looking back, Cyrus pointed the drumstick in his left hand at Natasha, giving her the *go* sign.

All attempts at stealthy concealment were shed, as Natasha rolled off the scraped elbow she'd landed on. Prior to this, even moving the inches necessary to bring relief to her pain would have threatened to create sound from her guitar and paint them all as targets.

Rolling onto her back, she brought the guitar to rest on her right hip. Natasha had lost her pick but that didn't matter. Without giving the system time to register feedback from her motion, she raked the tips of her bare fingers across the guitar strings. The silence of the deserted bar was shattered, as Natasha launched into a ferocious riff that literally thundered through the room. Not only had the instruments remained functional on backup power, but the entire array of speakers was still online.

Natasha had hit only her fourth note when Cyrus shoulder-rolled onto the stage; spinning, he came instantly to his feet. As he'd hoped, both his target and Moses across the room, had been caught off-guard by Natasha's tumultuous auditory assault. Thanks to the towering speakers that flanked the stage, the sound seemed to be smashing in on them from all sides.

That second of delay in reaction was exactly what Cyrus needed. He was on the first gunman before he could fully recognize his presence. In a single violent motion, Cyrus parried the man's assault rifle away with his left hand while he drove a drumstick through the man's heart with his right.

Cyrus looked into the killer's eyes, and noted the grasp of truth that was displayed in that moment; the moment where the man knew his life had come to an abrupt end. Even as he did, Cyrus pulled both lapels of the killer's jacket into his right fist, bent at the knees, and twisted his hip into the man's dying body for leverage. The killer sagged against him while he shifted his stance to hold the man's body upright.

At that moment, a barrage of bullets struck the body of his human shield. Peeking around the corpse's shoulder, Cyrus spied Moses moving laterally in an effort to change his vector and defeat the improvised shield. Cyrus twisted the upright corpse in order to keep the dead man between them. At the same time, his left hand groped blindly for the man's weapon.

As he turned, Cyrus felt his foot kick something and heard it slide a few inches across the floor. He realized instantly that he'd kicked his attacker's MP5. Understandably, the man had dropped the weapon the moment he'd been stabbed through the heart. It had somehow slipped from the man's shoulder sling in the jostle.

Curses filled Cyrus's mind. His shield was quickly outliving its usefulness. When it fell, so would he. Then, an idea hit him, like a bolt from the blue. Fighting fatigue, he hoisted the man higher and glanced around the man's shoulder to adjust his direction once more. Reaching blindly, Cyrus nearly laughed aloud when his hand slapped against the sidearm that was strapped to the hip of the corpse.

Pulling the gun free, Cyrus charged to the front of the stage. At the edge, he let the dead man's body fly and did his best to fling the tumbling form at Moses. At the same time, Cyrus stepped from the stage and fell three-feet straight down. As soon as his boots impacted the tile floor, he dropped to one knee. His weapon was already raised. He opened fire on Moses, stitching the man across the torso as quickly as he could cycle the trigger. The rapid-fire sequence was concluded with a single gunshot to Moses's face, just in case he was wearing body armor.

Moses spun and crumpled to the floor with a wet splat. A moment later, Cyrus was on him. His first intent was to check the man for a pulse, but it wasn't necessary. Moses lay face down, the back of his head pointed at the ceiling—most of it, completely missing.

Cyrus quickly rifled through the man's pockets, finding nothing to identify him but relieving him of two additional magazines, as well as his sidearm.

"Time to go!" Cyrus called to Natasha.

While he waited for her to extract herself from the mess behind the stage, Cyrus slapped a fresh magazine into the first of the two confiscated pistols. When Natasha reached his side, he slid the extra gun into her hand and took her by the elbow— gently leading her toward the door as if it was the most normal thing in the world.

Chapter 46

The Cuban
1:19 am

A dark figure stood cloaked in the shadows at the end of an alley a block and a half away from *The Cuban*. The man wore a long dark coat and a fedora that he kept low on his brow to better conceal his identity. The outfit was cliché, but he considered that one of its charms. It suited his image as the 'puppet master' behind all that was happening. Even though he had worked hard to conceal his identity from everyone hired for the current operation, he still found amusement in his shadowy attire, even if no one would even share in his levity.

Though he should never have been on the island in the first place, he reasoned that it had become a necessity when those he'd hired had failed to kill Cyrus Cooper on the train outside of Paris. He shouldn't have been surprised, but at the same time, Cooper shouldn't have been expecting resistance. Not only had he survived the train, but also successfully infiltrated Doctor Voss's compound.

That was impressive work. Still, the need to eliminate Cooper was unavoidable. As such, he had sent another team into the bar to dispatch him. Had it not been for his own man inside the Voss compound, he would never have known that young Cyrus was about to make his way beyond the walls of the facility. For as useful as his man inside had been, he had not known how Cyrus would escape the facility, or where he would emerge.

Pulling the collar of his coat tight against the cold, he focused on the distant entrance to the bar. He'd personally watched Cooper enter the establishment. As he suspected, the young man had somehow bypassed the men who had been assigned to watch the perimeter of the compound. He'd been forced to contact his agents directly and alert them to their oversight. It was frustrating, but it only reinforced his earlier decision to eliminate the hired team once the operation was complete.

Shoving his gloved hands deep into the pockets of his coat, the man flexed his fingers in hopes of returning some degree of feeling to his extremities. It was only a matter of time now. He'd watched the second of the hired gunmen enter the bar only minutes before. The operation was clearly underway, as illustrated by the rush of drunken, screaming people spilling from the entrance of the building.

The distant sound of automatic gunfire was unmistakable. The dark figure watched those fleeing the building, looking for any sign of Cyrus Cooper among the pathetic mass. Though it was unlikely that Cooper would make it past the pair of experienced killers, if anyone knew how resourceful young Cyrus could be, it was him.

When the stream of those fleeing the bar finally ran dry, the figure fought the urge to move closer; he was already risking too much standing on a public street. That he was even on the island, using one of his numerous sets of fake identification, was reckless enough.

Another burst of gunfire erupted from inside the bar and the dark figure felt a grim smile spread across his face. That was it, he realized. The crowd had been cleared, and his men were finally getting down to business.

It won't be long now.

Another rapid series of shots; these from a handgun and not an automatic, sounded from inside the bar. The figure fought an almost overpowering urge. Those who had fled the scene were long gone. The surrounding area was deserted. No sirens could yet be heard, so emergency services would still be minutes away. There was minimal risk of exposure if he were to move just a *little* closer...

Just as he stepped from the curb and was about to make his way across the street, a pair of figures emerged from the front of the bar. Ducking back into the darkness, the man quickly checked his surroundings to be sure no one had seen him.

He was still alone.

His eyes returning to the action, he expected to see the two men he'd hired making their escape from the scene of the crime. This part of the operation was finally over, he thought. He could move ahead with the remainder of the mission without fear of Cyrus Cooper's interference.

The smug smile was snatched from his face when he watched the pair of figures move quickly across the parking lot, one of them waving a gun defensively, while guiding the other by the arm.

No!

The dark figure nearly cried out when he realized that it was Cyrus Cooper and Natasha Voss. He watched, impotently from the shadows, as Cooper slipped into the driver's compartment of a small, four-wheel drive pickup truck. A moment later, and the vehicle was hot-wired. Only seconds more, and the targets had disappeared into the night.

The dark figure was confounded by the turn of events. It most certainly meant that the men he'd hired were dead. But he knew for a fact that the young man had entered the bar unarmed. Once more, just like on the train, Cyrus had managed to get the better of his opposition.

That brought a greater, and potentially more troubling question, to his mind. When on the train, Cooper had believed that the assassination team's objective had been to retrieve the technology destined for Doctor Voss. He had no idea that he'd been the team's target the entire time. But now, after surviving this new attack at the bar, would Cooper see the truth—or would he suspect that the gunmen had been after Voss's daughter? He'd gone to the trouble of fleeing the bar with her, after all…

So, there was hope.

Pulling his phone from the pocket of his coat, he tapped the pre-programmed speed-dial. "I hope you're ready," he said, as soon as the line was picked up. "The target is on his way to you now. Don't mess this up."

If many years in the profession had taught the dark figure anything, it was to have a contingency plan. And when Cyrus Cooper was involved, it was good to have more than one. The young man was extremely unpredictable.

Extremely, *but not always.*

After disconnecting the call, the figure twisted the phone between his two powerful hands and shattered it into dozens of pieces. Turning, he walked slowly up the street, dropping the wrecked device into a curbside storm drain.

The night wasn't over yet, and Cyrus Cooper would not live to see daybreak.

To be continued...

Cyrus Cooper will return in...

Rogue Faction Part 2

A Note from Xander Weaver:

Thank you for reading Rogue Faction Part 1. I hope you've had as much fun reading it as I've had writing it. If you did, please show your support by posting a review with your online retailer of choice. Those reviews make a difference to new readers, and they can make a real difference when it comes to spreading the word about my work. Just a brief statement explaining what it was that you enjoyed most is all it takes.

Your time and effort is sincerely appreciated.

Thank you!

—Xander Weaver

Acknowledgments:

A great deal of time and effort goes into the release of each and every book. And while I am the 'captain of the ship' when it comes to the creation of the story, the final product has been honed and refined by a number of talented and generous friends. This book is better thanks to their efforts, and I become a better writer thanks to their continued support.

First, thanks must go to Amy Lignor for her work as Editor. This is our second project together and I consider myself lucky, once more, to have her on my team. She brings a level of polish and refinement to the final draft that I find profoundly satisfying.

Before the book ever reaches an editor, multiple drafts are inflicted on several brave souls. These daring individuals, my beta readers, see a version of the manuscript that is often very different from the final release. They watch for errors, check for continuity, count the bullets and bodies, and keep me from making foolish mistakes. But most of all, they offer constructive feedback. Different specialties, skills, talents, and personalities make these people ideal beta readers, and I am lucky to have their support. Special thanks go to Jamie Dresser, Seeley James, Wayne and Terri Manke, and Tom Nielsen. And thanks to Dan Barbier for help with the French translations.

The cover design is once more thanks to Lee Roesner from Paradigm Graphic Design. After putting countless hours into a manuscript, it's crucial to have a cover that properly represents the story being told. Lee has the kind of talent and imagination that makes complicated design look easy. And his work speaks for itself. I couldn't be happier with the final cover art.

Last, but certainly not least, I want to thank my wife, Carrie. She's the first person to read my books and the first to help me begin refining them into something special. The amount of time and energy she puts into each initial draft is astounding. She sees a version of each book that I'm not willing to share with anyone else, and she helps me turn them into something I can be proud of. I wouldn't do this without her.

Thank you, Carrie. For being my friend, but also for being my wife!

Newsletter:

Want to hear about the latest book release, contests, and giveaways?

Join the newsletter:
XanderWeaver.com/newsletter

About the Author:

Thank you for reading, "Rogue Faction Part 1." The story was simply too much to cram into a single novel, so this tale will conclude with *Rogue Faction Part 2*. That book will pick up right where this one leaves off and is packed with as much—if not more—adventure and mayhem. I'm very excited about both releases.

As a lifetime fan of thrillers, as well as science fiction, I love the opportunity to blend both genres to create excitement and adventure that includes a sci-fi 'kick'. Part 2 of this story is set to be released soon after this book, so look for it in the near future.

If you would like to be notified of future book releases in advance, you can sign-up via my website at www.XanderWeaver.com. And you can rest assured that your personal information will never be sold or traded.

While I'm working on the newest thrill ride, I frequently post updates to my Facebook (Weaver.Books) and Twitter (@XanderWeaver) pages. Follow the progress and join in the fun!

Other books by Xander Weaver:
Book One: *Dangerous Minds*
Book Two: *Rogue Faction Part 2*

For more information, please visit:
www.XanderWeaver.com